LOST SOULS FOREVER

A NEARLY DEARLY DEPARTED CLUB NOVEL

ANTHONY GRACE

Copyright @ 2023 by Anthony Grace.

The right of Anthony Grace to be identified as the author of this work has been asserted in accordance with the Copyright, Design and Patents Act 1988.

All rights reserved.

This book, or any portion thereof, may not be reproduced or used in any manner whatsoever without the express, written permission of the author, except for the use of brief quotations in a book review.

The characters in this book are entirely fictitious. Any resemblance to actual persons living or dead is entirely coincidental.

CHAPTER ONE
THE COUNTDOWN

Impetus Stokes sat in the corner of his cell and contemplated his future.

Time, as is its very nature, was ticking. If he wasn't careful, he'd be late. *Too* late. And that was simply unacceptable. Especially when the stakes were so high.

Because this meant more to him than anything. More than life itself, if that was possible.

Impetus had been incarcerated in HM Prison Stainmouth, category B status, for almost two years now. Two years into a seven stretch for robbery. The sheer ridiculousness of it always brought a smile to his face. Is that all he was? A petty thief with envious eyes and fast fingers? Maybe his imprisonment would be easier to stomach if that was true. Just another knuckle dragger with nothing upstairs.

Until a few days ago, Impetus had been fully prepared to see out his sentence. Do the crime, do the time as the old cliche went. Head down, nose clean, no eye contact with those of an unpredictable disposition.

He was less prepared, however, when he received the bad news.

No, not bad. That didn't do it justice. This was devastating. Beyond tragic. It was also the catalyst for change. From that moment forth, Impetus had set the wheels in motion. Talk and they will listen. And, sure enough, they had. With wide eyes and open ears.

A knock at the cell door brought him back to reality.

'Enter.'

The door creaked open and a shaven head appeared in its place. Dark eyes, sunken cheekbones and patchy stubble. Early twenties, but ageing fast. A life lost to petty crime. Drugs. Assault. You name it. Such a waste, thought Impetus. Misguided, yes. Naive, almost certainly. A hardened criminal, anything but.

The shaven head smiled, softening his features. Everybody called him Lip. Friends and family. Even enemies, of which there were plenty.

Impetus, as had long been the case, wasn't so easy to categorise.

'Good day to you, Phillip. How can I be of assistance?'

Lip was bouncing up and down on the spot, unnaturally excited for a bleak Sunday afternoon. 'Poker in the dayroom, Mr Stokes. There are five of us. Me, Craggy, Benno, Moist and Double Decker. We could always shift up for a little one, though.' Lip pulled a face. 'Not little. Just ... erm ... perfectly formed. No offence intended.'

'None taken.' Impetus took a moment to mull over the invitation. Contrary to popular opinion, poker was a game of skill. A professional player would always mitigate the luck aspect by consistently making mathematically superior decisions. Craggy, unsurprisingly, didn't make mathematically superior decisions. But then neither did Benno or Moist. Double Decker could barely count his toes, whilst Lip just enjoyed the social side of things. It could've been tiddlywinks or hopscotch for all he cared. Anything was better than being locked up all day.

They were no competition. Not for someone like Impetus Stokes. Also known as the Imp. Cunning and calculating. Devious and determined. The biggest brain on their wing. The biggest brain in the smallest body.

'Be a shame for you not to put in an appearance,' said Lip.

'Yes, it would, wouldn't it?'

Lip hadn't finished. 'You'll win, of course. You always do.'

'True. And yet ... it's a kind offer, Phillip, but on this occasion I'm afraid I'll have to pass.'

'Oh.' Lip stared at him. 'You alright? You look ... I don't know ... worried.'

Impetus forced a smile. 'Your concern is most gratifying. I am, however, in perfect spirits.' A momentary pause. That wasn't enough. Lip would need something more convincing. 'I've one of my heads,' said Impetus, pressing a forefinger against his temple. 'It's pounding. I wouldn't make for good company.'

'Shit.' Lip checked himself. 'Sorry, Mr Stokes. That slipped out by accident. I know you don't like ... listen, maybe I could fetch Karim. He can give you one of his special massages. He's got magic fingers, that boy. Fixed Bunker's knee first time—'

'That won't be necessary,' said Impetus sharply. *Too* sharply if he was being honest. Time to pivot. 'You're a fine young man, Phillip. Don't let anybody tell you otherwise.'

'If you say so.' Lip lingered in the doorway. 'Anything else? Cup of tea? Coffee? Reckon I could rustle up a couple of biscuits if I look hard enough—'

Impetus raised a hand. 'I'm good, thank you. My head will pass, of that I am certain. There is one thing you can do for me, though. Under no circumstances am I to be disturbed. Not for an hour or two, at the very least. Can you inform the others?'

Lip nodded, eager to please. 'I'll spread the word. Right, you get yourself better, Mr Stokes. See you later.'

Unlikely, thought Impetus.

He waited for Lip to close the door. For his footsteps to fade away. Peace at last.

Reaching into the pocket of his joggers, he carefully removed the white pill from its resting place and rolled it around his fingertips. It was smaller than he expected. Chalky to the touch. Ready to dissolve when the need arose.

The instructions were clear and concise. Three simple words. *Swallow it whole.*

I don't think so somehow ...

Climbing to his feet, Impetus walked over to a wooden desk in the opposite corner of the cell. He had stolen a plastic knife from the canteen only that morning before quickly concealing it. Thankfully, it was still there, stuck to the underside of the desk with a lump of chewing gum he had found in the corridor.

Impetus removed the knife, wiping it clean on his joggers. He placed the pill on the desk and, brow furrowed, sliced it in two. Without overthinking things, he took the left half, dropped it to the floor and stamped on it, grinding it into oblivion. Then he took the right half and a mug of water and sat back down again.

This was the last resort of a desperate man. Whichever way he looked at it, he was placing far too much faith in people who should never be trusted. Bare-faced frauds who reeked of dishonesty. The Governor for one. The police for another. No, not your bog standard bobby, but those at the top. Those who lied for a living from the comfort of their private clubs and chauffeur-driven limousines. Impetus knew he was scraping the barrel, but it was still a barrel that needed to be scraped.

What was left of the pill was crumbling beneath his fingers. It was now or never.

Placing it on his tongue, Impetus took a gulp of water and swallowed. It vanished in an instant. There. He had done it. No turning back now.

He rested his head on the wall. Closed his eyes and let his mind wander. If things went to plan, if they were telling the truth, he would be dead in a few minutes.

He started the countdown to oblivion.

See you on the other side.

CHAPTER TWO
MONDAY

Agatha Pleasant didn't have to look too hard to find the Chief Constable of Stainmouth Police Force.

He had requested … no, demanded … no, ordered her to meet him deep in the woods at the bottom of his garden.

Not weird at all. Perfectly normal.

It was early morning, predictably grey, stubbornly overcast. Despite the gloom, Clifford Goose still stuck out like a fly on a wedding cake amongst the bushy undergrowth and rampant greenery that surrounded him. Dressed in a florescent yellow waterproof jacket and matching wellies, he was cuddling up to a huge, sprawling tree, his legs straddling the trunk. A pair of binoculars were clutched tightly in one hand. Nothing wrong with that. Less acceptable perhaps was the whereabouts of his other hand. Planted firmly in his trouser pocket, it seemed to be shuffling up and down with a disturbing regularity. Agatha let her eyes drift elsewhere as she edged closer. Tried desperately not to dwell on that particular image for fear of where her imagination might lead her.

'I never had you down as a keen ornithologist,' she said, creeping up behind him.

'Chuffin' hell, woman!' Spinning around in shock, Clifford Goose almost took a tumble before he steadied himself against the trunk. 'I nearly bloody wet myself!'

'As long as that's all you nearly did,' said Agatha, trying to hide her disgust. 'I thought you knew I was coming.'

'I did ... I do.' Goose pulled his hand out of his pocket and placed it on his heart, checking the rhythm. 'What did you just call me again? An orni-whatsit? Sounds contagious.'

'An ornithologist,' repeated Agatha. The bewildered look on Goose's face suggested a little more would be required. 'An expert on birds.'

'I'm not a flippin' expert,' muttered Goose, lifting the binoculars to his eyes. 'I just like watchin' them. It calms me down. Settles my nerves.'

Agatha sneered. 'Why do *your* nerves need settling?'

'I had a heavy night.' Goose burped loudly, as if to emphasise his point. 'About four too many at a charity dinner. Some feminist thing. Women's rights in the workplace ... equality ... the menopause ... that sort of bullcrap. They made me the guest of honour, believe it or not. I had to do a speech and everything. Now, I'm not one to brag, but the lady folk were lapping it up. Even the hairy armpit brigade gave me a standing ovation.'

Agatha rolled her eyes. 'I can imagine what you told them. That you've always been a fan of women from the moment you first met your mother.'

'Bloody hell! Were you there?' gasped Goose. 'I didn't see you. You are a sneaky little sod, though, so it wouldn't surprise me.'

'No invite, I'm afraid. My loss.' Agatha hopped awkwardly from toe to toe. Small talk wasn't even her thing with people she tolerated. With Clifford Goose, it was practically unbearable. 'So, what seems to be the problem? Surely I'm not here to nurse your hangover—'

'I've got a job for you,' said Goose gruffly. 'Something for your team of highly skilled specialists to dig their teeth into.'

Agatha fought hard to conceal a smile. Her team of highly skilled specialists was actually a warring rabble of fumbling amateurs. A little harsh perhaps, but not far off it. An ex-police officer, a former drug dealer, a bare-knuckle boxer and a trainee data analyst. Two men, two women. Four different worlds squeezed together under one roof. Light the fuse and watch it blow. Or just fizzle out. Either was possible.

Her Nearly Dearly Departed Club. A work in progress. Slow progress admittedly. Chronically slow. At this rate, she would have retired before they had even finished their training.

'Bugger me backwards! Is that a Lesser Spotted Woodpecker?' Goose stared with such intense concentration that a vein popped out of his forehead. 'Ruddy crisp packet,' he muttered, answering his own question. 'One of those fancy ones. You know the kind. Pickled caterpillar. Hummus and bird shit. What's wrong with good old cheese and onion? You know where you stand with cheese and onion. On solid ground. No confusion. Right, where was I?'

'The job,' said Agatha, keen to get things back on track. 'You know my team's already working on another of your little ... *assignments*, don't you? They're out there even as we speak—'

'Well, reel them back in,' said Goose, waving his free hand dismissively. 'That thing can wait. This, however, cannot. I need you to crack on. Get straight to it. This afternoon, to be precise.'

'Short notice,' said Agatha.

'Tough titties,' Goose shrugged. 'It only landed on my desk over the weekend and now I'm passing it on to you. That's how these things work, after all. And it's also why you're still here. In Stainmouth. You're at my beck and call. When I say jump, you say—'

'Just tell me what you want me to do,' said Agatha.

Goose crouched down. Shifted the binoculars to his right. 'I need you to pick up a man. No, not like that. You don't have to put on your best frock and talk dirty. He's in prison. Collect him at two o'clock this afternoon. It's strictly hush-hush, so don't go blabbing it to all and sundry. I know what you women are like. Love a gossip ...'

Agatha ignored that. 'And after we've collected him?'

'Sit on him for two days,' said Goose. 'Take him somewhere safe and don't let him out of your sight. I'll call you Wednesday and we'll go from there. When it comes to picking him up, get yourself a van. Something spacey. The more room, the merrier.'

'Why?'

'You'll need to fit the coffin in.' Goose turned slowly.

Smirked. 'Oh, did I forget to say? The man you're going to collect is no longer with us. He's dead. I hope that's not a problem.'

CHAPTER THREE

Clifford Goose was wrong.

The *thing that could wait* could not. Largely because it was already underway. The wheels had started to roll. Not only were the Nearly Dearly Departed Club in position, but they were also ready to strike.

Almost ready.

First, they had to decide who was going to knock the door down.

It was a choice of two polar opposites. The ex-police officer and the former drug dealer. Lucas Thorne and Tommy O'Strife. Between them, they made up one half of Agatha Pleasant's warring rabble. The male half. Raging testosterone and a fragile ego the only things they really had in common.

'Let me do it.' An irritatingly buoyant Tommy dangled a foot in mid-air. Aimed a high kick at nothing in particular. 'Did you see that? It was Bruce Lee-esque. Give me a chance and I'll smash that door clean off its hinges.'

Lucas shook his head. 'And what happens if you miss?'

'Miss? It's a bloody door!' snorted Tommy. 'I could hit it with my eyes closed.'

'You're not aiming for the door – you're aiming for the lock,' explained Lucas. 'Kick the door and the wood splinters, but little else. Smash the lock and the door swings open. Easy when you know how.'

'Easy when you know how,' echoed Tommy childishly. He pushed against the other man with his shoulder. 'Budge to one side and let me show you what I've got.'

Lucas refused to shift. They were in the back garden-cum-dumping ground of twenty-three Barton Avenue. An end terrace with a tall wooden fence surrounding the property, it was slap-bang in the centre of Stainmouth. The mucky middle, as it was often referred to. The other two members of the team – Mercy Mee and Rose Carrington-Finch – were guarding the front door. Or just standing idly, waiting for something, anything, to happen. Either way, they had a role to play. Not as big a role as the men, of course, a fact that both Lucas and Tommy repeated ad nauseam, if only to convince themselves.

Their instructions were so simple that even an ex-police officer and former drug dealer could understand them.

Get in. Locate the occupant. Make a citizen's arrest. And then drop him off at the nearest cop shop as soon as.

And yet ...

Lucas had questioned it immediately. The occupant – nicknamed Matty the Moon, surname undisclosed – was apparently well known to the local police. If that was the case, then why weren't they here now? It was on their patch, after all. You don't just pass a regular on to a bunch of amateurs. Not unless Matty was more than just a persistent offender. Maybe he was an unhinged psychopath who despised authority with a passion. That was probably worth bearing in mind when they finally entered the premises.

Don't stick your neck out. Not unless you want it removing from your shoulders.

'Have you tried the handle?' asked Tommy, out of the blue.

Lucas greeted the question with a look of pure contempt. 'Have you?'

'Course not. Wouldn't have asked if I had. It might be unlocked, though. Stranger things have happened.'

'No, they haven't. And it won't be.'

'It might.'

'It won't.'

'Prove it.' Tommy wagged a finger in Lucas's face. 'I've got in your head, haven't I? I can tell. That door handle is all you're thinking about now. You're obsessed.'

'I'm not,' argued Lucas. 'I couldn't care less about the sodding door handle. It's the last thing on my mind.'

He exhaled slowly. *Don't do it. I'm warning you. Do not grab that ...*

'Fine.' Lucas yanked down on the handle. As expected, the door was locked. 'Don't know why I bother—'

'No, I don't know why you bother either,' said Tommy. 'So move to one side and let a real man step forward. Knocking down doors is proper action hero shit. Right up my street. I've been dreaming about this moment all my life—'

'Sorry to burst your bubble, but not all dreams come true ...'

With that, Lucas lifted his boot and aimed a kick at the handle. It was a solid connection. To his relief, the lock put up little resistance.

'You can do the next one,' he said, as the door flew open to reveal a cramped kitchen. Any joy he felt soon passed, however, when he entered the property and drew breath. 'Jheez ... what the hell is that smell?'

Pushing his way inside, Tommy's first reaction was to squeeze his nostrils together. 'You been bathing in the sewers again?'

'Funny.' Lucas tried to resist, but it was no use. Like Tommy, he had to find a way to block out the rancid stench. 'Let's concentrate on the job at hand, shall we? We're not here to locate the source of the smell. We're here for Matty the Moon.'

'What if they're one and the same?' wondered Tommy. 'Maybe Matty's wanted for crimes against the senses. Christ almighty, I think my eyeballs are melting!'

He hurried out of the kitchen, only to find himself in a narrow, poorly lit hallway. To his dismay, the smell had intensified.

'Where is he?' A desperate Tommy poked his head into the sitting room. At first glance, it was empty. He didn't bother with a second glance. 'We've got a limited window. It's not safe to stay in here too long. This toxic stink can't be good for our insides.'

Fair point, thought Lucas, pausing at the foot of the staircase. 'If he's not downstairs, then he must be—'

'You're a braver man than me if you want to go up there.' Tommy placed a hand on the banister, blocking Lucas's path. 'Is there anybody home?' he called out. He waited less than three seconds for a reply that didn't come. 'Right, there's no one here. Let's get out of this shithole before one of us drops dead—'

'Shush.' Lucas glanced up at the ceiling. 'Did you hear that? Sounded like a creaking floorboard.'

'It's just a rat.'

'That's one *big* rat,' said Lucas. Ducking under Tommy's arm, he took to the stairs. 'Let's not piss about, eh? Up we go then. Follow that stink.'

CHAPTER FOUR

Mercy Mee was sick of staring at the front door.

It was red. Mostly. The paint had chipped and peeled over time, leaving patches of wood exposed to the elements. Throw in a letterbox that was hanging off its hinges and a bent handle and it made for a sorry sight. If only she had somewhere else to look.

Or someone else to talk to.

Mercy turned to the woman stood beside her. Rose Carrington-Finch had once been a trainee data analyst. Back in her previous life. When she was *alive*. Now she was little more than a statue. 'You know you can speak, don't you?' said Mercy. 'We don't just have to stand here in silence.'

Rose chose to reply with the slightest of nods. Nothing more. And certainly nothing less because that would've been practically impossible.

'I'm heading down to the boxing club later,' Mercy continued. 'I fancy getting back in the ring. Working up a sweat. Why don't you tag along? Better than just sitting around.'

Rose exchanged the nod for a gentle shake of her head.

'It'll do you good,' insisted Mercy. 'Get you out and about, meeting new people. You can just watch. You don't have to actually box.'

Another shake.

Mercy blew out, frustrated beyond belief. This was too much. There was *one* way to get Rose talking, though. It was a little unkind, manipulative even, but desperate times and all that.

'You've not had any more of those dark thoughts, have you?' she asked matter-of-factly.

Rose stiffened. 'What dark thoughts?'

'You know what I'm talking about. Those dark thoughts that tip you over the edge.'

Rose took a breath. 'You're not very subtle. If you want to ask if I've thought about killing myself again, then just say it.'

'I think you just said it for me.' Mercy waited. 'Well, have you?'

Rose hesitated a moment too long before shaking her head. 'No, not really. I'm fine. I don't mind living here ... in Stainmouth ... with you ... and Lucas ... and Tommy ...'

'Now I know you're lying,' said Mercy. 'Even Tommy probably doesn't like living with Tommy.' She waited again. Gave Rose the chance to fill in the gaps. Continue the conversation.

She didn't.

'Bloody hell, you're hard work sometimes,' moaned Mercy. 'Still, as long as you're all good.'

Rose chewed on her bottom lip. 'I didn't say I was good. I said I was fine. There's a big difference—'

'Hold that thought.' Mercy pointed up at the house. 'We've got company. And, unless I'm mistaken, it's completely naked!'

Rose followed her gaze, surprised to see that there was a man climbing out of the top-floor window. Bare bottom first, he was exiting backwards, none the wiser as to what lie beneath him.

That soon changed, however.

'I wouldn't do that if I were you,' Mercy called out. 'It's a long drop and we're not prepared to catch you.'

The man glanced over his shoulder. At the same time, his foot slipped straight off the window ledge and his knee scraped against the wall. A scream followed. Loud enough to draw attention.

'Go back inside,' shouted Mercy, twirling her finger as she urged the man to retrace his route. 'Save us the bother of peeling you up off your own doorstep.'

Rose bent over, clutching her stomach. She was about to be sick. Still, at least it would blend in effortlessly with the man's flowing blood and splattered organs when he inevitably hit the ground.

'You can breathe easy now,' remarked Mercy, placing a hand on her friend's back. 'Nothing to see here.'

Rose lifted her head. Peered up at the window. As far as she could tell, the man had regained his footing, tightened his grip and then listened to Mercy's advice. He had changed direction. Rather in than out.

'What now?' she asked.

'Now we warn the others,' said Mercy, heading towards the back of the house. 'We may have got a bum deal, but they'll be in for a full frontal.'

Lucas was halfway up the staircase when a figure emerged from a room to his left.

A man. It was his chest hair that gave him away. Oh, and something else.

'Is that a willy?' wondered Tommy, peering over Lucas's shoulder.

'Why are you asking me?' said Lucas. 'You've got one yourself, haven't you?'

'Not that small. Mine would be a dangerous weapon in the wrong hands.'

Lucas barely had time to roll his eyes before the man disappeared into another room, slamming the door behind him. Lucas followed, bounding up the last few steps in a matter of strides. When he reached the top, he pulled on the handle. Locked.

'Is that you, Matty?' he asked, pressing his ear to the door. 'Matty the Moon?'

'Don't call me that,' panted a voice.

'Which bit? Matty? Or the Moon?'

'The Moon. It's not my fault. I can't help the way I am. It's a life choice, so stop judging me.'

'I'm not,' insisted Lucas. 'I don't know a thing about you.'

'I'm a naturist,' revealed Matty. 'An extreme naturist. I don't let clothes control me. And I don't believe in using man-made inventions if possible. I'd rather go back to a better, more liberated time.'

Tommy's cogs turned. 'Is that why you shit on the floor instead of using the toilet?' Silence greeted his question. 'Oh, you do, don't you? That's why it stinks so bad in here.'

'Just put on some clothes and open the door,' said Lucas firmly. 'The sooner you come out, the sooner we can get out of here. The sooner we get out of here, the sooner we can breathe again.'

Matty snorted. 'You've not been listening, have you? I couldn't do that even if I wanted to. I don't own any clothes. And that's why they don't like me leaving the house. The police, I mean. They say I'm a threat to society.'

'You're a threat to our nostrils,' moaned Tommy.

Lucas, for once, had to agree. 'Right, enough is enough. You've got three seconds to unlock this door. If you don't, we'll knock it down and drag you out by your ... your ...'

'Testicles,' finished Tommy.

Matty yelped in horror.

'And, in case you're wondering, it'll be *me* who knocks the door down,' continued Tommy, squeezing in front of his companion. 'It's my turn. You promised, Lucas.'

The three seconds were up.

Lifting his foot, Tommy leant back and karate-kicked the door with unexpected accuracy. To Lucas's surprise, it crashed to one side. Even more surprising was the sight of a naked Matty stood nervously by an open window. He had simply switched from front to back. Same plan, different room. One leg in, one leg out. Genitalia resting on the window ledge.

'I'll jump,' he said, voice trembling.

Lucas dismissed that with a shake of his head. 'You won't.'

'I will.'

'No, you really won't.'

'I will ... I'm going to ... don't make me—'

'Oh, just do it then!' blurted out Tommy. 'Go on, I dare you. Put us all out of our fuckin' misery.'

So he did.

Before their very eyes, Matty the Moon swung his other leg out of the window and vanished from sight.

Lucas threw his hands up in despair as he rushed across the room. 'Why did you tell him to do that?'

'I was calling his bluff,' muttered Tommy. 'Seems like his bollocks are bigger than they looked.'

Lucas poked his head out of the window. He could see Matty. He was still in one piece, all parts intact, albeit some in a worse condition than others as he scrambled to his feet.

Lucas's response was to turn around and push past a bewildered Tommy. He was out the door in seconds. Down the stairs and back through the house. By the time he got outside, Matty was halfway over the wall at the rear of the property. He had escape in mind. And he wasn't far from it becoming a reality.

Lucas lunged forward and grabbed him by the ankle. The naturist screamed, before instinctively lashing out with his other foot. Whether he meant to or not, he caught Lucas hard on the side of his head. Heel on bone. The pain was sharp and sudden, leaving Lucas with little choice but to let go. Free of his grasp, Matty didn't hang around to apologise. He was gone a few seconds later. Up and over. Disappearing into the next neighbourhood.

Lucas, meanwhile, wasn't going anywhere. Staggering backwards, he closed his eyes as a shrill, ringing sound attacked his senses. He tried to blank it out. To his relief, the ringing began to fade after only a few seconds. A voice replaced it. Not exactly warm and friendly, but familiar.

'That looked painful,' said Mercy, as she wandered up behind him. 'Are you okay?'

'Not sure. Ask me again when I can see properly.' Lucas climbed gingerly to his feet. 'Matty's legged it.'

'Don't worry about him,' said Mercy, waving her phone in the air. 'I've just had a call. We've got bigger fish to fry. No time for tiddlers.'

An unfortunate image of a naked Matty the Moon floated around Lucas's thoughts. 'Go on.'

'It was Miles,' explained Mercy. 'He wants us to meet him back at Cockleshell Farm as soon as possible. Agatha's got a new job for us.'

CHAPTER FIVE

Miles was Agatha Pleasant's right-hand man.

Her number two. The one sane voice in an unpredictable world. Agatha trusted him emphatically. He felt the same way about her. She was a legend in their field. She had never put a foot wrong.

Until now.

Her most recent project.

Her Nearly Dearly Departed Club.

Four random strangers, raised from the dead – or as close to death as you can possibly be – before being dropped into a world they had no concept of. Early evidence had suggested they were barely fit for purpose. Inadequate for the job at hand. Agatha was persistent, though. Give them time and they would prosper. Miles had his doubts. Of course he did. Doubts that he had raised on numerous occasions. Doubts that had been largely shunted to one side and ignored.

Still, there were only so many times you could fall flat on your face before you stopped getting back up again. Sense would surely prevail eventually.

Wouldn't it?

'So ...' Miles stopped pacing the sitting room carpet at Cockleshell Farm and studied the four faces that were staring back at him. 'Does everybody understand what's expected of them?'

Mercy, perched on the edge of the sofa, was the first to reply. 'Go to the prison and collect a man—'

'A *dead* man,' said Lucas, sat beside her.

'Ok, dead man,' continued Mercy. 'And then bring him back here for a couple of days. Don't let his coffin out of our sight.'

'Tommy could always climb inside and keep the corpse company,' Lucas suggested. 'Safe in the knowledge that there's no chance he could bore them to death with his shit banter and vaguely sexist chit-chat.'

Tommy, sprawled out on the armchair, turned up his nose. 'Sounds a bit perverted, if you ask me. I'm no fan of nepo ... nico ... noca—'

'Necrophilia,' said Lucas.

'Oh, you seem to know a lot about it,' Tommy grinned. 'I just hope Proud Mary doesn't drop dead one evening. You'd be all over her like a rash—'

'No one will be going anywhere near the corpse.'

Agatha stepped out of the corner of the room. Until then, she had let Miles do the talking. Sometimes, however, it was necessary to assert herself. 'Two days,' she said, holding up the required amount of fingers. 'That's all. It's neither complicated nor difficult.'

'Just weird,' said Mercy.

'*Very* weird,' said Lucas.

'*Kinky* weird,' added Tommy, largely because he knew it would get everyone's back up.

Agatha shrugged. 'What can I say? The Chief Constable *is* weird. I don't know ... maybe it's a test. Maybe he's assessing us. Whatever, ours is not to reason why. Any more questions?'

'Transport,' said Tommy, his hands clasped around an imaginary steering wheel. 'We can't just walk casually down the street with a coffin.'

'You won't have to.' Miles gestured over his shoulder. Towards the farmyard. 'There's a van out the back. A white Transit. It'd struggle to pass its MOT, but it's all I could lay my hands on at short notice.' He tossed the keys to Lucas. 'There's only one set, so don't lose them.'

Lucas caught them one-handed and stuck them in his pocket.

'I suggest you work in pairs,' said Agatha. 'Mr Thorne and Mr O'Strife. Miss Mee and Miss Carrington-Finch. You did such a good job with our extreme naturist this morning, it'd be a shame to mix things up. Any objections?'

'Yes,' said Lucas and Tommy in unison.

'Sounds good to me,' said Mercy, smiling at Rose. Rose thought about smiling back, before deciding against it.

'Splendid.' Agatha nodded at Miles as she turned towards the door. 'If there's nothing else I'll be on my—'

'Whoa there, cowgirl!' Leaping up off the armchair, Tommy hurried across the room so he could block Agatha's exit route.

'I've been thinking—'

'Don't,' said Miles. 'You'll get a headache.'

'Yeah, right, hilarious,' groaned Tommy. 'No, I've been thinking—'

'Or a nosebleed,' said Miles. 'Best not to let that brain of yours work too hard. Besides, why break the habit of a lifetime?'

Tommy waited. 'Is that it? Have you finished? Are you going to let me speak now?'

Miles pressed on towards the door, knocking Tommy against the wall as he did so. Tommy's response was to bounce back in a flash, ready for a confrontation that had erupted from nowhere.

'Behave,' said Agatha, placing a hand between the two men. 'Now, Mr O'Strife, if you've got something troubling you, then it's only fair that you're allowed to get it off your chest. I'm sure you wouldn't deliberately waste our time.'

'Definitely not,' insisted Tommy. 'No, I've been thinking ... and don't just jump in and shoot me down ... but maybe ... you know ... I ... no, *we* ... we're due a pay rise.'

Agatha greeted the request with a sigh. 'Oh, it seems I was wrong. Time wasting is clearly on the agenda.'

'What do you mean?' snapped Tommy, rearing up. 'We want a pay rise. What's so bad about that?'

'We'd have to pay you for a start,' said Agatha. 'And we don't. What you get are expenses.'

'Adult pocket money,' added Miles, a smirk forming on his lips.

Tommy refused to bite. 'Well, can I have some more adult

pocket money, then? Thirty quid a day is barely enough to wipe my arse with. I'd get more for doing a paper round—'

Agatha raised a hand to silence him. 'Let me remind you, Mr O'Strife, if it wasn't for me, you wouldn't need any money at all. Not a single penny. Everything's free in Heaven.'

'And Hell,' said Miles. 'Why do you want more money, anyway? You've got free board here at Cockleshell Farm. Proud Mary cooks and cleans for you. New clothes ... toiletries ... what else do you need?'

Tommy shuffled about on the spot. 'I don't know ... what if I want to take a girl out?'

'I don't want you to take a girl out,' said Agatha matter-of-factly.

'Who are you? My mother?'

'Yes,' replied Agatha. 'To all intents and purposes, I am.'

'I'm not your dad, though,' said Miles hastily. 'I don't want you asking me about the birds and the bees.'

Agatha made to leave the room. Stopped mid-step. Was that too harsh? Perhaps. Maybe it paid to tread more carefully. A softly softly approach. This whole dead-not-dead thing was still new to everybody. There was no need to rock the boat for the sake of a few pounds.

'I have a compromise for you,' began Agatha, resting a hand on Tommy's shoulder. 'Prove to me that you can successfully take care of the coffin and I'll raise your expenses.'

'Bit extra for a comic and a few sweeties,' remarked Miles.

Agatha glared at him. An unspoken warning. 'So, how does

that sound, Mr O'Strife?'

'Like music to my ears,' beamed Tommy. He stepped to one side. Ushered them out of the farmhouse. 'You can put your faith in me, Pleasant Agatha. That dead body won't even bat an eyelid whilst I'm on the case.'

CHAPTER SIX

The white Transit van pulled up at the rear gates to HM Prison Stainmouth at precisely five-to-two.

'We're early,' said Tommy, unclipping his seat belt so he could lean back and put his feet up on the dashboard. 'I've never been early in my life. It's unnatural.'

'Don't sweat it. They'll be out in a minute.' Lucas lowered his window and stared at the prison walls. Ignoring what it was, who it held captive, it still looked like a grim, soulless place. 'You ever been in there?'

Tommy screwed up his face. 'We've only been in Stainmouth a few weeks, mate. I think you would've realised—'

'Not *that* prison,' sighed Lucas. '*Any* prison. But I'm guessing you knew that when you came out with your stupid reply.'

'Prison? Moi?' Tommy rolled his eyes theatrically. 'You must have me confused for someone else. I wasn't just a petty crim in my past life, you know. Some brainless repeat offender, in and out of jail, too dumb to stop myself from making the same mistakes. No, I was the real deal. Top of the tree. Numero uno.

You don't get banged up when you're running the show.'

Lucas snorted. 'I'm calling bullshit.'

'Call it what you like,' shrugged Tommy. 'I know what I was ... what I still am. Doesn't matter what you think. What any of you think.'

'If you say so.' Lucas nodded towards the prison. 'Still looks like a right hellhole, though. Wouldn't wish a life-time stuck in there on my worst enemy.' He side-eyed Tommy. 'Not even you.'

Tommy was about to deliver his own pithy reply when a discreet door built into the prison wall creaked to one side. Two men appeared in the entrance. Their uniforms suggested prison guards. As did their stern features and serious demeanours. Between them, they were pushing a long trolley which was carrying a wooden coffin.

'Leave this to me.' Lucas climbed out of the van and walked towards the guards. He met them halfway, greeting them with a smile. 'Afternoon. We'll take that off your hands, gents.'

Neither guard let go of the trolley. 'You're not from the mortuary, are you?' said the bigger of the two.

'No, we're not,' admitted Lucas. 'We're ... erm ... private contractors.'

'You got any ID?'

Lucas tried not to laugh. If only they knew. 'No, that's one thing we definitely haven't got.'

'Then we've got a problem.' Both guards crossed their arms as if it was some unwritten rule when dealing with a sticky situation. 'We can't just hand over a dead body to any old ... private contractors.'

They had come to a standstill. Lucas had to say something to move things forward. Something persuasive. Insightful. Because if he didn't ...

He felt a shove in the back as Tommy pushed past him and strolled right up to the two guards. 'Say hello to the organ grinder,' he began. 'Don't listen to my companion; he was born boring. I, however, prefer to get straight to the point. Correct me if I'm wrong, but you're supposed to be meeting someone out here at two, right? Well, look around. I don't see anyone else hanging about, do you? Now, the way I see it, you've got two choices. You can either let us have the coffin and we'll be on our way, or you can fetch your Governor. Drag him out here and waste his time. I'm sure he won't mind.'

'*She,*' said the smaller of the two. 'The Governor's a woman. But you're right. She'll do her nut if we disturb her for no reason.' The guards put their heads together. Cue whispering. 'Okay. You can have the coffin,' said the smaller of the two. 'But if this is a trick—'

'Do we look like body-snatchers?' laughed Tommy. 'And we're not going to do anything sexual, if that's what you're thinking.' He glanced at Lucas. 'Well, he might. I can't be certain. Who knows what rocks his boat?'

'Give it a rest, dickhead.' Lucas reached out and grabbed hold of the trolley. Neither of the guards objected, so he pulled it towards him. 'Are you going to help?' he scowled at Tommy.

Tommy did just that, albeit with a grin on his face that he had no intention of concealing. 'We'll mark that down as a victory to me, shall we? The first of many.'

Silently fuming, Lucas loaded the dead man into the back of the van. He was about to close the doors when Tommy stopped him.

'Notice anything strange about that coffin?' He didn't wait for Lucas to reply. 'It's a bit small, don't you think?'

'Not our problem.' This time, Lucas slammed the doors with a satisfying *clang*. Climbing into the driver's seat, he started the engine. 'Get in before I change my mind.'

'About what?' Tommy had barely opened the passenger-side door before the van began to move. 'Oh, it's like that, is it?' He pulled a face at his disgruntled driver as he finally clambered inside. 'You're in a massive grump because I sweet-talked those two guards and now you're going to blank me. Very grown-up. Very mature. Well, two can play that game …'

Tommy turned to face the window. Clamped a hand over his mouth.

They drove in silence. But not for long.

'Oh, I can't stay mad with you,' said Tommy, swivelling around in his seat before they had even left the prison grounds. 'Can I put some tunes on?' Lucas remained stone-faced. 'I'll take that as a yes.'

Tommy stabbed at a button on the dashboard. There was a slight delay before the radio kicked into life. Pounding drums and screeching guitars. Howling vocals from a poodle-permed wannabe. Heavy metal from the last century.

'Yeah, I like this one,' said Tommy, tapping the beat out on his legs. 'I used to know this girl who was bang into music like this. It used to drive her wild. She was like a woman possessed. She'd rip my clothes off and ... what's wrong now?'

Brow furrowed, Lucas glanced over his shoulder. 'What's that noise?'

'Alright, Granddad,' sniggered Tommy. 'It's not that loud—'

'Not *that* noise.' Lucas prodded the same button and the music came to an abrupt end. 'Can you hear it? That banging sound? It's coming from the back of the van.'

Tommy dismissed it with a flick of his wrist. 'It'll just be the coffin sliding about a bit. We didn't fasten it down, did we? We just tossed it in and hoped for the best.'

Lucas nodded. Fair point. Except they were driving in a straight line now, no corners or tight bends to manoeuvre. And still the banging continued.

It didn't take Tommy long to come to the same conclusion. 'You know what I said about the coffin sliding about? Well, I was—'

'Wrong,' finished Lucas. He flicked the indicator. Began to slow down.

'What are you doing?' asked Tommy.

'Pulling over,' said Lucas. He brought the Transit to a halt in a lay-by at the side of the road. 'Let's open her up and take a look in the back. See what all that noise is about.'

CHAPTER SEVEN

Mercy should really have been resting.

Either laid out on the sofa or tucked up in bed. Fast asleep. Recuperating before her night shift guarding the coffin. Just like Rose, who had locked herself away in her room for the past few hours.

And yet Mercy wasn't doing anything of the kind.

If anything, she was doing the exact opposite.

Early afternoon, feeling restless, Mercy had kept a promise she had made a few weeks ago and headed down to the Come Fly With Me boxing club. She had run there. Cockleshell Farm to the centre of Stainmouth. Four miles. Maybe four-and-a-half. More than enough to get the heart pumping. A perfect warm-up for what was to come.

An afternoon in the ring.

As she'd hoped, the members of the club had welcomed her warmly with open arms. Open arms *and* clenched fists. To a man, they had practically been queuing up to spar with her. She had started with the biggest, Eddie, an old acquaintance, and then moved down the ranks, offering advice along the way.

Tips and tricks of the trade. Constructive criticism. As far as she could tell, everybody had listened. Everybody had benefited. Everybody had gone home happy.

Job done. Satisfaction guaranteed.

About two hours in, Mercy had taken a break. She had barely wiped the sweat from her forehead, before the club's owner, Nimble, a short man in a red tracksuit and flat cap, had sought her out.

'Word in your shell-like, my dear,' he said, sneaking up behind her. 'You're a woman, right?'

Mercy nodded. 'Well spotted.'

'I mean, you're not exactly the soft and gentle kind,' continued Nimble clumsily, 'but you're still a woman with ... erm ... womanly ways.'

Mercy frowned. She didn't like where this was heading. 'You're not asking me out, are you?'

'I wouldn't dare,' said Nimble hastily. 'Not that there's anything wrong with you. You're very pretty. I just wouldn't like a bird ... sorry ... *girlfriend* who could beat the living daylights out of me.'

'You know that hole you keep on digging?' said Mercy. 'You should probably think about putting that spade down now.'

Nimble held up his hands. 'Consider me spade-less. Listen, to cut a long story short, I need your help. There's a boy over there, in the locker room. Solomon. Good kid. Respectful. Polite. Decent boxer, too. But he's got problems. You can just tell, can't you? There's something hanging over him, weighing him down.

He used to be quiet before, but now he's practically mute. I've tried to talk to him, but he just clams up. One-word answers. Nothing more. Some of the other lads have tried as well, but it's always the same. He shuts down. Avoids eye contact. Now, I know what you're thinking. This is a boxing club, not the scrabble society. Young men don't want to talk about their feelings. Not when they're full of—'

'Macho bullshit,' chipped-in Mercy.

'Yeah, something like that,' said Nimble. 'And that's why I hoped that you, a woman, with your aforementioned womanly ways, could—'

'Do the job on your behalf?' finished Mercy.

Nimble fiddled awkwardly with his zip. 'Yeah, in a nutshell. Just try to talk to him. Get him to open up. So ... is that a yes?'

Mercy blew out. 'I'm hardly going to say no, am I?'

'Excellent.' A grinning Nimble rubbed his hands together. 'I knew you wouldn't let me down. You're one of the good 'uns. No time like the present either.'

'No, I guess not.' Mercy was about to make her way towards the locker room when Nimble skipped in front of her.

'You know that thing you were on about earlier,' he mumbled. 'Me asking you out—'

'No,' said Mercy firmly.

Nimble threw up his arms. 'You don't even know what I'm going to say.'

'It's still a no,' insisted Mercy. 'You need someone more your own age ... and height.'

'Suit yourself,' shrugged Nimble. 'You don't know what you're missing, though. Nimble by name, nimble by nature. You'd soon change your mind if you saw me doing cartwheels in the nude.'

'It's a chance I'm prepared to take,' said Mercy, back on the move.

Nimble let her pass with a smile and something that half-resembled a curtsy. He was a curious little man, thought Mercy, as she swerved around him. Good natured, though. Easy to talk to.

Unlike the nut she was about to crack.

CHAPTER EIGHT

Lucas jumped out of the Transit and made his way around to the back doors.

He was about to pull them open when Tommy appeared beside him. 'Wait! You don't know what's in there.'

Lucas responded with a frown. 'I know exactly what's in there. A coffin with a body inside.'

'You hope. What if there's something else, though? Something spooky? Something supernatural? Something that could ... oh, don't mind me. I was only talking.'

Lucas, not in the mood to be held up by idle chit-chat, had already opened one of the van doors. Yes, he was barely listening, but that's not to say he didn't take Tommy's warning seriously. Leaning forward, he poked his head in first and looked around. Sure enough, there was nothing in there except the coffin. The banging had stopped, too. Panic over.

'Strange.' Lucas opened the other door so he could climb inside. 'Maybe it was something else. The brakes. Tyres. Suspension—'

'A ghost?' said Tommy, before adding an inane *woo-woo* noise that managed to irritate Lucas far more than it should have.

'We're the only ghosts around here,' he muttered under his breath. Crouching down, he placed his hands on the coffin and tried to ease it to one side. It was still heavy, despite its size. There was no way it could've moved around by itself. Not at the speed they had been travelling.

Lucas was all set to climb back out the van when the banging sound returned.

'Don't piss around,' he snapped, fixing Tommy with a steely glare.

Tommy lifted his hands. 'This has got nothing to do with me.'

Both men stared at the coffin. Right on cue, it began to violently shake. It was enough to send Lucas staggering backwards, his body crashing against the side of the van.

'Steady,' said Tommy, offering support with an out-stretched arm. 'You'll do yourself an injury.'

And just like that, the coffin stopped shaking.

'What's going on?' cried Lucas, struggling to comprehend what had just happened.

'Only one way to find out.' Tommy disappeared from view. He returned a few seconds later carrying a small cloth bag that was tied up with string. 'I spotted this earlier in the glove compartment when I was searching for biscuits. Thought it might come in handy at some point.'

Tommy placed the bag in the back of the van and emptied its contents. There was a wrench. A screwdriver. A crowbar.

Swirling a finger, he pretended to select the crowbar at random.

Lucas didn't flinch. 'What do you expect me to do with that?'

'Open the coffin,' said Tommy matter-of-factly. 'Whatever's in there, it wants to get out.'

'I know the feeling well.' Lucas reluctantly took the tool and set to work. He tried not to think about what he was doing, but it was impossible to ignore. 'You can go to Hell for doing something like this,' he grumbled, loosening the lid with every nail he removed.

'We were in Hell the moment we woke up in Stainmouth,' remarked Tommy. 'That's punishment enough for anyone.'

Lucas steadied himself as the final nail fell into the back of the van.

'Go on then,' urged Tommy. 'Take it off and free the spirits.'

Lucas scowled at him. 'I'm going to. Give me a chance.'

'Yeah, well, chop-chop,' said Tommy, leaning in for a closer look. 'This is too much. The anticipation is making my balls tingle.'

Lucas knelt down. He was about to remove the lid when his worst fears came true.

The lid removed itself.

Right before his eyes, as if pulled by some invisible force, it slid to one side and landed in the back of the van.

Lucas scrambled to his feet, fearful of the unknown.

When he looked again, there was a body rising from the coffin.

A man. Middle-aged. Small and slightly built. An old face on a tiny body. A thick head of fair hair and reading glasses. Suited and booted. Laid to rest in his finest Sunday attire.

This was a Monday, though. And the man was still alive.

'Shit!' Tommy backed away from the van, dangerously close to the cars that sped past him. 'He's not dead!'

'Really? I hadn't noticed,' scowled Lucas.

The man sat up. Just like the coffin he had been trapped in, he was shaking uncontrollably. Struggling to catch his breath.

Reaching out, Lucas rested a hand on the man's shoulder. 'Whoa! Calm down. It's okay.'

The man ignored him, choosing, instead, to reach over for the crowbar. He launched it a second later, sending it arcing through the air. Tommy covered his head, relieved to hear the tool land in the bushes somewhere beyond the lay-by. When he looked again, the man was up and out of the coffin. With a little shimmy, he swerved Lucas's last gasp attempt to grab him and leapt out of the van. He had barely touched down before he was back on the move. Without a second thought for his own safety, he half-limped, half-scampered, straight into the road.

Straight into trouble.

Trouble being a silver Subaru that didn't see him coming.

CHAPTER NINE

Mercy wandered casually into the locker room.

There was only one other person in there. The youth called Solomon. Sat on a long wooden bench, he was sipping at an energy drink whilst staring vacantly at a blank brick wall. Mercy gave him a quick once over. He was late teens, at a guess. Eighteen or nineteen. Tight dreads and a smattering of patchy stubble. Long and lean. Flailing limbs hidden beneath a baggy, black tracksuit.

'You okay?' Mercy tried to make it sound natural. She only half-succeeded.

Not that Solomon seemed to notice. His only response was the slightest of nods, the wall still the focus of his attention.

'Fancy a few rounds?' Raising her fists, Mercy threw a combination of punches at thin air. 'I'll go easy on you. I promise.'

Solomon shook his head.

Bugger.

'I'm Mercy,' she said, trying to find another angle.

'I know.' A silence fell upon the locker room. 'I'm Solomon,' he said eventually.

Mercy nodded. What now? Gently, gently? Not a chance. Better to get straight to it. No point pissing about. 'Nimble reckons you've been off it recently. Not yourself. Quiet. Withdrawn—'

'He had no right to tell you that.' Solomon stood up. Not angry as such. Offended, if anything. 'What's it got to do with you?'

'Nothing,' shrugged Mercy. 'Not really. Except ... Nimble's worried. He clearly cares about you. About *all* of you. And that's why I stupidly agreed to come and have a chat. He thought you might open up to someone not quite so ... erm ... ball heavy. Now, you can either tell me to get lost ...' Mercy waited for the inevitable reply. Surprisingly, it didn't come. 'Or we can start again,' she continued. 'Get to know each other. And then you can tell me what the problem is, preferably before I get frustrated and beat it out of you.'

The slightest of smiles crept across Solomon's features as he sat back down again. 'I'm fine. It's just ... you know ... other stuff. Away from here. At home.'

'I'm all ears.' Mercy joined him on the bench. Waited for Solomon to fill in the gaps. He didn't, though. 'I've been in places like this all my life,' she said, looking around her. 'It's a testosterone ticking timebomb. Survival of the strongest and all that nonsense. Thing is, I'm not like the others. I'm not trying to prove how tough I am. Anything you tell me now goes no further. I won't repeat it back to Nimble. Not if you don't want me to. You can trust me. And who knows? Maybe I can help—'

'It's my step-dad, Errol,' Solomon took a moment to choose his words carefully. 'It was bad before, when my mum was still alive. Now it's unbearable.'

Mercy mulled it over. 'It's an awkward relationship, having a step-family. Maybe he's just struggling to deal with your mum's—'

Solomon jumped back in before she could finish. 'It's not like that. Not at all. He used to hit my mum. All the time. She denied it, but I knew. It was horrible, but I was too young to do anything about it. That's why I started to come here. I wanted to get stronger. Learn how to protect her. She died before I got the chance, though. After that, Errol took his anger out on me. He flies off the handle at the drop of a hat.' Solomon rolled up his sleeve. There were two red burns on his forearm, trying to scab over.

'Nasty,' said Mercy. 'How did you do that?'

Solomon shook his head. 'I didn't – *he* did. He stabbed me with his ciggie. Said I was disrespecting him. I had barely said a word, though.' Solomon lowered his sleeve, but then pulled up his top. His ribs and stomach were covered in a variety of bruises. 'He hits me all the time,' he mumbled. 'Mostly when I'm not ready. I want to fight back, I really do, but ...' Solomon tailed off.

'Go on,' said Mercy. 'Please.'

Solomon turned his face away so he could wipe his eyes. 'He's bigger than me. Bigger, stronger, meaner. I'm worried that if I retaliate, he'll hit me even harder. I'm screwed, aren't I? There's nothing I can do.'

Mercy could feel her blood beginning to boil. Solomon was right. What could he do? He was trapped in an impossible situation, left with little choice but to soak up the abuse and put on a brave face?

No.

There had to be another way. This man, this vile excuse for a human being, couldn't just get away with it.

'I'd move out if I could, but I can't afford it,' said Solomon. 'I only work part-time. I'm combining it with a course at college. Sports coaching with kids. You know, going into schools and stuff. The money's terrible at first, but it'll get better once I've qualified.'

Mercy nodded. She understood alright. Understood how hard it was to make a living when you were young. Short-term struggle for long-term gains. Either that or reject the system completely. Bend the law until it snapped in two. She had done that herself, of course. But then that was how she had wound up in Stainmouth.

'Tell me I'm not fucked,' said Solomon, out of the blue.

Mercy fiercely shook her head. 'You're not fucked. I'll sort it.'

'Really?' Solomon looked at her properly for the first time. 'How are you going to do that?'

'Give me your address,' said Mercy. 'I'll go round. Have a word. Your step-dad, Errol, he doesn't have to treat you like a son – he doesn't even have to like you – but he can't hurt you.

That's unacceptable.'

'What if he won't listen?' said Solomon, clearly not convinced.

'Oh, he'll listen,' insisted Mercy. 'I'll make sure of it.'

Solomon stood up and walked over to a small table in the corner of the room. He found a pen there and some scraps of paper. When he had finished writing, he folded the paper and handed it to Mercy.

'I'll be round as soon as I get the chance,' she said. 'Just keep your head down until then and stay out of his way. Here, pass me that pen ...' Mercy ripped the paper in half before taking the pen from Solomon. 'That's my number,' she said, handing him one half. 'Call me if things get too much to bear.'

Solomon nodded. 'I will.'

'Good.' Mercy climbed up off the bench and walked towards the exit. The grunts and groans grew louder the closer she got. Young men huffing and puffing as they pounded the pads, the bag, or just each other. 'Fancy those few rounds yet?' she asked, stopping in the doorway.

Solomon's shoulders slumped as he sat back down again. 'No, you're okay. I'm not in the mood.'

Mercy studied him for a moment. Poor kid. He didn't deserve that. But then no one did.

One way or another, she would stick to her promise.

She would sort it.

CHAPTER TEN

Miles moved the phone away from his ear.

His brain was spinning, struggling to make sense of what he had just been told.

The dead had awoken.

That was only half of it, though. The dead had awoken ... and then managed to go straight back to sleep by walking blindly into passing traffic.

'You still there, Millie?'

Miles stirred. Lifted the phone to his ear. 'Yes, I'm still here. And don't call me Millie. It's not funny. Not in the slightest.'

'It's not supposed to be,' insisted Tommy, trying not to laugh. 'I was being affectionate. I thought you'd like it.'

'No, you didn't,' argued Miles. 'You knew it would annoy me. Much like everything you've just told me, in fact. Only you and your bumbling pal could fail to transport a coffin from one location to another without something going horribly wrong. Where are you now?'

'At the hospital,' said Tommy. 'Well, in the corridor. The runaway corpse is being given the once over by the doctor. He was out for the count last time I saw him. If he wasn't dead before, he probably is now.'

Miles processed that particular nugget of information. 'Right, stay where you are and don't let that body out of your sight. I'll call Agatha. See what she has to say on the matter ...'

Shit.

That was the first word that passed Agatha's lips. Followed swiftly by several other mumbled expletives that Miles could barely make out.

'Sorry,' she said. 'That was unprofessional of me. Sometimes you have to get it off your chest, though. Better that than keep it stored up.'

'Don't worry about it. I've heard worse.' Miles took a moment to mull things over. 'You don't think this is a set-up, do you?'

'A set-up?' Agatha only repeated it to buy herself some time. The assignment had seemed decidedly dodgy right from the very beginning. And now this. Dead, alive, and maybe dead again in a matter of minutes. What was that? An unfortunate occurrence? Or had Goose and his cronies planned it all along?

'I don't know,' she sighed eventually. 'I mean, let's think about this logically. What good reason would anybody have to set us up?'

'They don't like us,' offered Miles. 'All those at the top. The Stainmouth establishment. Maybe they see us as a hindrance. An unnecessary inconvenience interfering in their business, sticking our noses into places we shouldn't.'

'You think they don't want us here?' Agatha snorted. 'They're not the only ones. *We* don't want us here either.'

'True. But with familiarity comes contempt. They didn't know us when we first arrived. They do now.'

'Okay, I get it. I suppose there are lots of reasons somebody might object to us. Well, one *somebody* in particular. Just give me twenty minutes, will you, Miles? Then we'll come and get you. I've got a call to make first. As things stand, we're completely in the dark. Questions need to be asked if we want to see where we're heading.'

And that was that. Conversation over. Without thinking, Miles stuck his phone back in his pocket and walked towards the door to his hotel room. 'Yeah, questions need to be asked,' he grumbled under his breath. 'Just don't hold your breath waiting for an answer.'

'What in the name of buggery are you chirpin' on about, woman?'

The Chief Constable, Clifford Goose, had dragged himself out of a surprisingly vigorous massage for this. A delirious phone call with the not-so pleasant Pleasant. Who did she think she was? Throwing around accusations? Pointing painted fingernails in his direction? No, she had a lot to learn if she was going to set up camp in Stainmouth. Starting with …

'Respect,' boomed Goose.

'You can stick your respect,' said Agatha sharply. 'Let's just concentrate on the truth, shall we? Who was ... *is* the corpse?'

Goose weighed it up. Give a little, not a lot. Just enough to shut her up. 'His name is Impetus Stokes. Also known as the Imp. He was doing seven years in prison for robbery when he passed away—'

'And yet he didn't, did he? Pass away, I mean.'

'Apparently not. Accordin' to you and yours, it was just an unusually deep slumber. The Sleeping Beauty of Stainmouth. Which one of you woke him up with a sloppy kiss?'

Agatha could feel the hairs prickle on the back of her neck. He was mocking her. Making light of a serious situation. 'Why were we collecting him?'

'S.A.S,' barked Goose. 'Safety and security. We had reason to believe that some notoriously heavy undesirables might try to take a pop at him.'

'At a dead body?' Agatha shook her head. 'Why?'

'Why not? The mind of your commonplace criminal is not something I choose to analyse on a daily basis. Now stop wittering, woman, and listen. I'm not wetting my knickers, so why are you? Just keep your peepers fixed on Stokes—'

'Shouldn't be too difficult. By the sound of things, he's in a bad way.'

'Good.' Goose checked himself. 'No, not good. Just easier, that's all. Right, I'll get back to you when I feel the need to talk some more—'

'We haven't finished yet.'

'One of us has.'

'Do not hang up, Clifford.'

'I've got to get back to work, Miss Pleasant. Gunther is waiting for me.'

'I'm warning you ...'

'Goodbye.'

Agatha stared at her phone. He had gone. How dare he, the ignorant pig?

Her first thought was to call him back. Thankfully, that thought soon passed as she drew breath, swept her emotions to one side and re-focussed. Dead or alive, nothing had changed. Impetus Stokes, for the time being at least, was under their care.

They had a job to do.

CHAPTER ELEVEN

Lucas pressed his nose up to the window.

Three floors up in a private room, he had a perfect view of the Stainmouth County Hospital car park. At first glance, space was at a premium. You either got lucky or you didn't. Not that Lucas cared either way. He had barely noticed the tricky manoeuvres and occasional road rage as drivers fought for an opening. No, his gaze was fixed primarily on one car in particular. A black Ford Focus. Eight years old, but still in good nick. Decent, yes, but not something that would ever grab anybody's attention. To your average passer-by, it was bog standard. Run of the mill. Boring.

And that was the problem.

'Can't you just use a tissue like a normal person?'

Lucas turned back into the room. 'What are you talking about?'

'You,' grinned Tommy. He was over by the door, balanced precariously on the back two legs of a plastic visitor's chair. 'I don't like you wiping your nose on the window. If you haven't got a tissue, try using the bed covers. I'm sure matey boy here won't mind. He's got more important things to worry about than snotty sheets.'

Matey boy – also known as the runaway corpse – was flat on his back, only half-filling the single bed that took up much of the floor space.

'I was watching, not wiping,' said Lucas, resting a hand on the glass. 'There's a car down there.'

Tommy's eyes widened. 'A car? In the car park? Wow! Wonders will never cease!'

'A black Ford Focus,' continued Lucas, refusing to bite. 'It arrived at the same time as we did and has been parked up ever since. There are two men inside who haven't moved an inch. Big men. Middle-aged. Fifties. Maybe more. Proper goons. They're just sat there, staring at the entrance.'

'And?'

'And it's strange, don't you think? No one comes to a hospital to take in the sights. And it's even stranger when you consider they've been following us.'

Tommy gazed up at the ceiling. Rolled his eyes. 'Well, that escalated quickly, didn't it? Not like you to over-think things. They're probably just ambulance spotters or something. Now, why don't you take the strain off your size tens and chill out before you give yourself a heart attack?' Tommy looked on in disbelief as Lucas squeezed past the bed and marched towards the exit. 'Where are you going now?'

'The car park,' replied Lucas, refusing to slow as he opened the door and stepped outside. 'Don't miss me too much.'

'No chance of that happening.' Tommy waited for the door to close before he stretched his arms above his head and yawned. Ah, that was better. A bit of privacy for a change. Well, practically. There was still the napping gnome, of course, but he wasn't the most demanding of patients. Not in his current state, at least.

Tommy yawned again. Mercy and Rose would be here soon to relieve them of their duties. That was the plan. After that, he'd be his own boss. In control of his destiny. A quick cat nap now and he'd be ready for the night ahead. What day was it again? Monday. Not the liveliest in all honesty. A bit of a damp squib. Still, he could always hit the town early. Get straight on it. Draw them in with his wit and repartee. Oh, and good looks. Obviously. That was his USP, after all. Within minutes, he'd be the centre of attention. Monday's main event.

Gather round, one and all. Welcome to the wild and wonderful world of Tommy O'Strife.

Or maybe he would just stay in. A couple of sherries with Proud Mary at Cockleshell Farm. A nature documentary and buttered crumpets. Yeah, that was more like it. Why dream big when you can settle for the mundane?

Tommy groaned out loud as the handle dropped and the door to the private room opened.

'That was quick,' he muttered, refusing to turn around. 'What happened? Did the big, bad men tell you to keep your beak out, you nosey prick?'

'And which big, bad men would that be?'

The voice was clear and concise. And didn't belong to Lucas.

'Bloody hell!' Tommy rocked forward on his chair. Almost fell off as the legs skidded across the floor. 'You scared the shit out of me!'

'Nice to see you too, Mr O'Strife,' said Agatha. She was standing in the doorway, arms crossed, deadly serious. Miles was slightly behind her, trying not to smile. 'Mr Thorne, however, seems to be conspicuous by his absence,' she continued. 'Any ideas where he might be?'

'He's using the facilities.' Tommy pointed between his legs as if it needed explaining. 'Weak bladder. Not like me. My bladder's up there with the best of them. I'm like a human camel. I store my water in my humps.'

'Lovely,' said Agatha, trying not to dwell on that particular image. 'And did Lucas arrange to meet these big, bad men you mentioned in the lavatory, or was he just hoping to get lucky?'

Tommy held up his hands. 'You've got me. All that bladder stuff was a load of old bollocks. Nah, Lucas has gone downstairs. To the car park. There's a car there—'

'In the car park?' Miles put a hand to his mouth. Gasped in mock horror. 'Go figure.'

Tommy clicked his fingers in agreement. 'Yeah, that's what I said, but Lucas wasn't having none of it. It's the copper in him. The *ex*-copper. He always knows best. Well, he *thinks* he does.'

Miles squeezed past Agatha as he moved towards the window. 'Which car was it?'

'A black one,' replied Tommy.

'Helpful,' muttered Miles. Like Lucas, he pressed his nose up to the glass.

'A Ford Focus,' said Tommy, filling in the gaps. 'I tried to talk him out of it, but—'

'Decided to give up soon after and have a nice little sleep instead,' frowned Agatha.

'Just resting my eyes,' Tommy shot back. 'The brain, however, is always awake.'

'Pleased to hear it.' Agatha walked over to Miles. Laid a hand on his shoulder. 'Check up on Mr Thorne, will you? It's probably nothing—'

'*Definitely* nothing,' said Miles.

'But it's still better to be safe than sorry,' finished Agatha. 'I'll stay here with Mr O'Strife. Make sure he doesn't drop off again.'

Miles nodded. Left the room without another word.

'Just the two of us,' sang Tommy, settling back in his chair.

'*Three* of us.' Agatha pointed towards the bed. 'His name is Impetus Stokes. More commonly known as the Imp. Make yourself comfortable, Mr O'Strife, because we're not going anywhere until the dead decides to stir for a second time.'

CHAPTER TWELVE

Hurrying out of the hospital, Lucas tried to get his bearings.

The private room on the third floor was directly above the car park. Which meant he shouldn't have to look too hard to find ... ah, there it was. Hidden amongst the numerous Nissans and various Volkswagens. A perfectly ordinary, exceptionally unexceptional black Ford Focus.

Without breaking stride, Lucas veered towards it. He kept a steady pace. Not too fast, not too slow. The smooth, confident walk of a man at ease with his current situation. Yeah, whatever you say. Maybe he should try telling his heart that. Preferably before it burst out of his chest and rolled into the nearest gutter.

He had a plan of attack. No, not attack. That was the wrong word completely. Nothing so threatening. Little more than a gentle word should do the trick. Accompanied by a cheery demeanour and sympathetic smile. With any luck, it would all pass without incident. There was no reason to think the worst all the time. No need to listen to the over-active imagination of a suspicious mind. *His* suspicious mind.

And yet ...

Lucas had been here before. Plenty of times. Too many to count in all honesty. Routine, everyday situations that turned sour in the blink of an eye. A misplaced word or sideways glance that led to total chaos and bewildering confusion. With that in mind, surely it was best to suspect everyone rather than no one at all. Harsh perhaps, but it was a rule that Lucas had adhered to for much of his adult life. Both alive *and* dead. If they *looked* dodgy, then they most probably were. And the Ford Focus certainly looked dodgy. As did the two men sat inside of it.

And if he was wrong? Well, just apologise and move on. Sorry. My mistake. No harm done.

Lucas slowed his step as he drew level with the car. The two men were both sat in the front, staring straight ahead. They looked almost identical. Granite-faced. Balding heads shaven to the scalp. Matching woollen overcoats fastened to the chin. Brothers. Twins even. The only actual difference was the horn-rimmed glasses that the man in the passenger seat was wearing. The lenses were so thick they gave him an almost alien-like quality.

Which probably explains why Lucas chose left over right and opted for the driver instead.

Crouching down, he tapped on the window with his knuckle. It began to lower. Close up, Lucas knew that his assessment had been spot on. These were hard men cut from a different cloth.

'Can we help you?' That was the driver. His voice was gruff, tone flat. Not unfriendly. Just lacking even a modicum of emotion.

'I hope so.' Lucas forced a smile. Keep it light. 'I've not been spying – honestly – but you've been parked here for ages. There's nothing wrong with that, not in the slightest. It's just ... a bit ... odd.'

The driver didn't bat an eyelid. 'Odd?'

'Don't you think?' pressed Lucas.

'Do we think? Do ... we ... think?' The passenger with the horn-rimmed glasses leant over, eyes wild behind his lenses, before the driver restrained him with a firm hand on his chest.

'Allow me,' he said calmly. He turned back to Lucas. 'You've done us a favour, boy.'

'Boy?' Lucas sensed movement and stood up straight. Sure enough, the passenger with the horn-rimmed glasses had climbed out of his seat and was walking around to the driver's side of the vehicle. He was shorter than Lucas, but not by much. Stockier, though. Muscle not fat. Threat level way above average. 'I'm not here to cause trouble,' said Lucas hastily.

'And neither are we,' remarked the driver. 'We're law-abiding citizens. As honest as the day is long. But if there's one thing I can't stand, it's airing my dirty laundry in public. How about you hop in the back and we can discuss things further? In private? Just the three of us?'

'No. I don't think—' Lucas tried to edge away, but the passenger had blocked him in. There was nowhere to go.

'I do,' the passenger insisted.

Lucas felt a sharp, stabbing pain. He lifted his arm and looked down, surprised to see that there was a small handgun digging into his ribs. 'Whoa! There's no need for—'

'There's every need,' said the passenger. 'Just get in.' He pulled open the car door and bundled Lucas onto the back seat. 'Don't,' he warned, sliding in beside him. 'Don't shout. Don't scream. And don't you dare move a fucking muscle! We're going for a little ride.'

'That sounds nice, doesn't it?' The driver glanced at Lucas in his rear-view mirror as he started the engine. 'Whether you return in one piece, however, is entirely down to you, boy.'

CHAPTER THIRTEEN

Mercy slowed her step as she reached the driveway to Cockleshell Farm.

That was harder than she had expected. The warm-down from Come Fly With Me to Croplington. A few weeks ago she would've run that in her sleep.

A few weeks ago, however, felt like a different lifetime after everything that had happened.

When she was still *alive*, she used to train every day without fail. Work herself into the ground until she had nothing left to give. It was either that or come unstuck in the ring. Bare-knuckle boxing was brutal enough even when you were in the best of shape. Take your eye off the prize and some other fighter would knock the wind out of your lungs before the bell had even sounded.

Mercy leant against the door as she caught her breath. What was she now? In this, her new life? Some kind of undercover agent? A private investigator? Neither quite fit the bill. Just a puppet on a string, then. A body that Agatha Pleasant could move about wherever, whenever, she liked. Why, though?

Or rather, why Mercy?

There were millions of other people that Agatha could've chosen. What did she have that was so special? Yes, she could fight, but that was all. Barring her obvious street smarts, she wasn't particularly intelligent. She had no skills to speak of. Which got her thinking. Would anyone really miss her if she jumped ship and headed for home? Tommy had tried before, of course. Tried and failed. So, was that it? Give up at the first hurdle? Roll over and let them walk all over you? No chance. What was the old saying again?

If at first you don't succeed ...

Breathing back to something resembling normal, Mercy opened the door and wandered into the farmhouse. She had barely crossed the threshold, however, before her phone began to vibrate. She removed it from the running belt around her waist and studied the screen.

No caller ID.

She was about to answer when the vibrating stopped. A moment later, the wind caught the door and it slammed shut behind her. She jumped ... but nowhere near as high as Rose. Sat in the sitting room, she practically hit the ceiling as she leapt up off the sofa.

'Whoops.' Mercy raised her hands by way of an apology. 'You forget how blustery it is around here sometimes.'

Rose nodded as she sat back down again. She was shaking, though. Mercy could see that from the hallway.

'You on your own?' she asked, switching the phone from her

belt to her pocket. She looked around the room as she joined Rose on the sofa. 'Where did they put the coffin?'

'They didn't. You don't know, do you?' Rose waited for Mercy to shake her head. 'Miles called. Not long after you had left. There's been an accident. Nothing to worry about,' she added hastily. 'You're not going to believe this, though ...'

Rose was right; Mercy didn't believe it. Largely because it made no sense. The dead don't just wake up. Not when they've been prodded and probed for any sign of life and then dumped in a coffin.

'You should've called me,' said Mercy.

'I didn't think you'd want to be disturbed.'

'True. That's not the point, though.' Mercy pressed a hand against her phone. She thought it was vibrating again. Not this time. 'So, what have you been doing since you found out?'

'Nothing much,' shrugged Rose. 'Just thinking.'

Mercy tried not to show her concern. She didn't like it when Rose had time by herself. Dark thoughts led to dark actions. Dark actions with dire consequences. That was how Rose had *died*, after all. By thinking too much.

'Miles wants us at the hospital for eight.' Rose stopped abruptly, the worry clear on her face. 'I don't know how we'll get there—'

'Miles will have thought of something,' insisted Mercy. 'It's his job, remember.' She shifted slightly, surprised to find that on this occasion her phone really was vibrating. By the time she had removed it from her pocket, though, the outcome was much the same as before.

A missed call from *no caller ID*.

'Who was that?' Rose asked.

Mercy placed her phone down on the coffee table. 'Nobody.'

'It has to be *somebody*.'

'Yeah, obviously.'

'I didn't think anybody else had these numbers. Only the four of us. And Miles—'

'Oh, give it a rest, will you?' Mercy snapped as the frustration got the better of her. 'It's not important. Okay?'

She watched as a muted Rose visibly shrank before her very eyes. Her head dropped, her shoulders slumped, and her body disappeared into the sofa. And just like that, Mercy hated herself. Too blunt. Too harsh. Too much.

'Sorry.' Mercy stood up. 'I'm going for a shower. I'll be a different person when I come out. Well, I'll be less sweaty for a start.'

She was all set to leave when the same dull vibrations stopped her in her tracks.

Moving quickly, she snatched the phone up off the coffee table.

No caller ID.

This time, she answered. 'Hello.'

There was no reply. Not at first. But the background noise was intense. Crashing and banging about. A man shouting in the distance. Followed by a younger voice. Determined not to be overheard.

'Please ... you've got to help me.'

Mercy tensed up. 'Who is this?'

The call ended without warning. Mercy stayed where she was. Eyes glued to the screen.

'Is something the matter?' asked Rose.

Mercy hesitated. 'No. I don't think so. It was nothing. Nobody.'

She left the room without another word.

Rose held her tongue. Decided not to force the issue. If Mercy said it was nobody, then it was nobody.

Even if it wasn't.

CHAPTER FOURTEEN

Lucas peered out of the car window.

The Ford Focus was weaving its way through the meandering streets of Stainmouth. Emphasis on *mean*. Darkened back alleys and murky lanes. Unknown territory in a foreign land. Out of bounds at the best of times. And at the worst of times ...

Don't go there, thought Lucas. He closed his eyes. Drew a ragged breath. He had a horrible feeling that, one way or another, this was going to end badly. One way and the two big goons would beat him to a pulp before disposing of him like a used tissue. Another and they would put a bullet in his head and watch him die. Both were similar in so many ways, albeit with varying degrees of pain and suffering.

Unsurprisingly, neither exactly appealed.

The Focus ground to a shuddering halt, much to Lucas's dismay. There were abandoned garages on either side of him and a tall, wooden fence surrounded by trees straight ahead. No viable escape route. Your basic dead-end in the middle of nowhere.

'Get out.' The man with the horn-rimmed glasses waved the

gun in Lucas's face. 'Stand beside the car and don't do anything stupid.'

Lucas did as he was told. It was getting colder. And darker. A Stainmouth special. 'There's been a misunderstanding—'

'So you keep on saying.' The man with the horn-rimmed glasses lowered the gun and tucked it inside his waistband. Out of sight perhaps, but easy to reach.

'That's because it's true,' insisted Lucas. 'I've got no problem with you guys. I don't even know who you are.'

'I'm Sandy,' said the driver, joining them outside. 'And that's my brother, Maurice,' he added, gesturing towards the man with the horn-rimmed glasses. 'And you are ...?'

In the shit, thought Lucas. There was only one reason a couple of heavies would snatch you off the street and then willingly tell you their names. And that's because they were going to silence you forever. Most probably at the next available opportunity. Which was ... now.

Unless you could convince them otherwise, of course.

'And you are ...?' Sandy repeated.

This time Lucas didn't miss a beat. 'Police.'

Sandy's only response was a weary sigh. His brother, however, reacted differently. As if powered by an imaginary switch, Maurice clenched his fist and punched Lucas hard in the gut. Not once, but twice. Two quick shots without warning.

Lucas dropped to his knees as he gasped for breath. He hadn't been ready for that. That was his first mistake. Chances were, he couldn't afford another.

'You're not the police,' said Sandy, hauling Lucas to his feet. 'You know it. I know it. Even Maurice here knows it. Now, if there's one thing we both hate, it's being lied to. It's disrespectful. So, shall we try again? Who are you?'

'The ... police,' mumbled Lucas. 'I'm ... undercover.'

Maurice moved in, ready for second helpings, only to be warned off by his brother.

'This is getting tedious,' remarked Sandy. 'You're not the law, so stop pretending. We've been watching you. Coppers don't collect coffins from the back of a prison. And they certainly don't let the body inside go and play with the traffic. Very careless, that was. Most unprofessional. We followed your ambulance to the hospital, but that was where our trail grew cold. We lost you amongst the flashing lights and stumbling drunks. Funnily enough, we were about done when you came down to introduce yourself. Unlucky, son. A minute or two later and we'd have been long gone.'

Lucas steadied himself against the car. Decided to try a different approach now he could breathe again. 'Okay, my name is Lucas, but I'm a nobody. I just drive vans for a living. Take me back to the hospital and we can forget all about it.'

Lucas yanked open the car door. He expected Maurice would move fast to close it and, sure enough, he did. As soon as the man's hand shot out, Lucas slammed the door shut with as much force as he could muster, trapping Maurice's fingers inside. There was a moment's delay before the pain announced itself and he cried out in agony.

And in that moment's delay, Lucas made a run for it.

There was only one option, and that was the wooden fence. At a guess, it led into a garden. To a house. To civilisation. And if it didn't, well, it couldn't be any worse than his current location.

Lucas had hit top speed by the time he threw himself at the fence. He had almost clambered all the way to the top when two hands grabbed him roughly around the waist. Suddenly, he was heading the other way. Not up and over, but back down to where he had come from. He landed on two feet and spun around. He had barely raised his fists, however, before Sandy struck first. A knee to the groin was enough to disable Lucas immediately. The breath caught and his stomach turned as a dull ache washed over him. When he finally dared to stand up straight, Sandy was still there, but now he had company. Maurice had unpeeled himself and his fingers from the Focus. Those same fingers were now curled up by his side, blood dripping from the knuckles.

The fingers on his other hand, however, were holding the gun.

'Put that bloody thing away,' scowled Sandy. Grabbing Lucas by the neck, he threw him towards his brother. 'Get him in the car. If he won't talk to us here, then we'll take him to the Shooting Gallery. See how he likes that.'

'He won't,' muttered Maurice, dragging Lucas back towards the Focus. 'He won't like it one little bit.'

CHAPTER FIFTEEN

'What do you mean, he's vanished?'

Miles took a moment to compose himself. He had ignored the lift and opted for the stairs instead. Raced up to the third floor of the hospital as fast as his leather-clad feet would take him. Burst into the private room and blurted out a mumbled message that even he struggled to fully understand. That Agatha now wanted him to repeat it was hugely unfair under the circumstances. Not to mention downright impossible when you can barely breathe.

Still, an order was an order. Who was he to disagree?

'Lucas ... vanished.' Hunched over, hands on knees, Miles tried to suck in mouthfuls of air between every other word. 'Got down ... to the ... car park ... but he ... wasn't there.'

Agatha responded with a dismissive snort. 'Gone perhaps, but vanished? Bit over-dramatic, don't you think? He's not a magician. Maybe he's just wandered off. Entered via a different door. Got side-tracked. Maybe he's—'

'Using the facilities,' chipped-in Tommy. 'What did I tell you about his weak bladder? Trust me, he'll be dangling his little

Thorne over a toilet bowl right about now.'

Miles stood up straight. Puffed out his chest. He was feeling slightly more like himself. And slightly more like himself meant he was able to argue. 'There's something else. That car you mentioned. The black Ford Focus. It was just leaving the car park when I got downstairs.'

Agatha snorted again. Not so dismissively this time, though. 'What are you trying to say? You think Lucas has been kidnapped?'

'No ... I mean ... who knows?' shrugged Miles. 'Let's deal with the facts. Both Lucas and the Focus have gone. Make of that what you will.'

'You can track him though, can't you?' Tommy pointed an accusing finger in Miles's direction. 'Like you tracked me. With that thing you've put in my head. And don't say a brain because it wasn't funny the first time you said it.'

Miles shifted closer to Agatha. Spoke in a hushed tone behind his hand. 'He's right. I can't track Lucas here, though. I've not got the equipment. It's back at the hotel.'

Agatha nodded. 'Then that's decided. We'll go to your hotel and see if we can locate Mr Thorne. Mr O'Strife, meanwhile, can stay put and keep a close eye on our comatose friend here.' She frowned at Tommy. 'That's not beyond you, is it?'

'Do you really need to ask?' he grinned back at her. 'I can watch over a hospital bed in my sleep. No pun intended.'

'Miles will send the other two over to assist you forthwith,' said Agatha, turning towards the exit. 'Proud Mary can lend them her car. Just don't do anything silly before they get here.'

'As if,' said Tommy. He blew her a kiss, which she duly ignored as she left the room. Miles followed close behind, shutting the door on his way out.

Tommy gave it less than five seconds before he laughed out loud.

'So long, fuckers.' Not for the first time, he put his feet up on the bed, leant back in his chair and yawned. He took one last look at the patient and then closed his eyes. 'Sweet dreams, mister munchkin. Try not to disturb me if you wake up.'

CHAPTER SIXTEEN

Lucas could do nothing to stop himself from bouncing around in the footwell of the Ford Focus.

He had squeezed down there not through choice, but at gunpoint. Maurice was responsible for both. The gun and the pointing. All of a sudden, neither of the bald brothers wanted him to know where they were heading. A secret location perhaps, but they'd given it a name.

The Shooting Gallery.

Lucas shifted to one side as the Focus swung around a corner. He tried to steady himself by grabbing the closest thing to hand.

Maurice's leg.

'Get off me!' he growled.

Lucas was slow to oblige. He knew it was bound to stir up some kind of reaction or other.

And it did.

Maurice, still raging after having his hand trapped in the car, raised his other fist, ready to lash out. Lucas covered his head. Held his breath. He only relaxed when the goon didn't follow through with his actions.

The reason soon became clear, though, when the Focus came to a halt.

'We're here,' said Sandy, glancing over his shoulder. 'You two still the best of friends?'

'Inseparable,' scowled Maurice.

Lucas started to climb out of the footwell. He didn't get far, however, before a firm hand halted his progress.

'Stay down,' ordered Maurice. 'We need to put something over your head. Stop you from peeking.'

Sandy returned swiftly with a plastic shopping bag. He handed it to Maurice, who pulled it down over Lucas's face until it reached his chin.

'Can you see?'

'What do you think?' snapped Lucas.

Maurice's response was to slap him firmly across the face. Lucas winced. Not from the pain, but from the shock.

'That's what you get for a smart arse comment,' hissed Maurice under his breath. 'Next time it'll be twice as hard—'

'Let's save the violence until we're safely inside the Shooting Gallery,' said Sandy. 'We don't want any nosey neighbours belling the police now, do we? Some things are best kept private.'

Lucas felt the Focus rock as the other two men climbed out of the vehicle. Next thing he knew, he was being hauled out of the footwell and dragged along by his arm. Despite the makeshift blindfold, he could still sense the change in atmosphere as they moved indoors.

'Step,' said Maurice. Lucas processed the information a little too late and tripped. 'Don't you listen,' Maurice spat in his ear. 'I said step. We're heading upstairs.'

This time, Lucas lifted his feet. When they reached the top, Maurice pushed him firmly in the back, sending Lucas staggering forward. He somehow stayed upright. Thought about spinning around. Fighting back.

Instead, he turned slowly, fearful of what would happen next.

Two things.

A door closed. And the shopping bag was yanked roughly from his head.

Lucas blinked several times as his eyes adjusted to the light of a single exposed bulb. He was in an empty room. Bare walls and stripped-back floorboards. One window above a radiator.

'We found a rat in here once,' said Sandy, moving swiftly to close the curtains. 'A bit of company would be nice for you, wouldn't it?'

'I killed that rat,' said Maurice matter-of-factly. 'A dead man would be harder to get rid of, though.'

Lucas took a breath. They were trying to scare him. And it was working.

'Right, let's not stand on ceremony. Take a seat,' said Sandy.

Lucas looked around. Considered his options. Or lack of.

'On the floor,' said Sandy, reading his mind. 'Under the window.'

Lucas did as he was told. It surprised him when Maurice did the same. He was less surprised when he spotted a pair of handcuffs dangling from the man's fingertips.

'Keep still.' Lifting Lucas's wrist, Maurice cuffed him to a pipe that ran all the way along the wall beneath the radiator. 'On second thoughts, move around a bit. It'll give me a good reason to hurt you.'

Lucas sneered back at him. He'd had enough of this bullshit. The constant menace. The air of intimidation. 'What now?' he asked brusquely. 'What are we waiting for?'

The answer came, not from either man, but from downstairs. From the front door. Lucas heard it open and then close in quick succession. It was followed by the rhythmic beat of stomping boots. Whoever had entered was coming up the stairs.

Lucas watched as the door to the room swung open.

A bulky presence filled the entrance. A man. A bear of a man. Broad shoulders and a huge chest stuffed into a black woollen overcoat. A grey side-parting, dark eyebrows and scarred features that had seen more than their fair share of action. Similar in age to Sandy and Maurice, give or take a year or three.

A wrong 'un, decided Lucas. One of the old breed. Offended by anyone under the age of thirty with a tech addiction and a leaning towards social media.

'Who's this?' asked the man, jabbing a finger in Lucas's direction.

'Lucas, or so he says,' replied Sandy. 'We picked him up at the hospital.'

'Nice to meet you. I'm Frank. Frank DeMayo.' The man's

voice was markedly hoarse. Almost as if a lifetime of roll-ups and cheap whiskey had seriously damaged his vocal chords. 'You're looking a little confused, laddie. The DeMayo Diamond Gang? No? Didn't you do your research before my boys picked you up? I thought my name would've at least rung a bell or two.'

Lucas shrugged. 'Should it?'

Frank glared at the prisoner handcuffed to the radiator with a fierce intensity that could've halted traffic. 'For your sake, yes.' He edged closer. Stopped by Lucas's feet. 'I like to think I'm a fair man,' he began. 'Generous even. Play your cards right and that might be to your advantage. Neither of us wants to be here, Lucas, so let's move things forward, eh? Do as I ask and you can leave practically unscathed. Don't ... and you won't. It's that simple.'

Lucas nodded. Yeah, that wasn't so difficult. Hardly rocket science. And it wasn't as if he had anything to hide, after all. Well, not much. Only the whole Nearly Dearly Departed Club thing and nobody in their right mind would believe that, anyway. 'Go on.'

'You've got something I want,' remarked Frank. 'Something that's very dear to me.'

Lucas stopped nodding. 'Are you sure about that? Because I've not got that much—'

'Impetus Stokes.' Crouching down, Frank poked Lucas firmly in the chest as if to focus his attention. 'You've got him tucked up tight somewhere in that hospital ... and now I'd like him back!'

CHAPTER SEVENTEEN

Mercy was in the shower when Rose had taken the call.

This was no mystery mumbler, though, impossible to decipher.

No, this was Miles. Abrupt and direct. Straight down to business.

Get to the hospital.

'What's the hurry?' Wrapped in a towel, Mercy skipped from the bathroom to her bedroom whilst trying not to drip on the carpet. 'Didn't he bother to explain?'

Rose followed her to the door, but refused to cross the threshold. 'No. That was all he said. Get to the hospital. Then he hung up.'

'No please or thank you?' said Mercy, as she quickly dried herself.

'Nope.' Rose turned away, afraid of seeing something that she'd rather not.

At the same time, Mercy dressed as quickly as she could. 'Better get going then,' she said, squeezing past Rose as she made her way onto the landing. 'Maybe Proud Mary has got a tandem we can borrow.'

As luck would have it, the landlady at Cockleshell Farm met them at the top of the stairs. 'I've had my orders. I'm to give you these ...' She held out her hand and showed them a set of car keys. 'I've a Mini Clubman parked out in the yard. It's not exactly my pride and joy, but I'd rather it came back in something resembling one piece.' She took a moment to study the two women. 'There,' she said, placing the keys in Rose's palm. 'You look like the most trustworthy. Now, have you time for a spot of dinner or are you in a frantic rush like most young people these days?'

Young people. Mercy tried not to laugh. She didn't feel young. Not in the slightest. Not after everything she'd been through. It was the other part of the question that interested her the most, though. She was absolutely famished after her boxing session. And there was no way that would just fade away as the day turned to night.

'I mean, I am starving,' she replied.

Rose cleared her throat. 'I don't know if we've got time. Miles was quite insistent.'

'I've got a stew in the oven,' pressed Proud Mary, keen to prove that Miles wasn't the only one who could dig his heels in. 'A lovely bit of beef. Fresh vegetables. I can't eat it all by myself.'

Mercy nodded. Shook her head. Nodded again. 'I can smell it from here. It's only making things worse—'

'It won't take long to dish up,' said Proud Mary. 'You don't want to go out on an empty stomach. It's not healthy.'

Mercy could feel the heat from Rose's glare. She had taken the call, so didn't want to get on the wrong side of Miles. It was hard to argue with her logic. Worse luck. 'Thanks ... but no thanks,' she muttered. 'We've really got to go.'

'Suit yourself. The thing is ...' Proud Mary reached behind her and removed a plastic box from a side table. 'Can you take this to Thomas, please? He must've forgotten it on his way out. He's always so appreciative, though. Such a lovely boy. He makes it hard to say no.'

Mercy took the box. Lifted it up for a closer look. 'You've made him a pack-up. What's in it?'

'Thomas's ... erm ... favourite,' mumbled Proud Mary. 'I would never make it for myself ... it's not to my taste ...'

Mercy snorted. 'Knowing Tommy, it'll be something ridiculous like sugar sandwiches.'

That sentence alone was enough to make Proud Mary visibly cringe. 'It was what he asked for.'

'Oh, no way. That's unbelievable.' Mercy rolled her eyes at the elderly landlady as she took to the stairs. 'We might be late, so don't wait up.'

'Late?' Proud Mary jumped at the chance to shift the conversation away from Tommy's teatime treats. 'I've got a curfew. You can't just come and go as you please.'

'We know that,' said Rose, following Mercy down the stairs. 'We shouldn't be too long.'

'And if we are, you'll have to take it up with Miles,' shouted Mercy, already out of sight. 'We've got a job to do. We can't be shackled by curfews. The good people of Stainmouth are depending on us.'

'There are no good people in Stainmouth,' grumbled Proud Mary, as she set off down the stairs herself. 'Still, I guess that's why the four of you have been dumped on me ...'

The journey from Cockleshell Farm to the hospital passed largely without incident.

Or should that be passed *slowly* without incident?

Rose drove at a pace that would infuriate even the most patient of passengers, whilst Mercy gazed longingly at Tommy's pack-up, wondering just how hungry you had to be before sugar sandwiches became a viable option to snack on.

She was still none the wiser when Rose finally turned into the car park. It was seven o'clock. Visiting time.

'We're going to struggle to find a space,' muttered Rose, slowing to a crawl.

Mercy was about to offer some reassuring words – or just a grunt or two, whichever came first – when her phone caught her off-guard. *No caller ID* was lit up on the screen. He was back. Her mystery mumbler. It was almost as if he had never been away.

Mercy answered on the fourth vibration. 'Don't fuck around. If you've got something to say, then just say it.'

And this time, they did. Over a background of chaos and confusion, a panic-stricken voice spluttered and stammered and stumbled over words that didn't flow easily.

'Help ... you gotta' get me out of here ... I don't know what he's going to do next ...'

'Is that you, Solomon?' Mercy cursed herself. Of course it was. The boy from the boxing club was the only other person who had her number. How had it taken her so long to figure it out? 'What's wrong?'

'Please ... I'm not joking ... he'll kill me ... wait! He's trying to get in! I think ... no ... get away from me!'

A loud *bang*. An ear-splitting scream. And then the call ended abruptly.

'Mercy.' That was Rose. 'What's the matter?'

But Mercy wasn't listening. She was frozen in time. Paralyzed by the last few seconds. The fear in Solomon's voice was real. Sheer bloody terror. He wasn't faking it. Over-acting for attention. No, he was genuinely petrified. Rightly or wrongly, he believed he was going to die.

'Mercy.' Rose touched her on the arm. 'Who was that?'

Mercy continued to ignore her. Not intentionally. Her mind had shifted, though. From the here and now to somewhere else entirely.

The Mini was still drifting around in circles when Mercy flung open the door and scrambled out of the car. 'Move,' she said, rushing around to the driver's side.

Rose eased the car to a halt. 'I don't understand—'

'Get out. Now.' Mercy pounded on the window. Then she pulled open the driver's door. Grabbed Rose by the arm. The look of panic on the other woman's face, however, was enough to make her let go.

'Please,' said Mercy. 'I wouldn't normally ask. You know that.'

Rose unclipped her seat belt and climbed out of the Mini. She let Mercy push past her as she slid onto the driver's seat, albeit with one hand on the door so it couldn't be slammed shut.

'Mercy, you're scaring me,' she said, ducking her head inside. 'What's going on?'

'Just find the others. I'll be back before you know it.' Mercy hesitated. 'You trust me, don't you, Rose?'

Rose nodded. Took a step back so Mercy could close the door.

Without another word, the Mini was back on the move. Heading towards the exit. Towards Solomon. Towards the unknown.

Left stranded in the car park, Rose shuffled out of the road with Mercy's parting words ringing in her ears.

You trust me, don't you?

Yes, she did. She trusted Mercy unequivocally. She was the closest thing she had to a friend, after all. To family. If she couldn't trust her, who could she trust?

And that was the problem. Yes, she trusted Mercy.

It was just the rest of the world she wasn't so sure about.

CHAPTER EIGHTEEN

'I've never even heard of Impetus Stokes.'

It was hard to tell if Frank DeMayo was listening or not. The words may have sunk in, but the face remained the same. Cold. Impassive. Not that Lucas could do much about that. He was only being honest, after all. It wasn't his fault that the bear man and his grizzly companions didn't like what they were hearing.

'I'm telling the truth,' Lucas insisted. 'I swear. I don't know anybody called that. And it's not the sort of name you could easily forget now, is it?'

Frank turned to Sandy and Maurice, both of whom greeted his stare with a shake of their heads. 'My boys reckon you're lying out your arse,' he said bluntly. 'As do I. You had Stokes in the van. You let him out of the coffin. You called the fucking ambulance, for pity's sake! Don't tell me you don't know the Imp when you've spent all afternoon together.'

'Oh.' Lucas nodded. Slowly at first, before he picked up speed. 'You mean the dead guy, don't you?'

There was an echoing *crack* as Frank clapped his hands together. 'The penny drops ...'

Lucas switched the nod to a shrug. 'Today was the first time that I've ever met him. Not that we actually met. Not really. Only when he ... you know ... came back from the other side and got splattered by a—'

A sudden burst of movement was enough to cut Lucas off mid-sentence. It was Maurice. Bounding across the floorboards, he lifted his boot and stamped down hard on Lucas's left ankle without breaking stride. Lucas screamed out loud. Loud enough to reverberate around the empty room. Loud enough to be heard outside in the street.

Loud enough to enrage Frank.

'Do that again and there'll be repercussions,' he warned. 'And that's aimed at both of you!' He waited for Maurice to back away and Lucas to stop gasping for breath before he spoke again. 'Where's the key?'

Sandy and Maurice exchanged glances. Replied in unison. 'What key?'

'The key to the handcuffs.'

Maurice reached into his pocket. Held out his hand.

'People call me old-fashioned,' began Frank, as he took the key and waved it at Lucas. 'A dinosaur. Stubborn. Blinkered. Yeah, I get that. I'm a traditionalist. I don't like change. Those same people say I should move with the times. They say threats and intimidation don't work anymore. That I should try a bit of psychology. Mess with your mind. Bamboozle your brain. So, okay, let's give it a whirl, shall we? I'll try anything once. Listen, don't shit yourself, sunshine. I'm not going to play endless thrash metal on repeat. I just want to get inside your skull, that's all. Not send you doolally.' Crouching down, Frank positioned the key in the centre of the room. 'Oh, look at me,' he said, standing up. 'Mister Mind Games. Now, unless I'm mistaken, that key is just out of your reach. So close ... yet so far.'

Lucas leant forward so he could rub his throbbing ankle with his free hand. The pain, thankfully, was beginning to fade.

'I'll ask you again.' Frank placed his boot beside the key. 'Tell me the truth and I'll slide this across the floor. You can free yourself. Be on your way. Tempting, isn't it? A few words and you could be out of here.' Frank paused. 'We think the Imp is in the hospital, but that's where the trail ends. Which floor is he on? Which room? How many guards?' He paused again. 'And, yes, just in case you need reminding, the Imp is the dead guy you collected from the prison—'

'The not-so-dead guy,' muttered Lucas under his breath. 'Get your facts straight—'

The remark had barely left his lips before Maurice shot forward and stamped down for a second time. He switched ankle from left to right, sharing out the punishment.

The outcome was much the same as before. Lucas screamed as the pain shot all the way up his leg and through his body. Maurice hadn't finished, though. Leaning over, he was all set to swap stamps for blows when Frank grabbed him by the shoulders and flung him towards the door.

'Stand over there and don't move,' he barked. 'I don't work with loose cannons. From now on, you control your emotions or you'll be gone.' Rant over, Frank turned his attention to Lucas. 'As for you, you're either incredibly stupid or ridiculously brave. Whichever it is, I'm past caring. This Impetus Stokes problem needs to be sorted and sorted fast. You, however, can wait.' Frank nodded at Sandy, who joined Maurice by the exit. 'We're going now. Back to the hospital. I'm not like these two. I don't mind laying on the charm to get what I want. A bit of smooth-talking around the nurses should do the trick. I'm sure they'll be only too happy to tell us which room you've got Stokes stashed away in—'

'I haven't got anyone stashed away anywhere!' blurted out Lucas.

'Of course you haven't.' Frank opened the door and ushered the other two outside. 'We won't be long, I promise. Unfortunately, that'll be it. The end. I'll let Maurice off his leash and his ugly face will be your last living memory. Harsh perhaps ... but unavoidable. Still, that's life, I guess. Shit happens and then you die. No hard feelings,' Frank added, all set to close the door behind him. 'We'll be back soon.'

CHAPTER NINETEEN

Mercy wasn't entirely sure where she was going.

She knew the area, but not the individual streets. She had an address – seven Bartholomew Street – that Solomon had scrawled onto a slip of paper, but that was all. Maybe she should have asked. Sought directions. So bloody impatient. Rushing about like a maniac. She wasn't doing anyone any favours. Certainly not Solomon.

There was no point driving around in circles. Time was precious. Much like life itself.

Mercy pulled up by the side of the road. Lowered the car window. There was a couple walking towards her. A man and a woman. Younger than her, but not by much. Mid-twenties, give or take. Attractive in a clean, fresh kind of way. Hand in hand. Chatting. Smiling. Laughing. It was drizzling, but they didn't seem to care. Maybe they hadn't even noticed.

Oh, to be in love …

'Excuse me.' Mercy stuck her head out of the window. 'You don't know where Bartholomew Street is, do you?'

The couple came to a halt, the man first to break free from his companion's grasp.

'Yeah, I do. Let me think.' He stroked his chin as if to emphasise the point. 'You're not that far away ... take a left at the next turning, carry on and then when you get to the crossroads—'

'No, no, no.' The woman slipped in front of him. 'You're way off. Bartholomew Street is where Rob and Sally used to live ... we went there about a year ago ... before they moved to the Kingfisher estate ...'

Mercy tried to smile, but her knuckles were gripped tight around the steering wheel. Beyond impatient. Like a short fuse that had burnt too fast.

'Turn around and take the next right,' said the woman, sensing Mercy's agitation. 'You should see the sign after that. Don't listen to him,' she added, digging the man in the ribs with her elbow. 'He's terrible with directions.'

'I can always find my way around your body,' the man grinned. The woman gasped in shock before the two of them walked away. Still laughing and joking. Still side by side and hand in hand.

And still absolutely sickening, thought Mercy, as she started the engine. If that's what love does to you, then you can shove it.

Credit where credit's due, though. At least the directions were good. Mercy turned the car around, took the next right and there it was. Directly in front of her. The sign for Bartholomew Street.

She parked the Mini Clubman on the opposite side of the road, away from the streetlights. Climbed out and locked up. Took in her surroundings. The street was quiet. No traffic. No dog walkers. No kids hanging around looking for something to do. Number seven was well within sight. A small mid-terrace, neighbours on either side. Curtains drawn, lights on. Nothing special. A perfectly ordinary house on a perfectly ordinary street in a perfectly ordinary town. What did she expect? It was Monday evening. The dullest night of the week by any stretch of the imagination.

Satisfied that no one was watching her, Mercy set off across the road towards the house. How long had it been since she had taken that last call from Solomon? Ten? Fifteen minutes? Something like that. Was she too late? Too slow? She kept moving regardless. Through the gate. Along a short path. All the way to the ...

Shit.

Mercy stopped dead in her tracks. The front door to the house was slightly ajar. Just an inch or two, but open nevertheless.

That was the first warning sign.

And Mercy didn't have to wait long for the second. Shuffling forward, she poked her head around the door and peered inside. She couldn't see much beyond the hallway. Nothing unusual, at least. No, it was what she could hear that really disturbed her. It wasn't the echo of raised voices. Nor was it the shouts and screams of an anger-fuelled argument.

No, it was just sobbing.

Mercy listened carefully. It was coming from downstairs. Steadying herself against the door frame, she tried to settle her nerves. She had no wish to enter the premises. Not now. Not ever.

Suck it up, girl.

Mercy checked that the coast was clear before she slowly opened the door. She stopped when it was wide enough for her to squeeze through. Once inside, she closed it behind her. She was about to call out for Solomon, but decided against it. Better to err on the side of caution than announce her arrival.

She was stood in a darkened hallway flanked by doors on either side and a staircase straight ahead. She turned to her left and checked out the nearest room. The sitting room. The television was on, but someone had muted the volume. There was an upturned side table leant haphazardly against an armchair. Several half-empty beer bottles left to spill out over the carpet. That was the next warning sign. Bottles don't just topple over by themselves.

Mercy ducked out of the room. Turning to her right, she found herself in a narrow dining room. A rectangular wooden table and four chairs filled up much of the floor space. It was only when Mercy looked a little closer that she realised there were stains on the carpet. Red stains.

Patches of blood.

They were fresh and had barely soaked into the fabric. She followed their trail and saw red smears on the door that led to the kitchen.

That was more than a warning sign.

Mercy was shuffling now, fearful of what was to come. The sobbing was gradually getting louder. She was going the right way, if such a way existed.

She crept into the kitchen. Stopped mid-step.

The sobbing had died away, only to be replaced by a ringing in her ears. Suddenly she felt dizzy, lightheaded, as the room swirled and her vision dipped in and out. She had to keep her cool. Her focus. There would be repercussions now. Whether she liked it or not, she was involved.

She had wondered if she was too late as she walked towards the house.

A dead body sprawled out across the kitchen floor seemed to suggest that she was.

CHAPTER TWENTY

We'll be back soon.

Those were Frank's parting words. And yet Lucas had no wish to see him at all. Full stop. I mean, where was the incentive? Believe the threats and the big, burly villain was going to kill him. If not by his own hand, then by someone else's. Maurice's most probably. He was clearly the muscle. The unhinged maniac with a penchant for violence at a drop of a hat.

Lucas felt numb. This was insane. Even more insane was the fact that he should have listened to Tommy of all people. Way back in the hospital. *Take the strain off your size tens and chill out before you give yourself a heart attack.* Tommy had practically laughed at him when he said he was going downstairs to investigate. Well, who was laughing now? Not Tommy, that was for sure. Not if he was out trawling the streets of Stainmouth in search of his missing housemate. The same could be said of Mercy ... Rose ... Agatha and Miles ...

And Lucas. His own face was set somewhere between grim determination and absolute dread. What if this was it? Would he be missed? Did he mean that much to anyone anymore? Had he ever? The answer to each question was the same. Just the two words.

Probably not.

Lucas rubbed at his eyes with his free hand to clear away the dark thoughts. There was a time and place for wallowing in self-pity, and cuffed to a radiator in an empty house probably wasn't it. He had an hour, maybe two if he was lucky, before Frank and his boys returned. You could do a lot in that time.

Like getting the fuck out of there.

Shifting from his bum to his knees, Lucas lifted the arm that was attached to the pipe, counted down from three, and then pulled with all his might.

A *creak*. A *groan*. And then ... silence.

Lucas relaxed. The cuffs were predictably solid. Police issue at a guess. They weren't just going to snap. What about the pipe? Could he pull it off the wall? Highly unlikely if he was being honest. Still, he had to give it a go ...

Moving from his knees to his feet, Lucas turned around to face the radiator. Leant back on his heels. Tried to use his full weight to force the issue.

It didn't.

The pipe held firm as the cuffs dug into Lucas's skin. By the time he had stopped pulling, there were red lacerations running all the way around his wrist. Sheer bloody agony. Was it worth it? Not this time.

Think again.

No, don't think at all.

How could he have been so blind? Desperation, probably. Fear. Panic. Take your pick. Any or all of them were damn good reasons why he had ignored what was staring him straight in the face. Literally.

The key.

Frank hadn't just placed it in the centre of the room earlier – he had *left* it in the centre of the room. As hard as it was to believe, he had failed to pick it up before he departed. Shame on you, Frank DeMayo. Amateur hour at the hostage hotel.

Lucas's heart fluttered. The doubts had vanished. His way out of there was no longer a fantasy. It was well within reach.

Moving fast, he shuffled across the floorboards on his bum until his handcuffed arm was at its full length. Laying flat on his back, he stretched out his leg, pointed his toes and strained. There was no way he could make himself any longer. Lifting his head, he rested his chin on his chest and looked down at his feet. The key was to his left. If he could just drag it towards him, he could grab it with his free hand.

Put it like that and it sounded so simple …

Lucas lifted his heel and tried to place it on top of the key. To his horror, his leg spasmed and then fell without warning. The floorboards shuddered, and the key bounced. Lucas swore under his breath. The key had moved – that was a given – but how far?

Too far.

Not out of sight, but out of reach.

Lucas wriggled about on his back, but it was all to no avail.

He couldn't extend his body any further, not even a few inches.

He sat up, panting. A sudden burst of anger and he punched the floorboards. He had built himself up to breaking point. He had believed he could get out of there and one slight spasm had ruined everything.

Maybe cost him his life.

'Help!' he shouted. 'Anybody! Please! Ah, come on—'

Lucas stopped. Listened. The house was no longer silent. He could hear movement. Not the heavy stomp of Frank or one of his boys, but small, shuffling footsteps. There was somebody outside. On the landing. Hovering by the door.

'I'm in here,' Lucas called out. No response. Try again. 'I'm in here.'

The door handle rattled.

'You can come in,' said Lucas, a little too desperately. 'It's safe.'

The rattling stopped. A lingering silence followed.

'Please.'

The handle dropped and the door moved slowly to one side.

A wide-eyed Lucas refused to blink as he stared at the opening. His heart sank, however, when he saw who was standing in the doorway.

Or rather, who *wasn't* standing in the doorway.

CHAPTER TWENTY-ONE

Rose began to fret.

She hated being alone. Especially like this. Out in the open. In the middle of a jam-packed car park. Surrounded by strangers.

What was Mercy playing at? Leaving her there to fend for herself?

It was raining. Not exactly pelting it down, but fast enough to make Rose rush for cover under the entrance to the hospital. Without thinking, she removed her phone, tried to look busy. When she *did* think about it, she scrolled through her contact list. Stopped at *Lucas*. Carried on to *Tommy*. And then returned to *Lucas*.

A choice of two made easy because one of them was Tommy.

According to Miles, they were supposed to meet the other two at the hospital. *They* consisted of just her though, ever since Mercy had shot off into the distance. Not only that, but Rose had no idea where they were. In the waiting room? On a ward? Dumped in a corridor? Maybe they were deep undercover emptying bed pans. Nothing would've surprised her these days.

Her anxiety increased with every passing second. So many questions ...

Questions that weren't about to be answered any time soon if Lucas failed to pick up.

That wasn't like him. He was normally so reliable. She ended the call and tried Tommy. Different number, same outcome.

There was always someone else, of course. Miles. He was a font of all knowledge. What would he say, though, if she asked for help? *Figure it out for yourself, Rose. Use some initiative, Rose. Stop being the weak link, Rose.* Well, that was what they *all* thought. Fact. Within the Nearly Dearly Departed Club, she stuck out like a sore thumb on a manicured hand. The odd one out.

No, calling Miles was clearly a last resort. Better to ask someone else first. Preferably someone not quite so judgmental.

With the rain refusing to let up, she made her way into the hospital and looked around. It was heaving in there, rammed full of people in various states of poor health and not-so-wellbeing. Rose kept her head down as she pressed on towards the reception desk. There were two women there. Both were staring at screens, talking privately behind their hands. One was dressed in pale blue hospital scrubs, whilst the other wore a white blouse and black trousers. White Blouse had a face like a thunderstorm, so Rose shifted over to Scrubs. Waited patiently.

It was White Blouse who glanced up first, though. Worse luck. 'Name?'

'Name?' Rose struggled to process the question. 'My ... name?'

'Yes, obviously. It's really not that difficult.'

'No ... not at all ... it's just ... why do you need my name?'

White Blouse blew out, exasperated. 'We take your name, then you tell us what's wrong with you. After that you take a seat and at some point we'll call you through for a chat.' White Blouse forced a smile. 'How does that sound?'

Rose sensed movement behind her. The huffing and puffing of an ever-increasing queue.

'You've got to tell us something,' pressed White Blouse. 'Yeah, it's a Monday, but we're always busy in A and E.'

Rose could feel herself blush.

'Accident and Emergency,' said White Blouse, just in case it needed explaining. 'Shall we start again? Name?'

'There's nothing wrong with me,' Rose blurted out.

'Then what are you doing here?' White Blouse turned to Scrubs. Muttered under her breath. 'Honestly ... as if we've nothing better to do ...'

Rose hurried away from the desk with the eyes of the entire waiting room boring into her. She was ready to leave when she heard her phone *ping*. Moving to one corner, she removed it from her pocket. She had a message. From Miles of all people.

Room thirty-three. Third floor. Should've told you earlier.

Rose tried to control her breathing. Yes, he should've. It would have saved her the embarrassment.

Turning back into the waiting room, she found the courage

to lift her head and take in her surroundings. Her eyes ran around the perimeter of the room in search of a staircase. As luck would have it, they fell upon the next best thing. A lift.

Rose passed between the sniffing, coughing, groaning masses as she made her way towards it. The doors opened the moment she got there. The lift was empty. Thank goodness for that.

She stepped inside and pressed the button for the third floor. Took a series of deep breaths as the doors began to close. In ... and out. In ... and out. She repeated the process until her nerves had started to settle.

That all changed when the door shuddered to a halt. There was a leather boot preventing it from fully closing.

A leather boot belonging to a big, broad man in a woollen overcoat.

A big, broad man and his two identical companions.

CHAPTER TWENTY-TWO

Stood rooted to the spot, Mercy could do little but stare at the body.

Beside it, a pool of blood had formed on the tiled floor. It was leaking from a head wound. The cause of death.

Probable cause of death.

Mercy had to be sure. Shuffling across the tiles, she stopped when she was within touching distance of the body. Not too close, not too far away. Crouching down, she leant forward on her toes. A feeling instantly swept over her. It was relief. Sheer bloody relief.

The body wasn't Solomon. It was a man, yes, but this one was older, bigger. Less hair. More lines.

The relief soon passed, only to be replaced by an uncomfortable uncertainty. Okay, so it wasn't Solomon, but it was still someone. A person. A human being.

A *dead* human being.

Again, she had to be sure. Avoiding the ever-increasing pool, she moved from wrist to neck in search of a pulse that was impossible to find. She took a breath. Tried to swallow back the bile that was rising in her chest. Was this how she had looked? When she had *died* back in the barn?

Mercy was about to stand when the sobbing returned. It was close now. In the same room. Right behind her.

Leaping to her feet, she spun around, ready for any potential confrontation.

It was hard to tell if Solomon even knew she was there. Slumped between the units in the corner of the kitchen, his hands were pressed against his face, whilst his whole body shook uncontrollably.

Mercy moved towards him. Touched him gently on the shoulder. The last thing she wanted was to spook him. If he lashed out suddenly she would have to defend herself. If he screamed the bloody house down, she would somehow have to silence him.

Thankfully, he did neither.

Without removing his hands, he mumbled a sentence between sobs that Mercy could just about make out. 'What have I done?'

She gripped a little tighter. 'You did this?'

Solomon nodded repeatedly as the words began to flow. 'He wouldn't stop. From the moment I got home. Always on at me. Calling me useless. Selfish.' He was shouting now. 'What do you do, Sol? Why are you here? I wish you'd died with your bloody mother. I'm not your dad. I can't stand the sight of you—'

Mercy pressed a hand to his mouth. 'You need to calm down,'

she whispered. She waited for him to catch his breath, stop panting, before she spoke again. 'That's your step-dad, right?'

Solomon nodded. 'Errol. That's his name. *Was* his name.'

'How did he die?' pressed Mercy.

'I ... I ... I killed him,' Solomon stammered. 'It's on me. All of it. I couldn't stop myself. I'm going to prison, aren't I? There's no way out of it—'

'Tell me what happened.' Mercy pulled a wooden chair out from under the kitchen table. 'Sit down. I just want to know the details.'

Solomon staggered over to the table. Slumped down onto the chair. 'He'd been drinking,' he began slowly. 'I saw the bottle in his hand as soon as I got in. The empties gathered around him. He followed me all around the house. Shouting. Swearing. He even spat at me.' Solomon shook his head at Mercy. 'I tried to call you. Repeatedly. I thought you might be able to help.'

'I can.' Mercy glanced at the dead body. 'I *still* can. I will. Just tell me what happened next.'

'I came in here,' said Solomon, looking around the kitchen. 'I opened the fridge and he slammed it shut. I was about to say something when he hit me around the head. I cried out, but it didn't hurt. Not really. It was a poor connection. Errol knew it, too. He tried to hit me again, but I caught him first. An uppercut. Right under the chin.' Solomon took a ragged breath. Sucked in as much air as possible. 'He was drunk. Unsteady on his feet. He fell backwards and hit his head, first on the table, then on the floor. He tried to stand, staggered about a bit, and then collapsed. He couldn't stop spluttering. Wriggling about. And then ... he was still. Dead.'

'It was an accident,' said Mercy. 'Self-defence.'

'I'm not sorry,' insisted Solomon, trying to convince himself as much as anything. 'He was an evil man. Horrible to my mum and then horrible to me. The only thing I'm sorry about was that it was me who killed him.' Solomon was suddenly hysterical. 'What am I going to do? I'm a murderer. I don't want to go to prison—'

Mercy shook him by the shoulders. Hard enough to shock him into silence. 'You need to stop ranting and listen,' she said firmly. 'I think there's a way out of this, but you have to do everything I say. Are you cool with that?'

Solomon tried to control his breathing. 'Yes. I am. I don't understand, though. What's your plan?'

'You didn't kill your step-dad,' said Mercy. 'Someone else did.'

'Who?'

Mercy screwed up her face. 'Me.'

CHAPTER TWENTY-THREE

Agatha couldn't help but frown as she took in her current surroundings.

The Black Hart. A dingy-looking hotel to the north of Stainmouth. Supposedly three-star. Well, that was a downright lie. Agatha had expected more. Okay, nothing as grand or luxurious as her own choice of residence about a mile away. Just ... better. As in cleaner. Smarter. Not so grubby.

Was that too much to ask?

'I had no idea,' sighed Agatha. She had moved from the doorstep to the lobby to the lift to Miles's room as quickly as her feet would take her. Breath held. Careful not to touch anything. 'You should've told me.'

Sat at the table, hunched over his laptop, Miles turned to look at the older woman. 'Pardon?'

'Your room,' explained Agatha. 'No, it's more than just that. The whole hotel. It's ... I don't quite know how to put it ...'

'A complete shithole,' finished Miles. He gently shook his head as he returned his focus to the laptop. 'Well, *you* booked it for me.'

'I didn't,' replied Agatha. She took a moment to decide if that was even true. 'I mean, not really. I got someone else to book it. I think I told them to get something that befitted your standing in the organisation—'

'And they picked this dump? Charming.'

'Sorry,' said Agatha, cringing slightly. 'You're better than this.'

'I should hope so. Don't worry; I've stayed in worse. I'm barely here, if I'm being honest. Only to sleep. And I'm too busy to do much of that.'

'Busy? Doing what?'

'Working.' Miles's fingers flashed across the keyboard as if to prove his point. 'Always working ...'

'I'll see if I can fix you up with somewhere better,' said Agatha hastily.

'There's no need. Seriously. We won't be here that long anyway, will we?'

Agatha didn't answer immediately. Maybe she shouldn't answer at all. Pretend she hadn't heard. Plead ignorance.

'We won't, will we?' pressed Miles, much to Agatha's despair.

'I guess that would ... depend.'

'On?'

'On what you consider to be *that long*,' said Agatha cryptically. 'I mean, we won't be gone by tomorrow ...'

'But next week?' asked Miles hopefully. 'Next month?'

'Something like that.' Agatha, keen to steer the conversation in a different direction, barely took a breath before she asked a question of her own. 'How are you getting on?'

'I'm not.' Miles moved his hands from the keys to his face. Rubbed his eyes. Scratched his cheek. 'Something's wrong,' he moaned. 'I've tried everything, but Lucas Thorne has vanished off the system. His signal has gone cold. And if there's no signal, I can't track him.'

Agatha sat down on the bed. She stood up when it *groaned* and *grumbled* under her weight.

'Don't take it personally,' said Miles. 'It does that to me as well.'

'Mr Thorne can't just disappear,' began Agatha, moving around the room for a closer look at the laptop's screen. 'None of them can. We've both seen this system in action. It's foolproof. You do remember Mr O'Strife's bid for freedom, not to mention his subsequent setback, don't you?'

Miles nodded. Of course he remembered, not that he'd call it a setback. No, it was more of a life-threatening collision. Tommy, infuriated by his lot in life, had made a run for it. Not by foot; in four wheels. A Fiat 500, to be precise. A Fiat 500 that had been packed off to the nearest scrapyard after Tommy had driven it into a tree trunk on his way out of Stainmouth.

Not that Tommy was entirely at fault, of course.

Yes, he had crashed the car, but Miles had offered the helping hand with the aid of a hidden microchip in Tommy's neck that vibrated whenever it was activated. The shock, coupled with a pulsating pain equivalent to a rocket grade migraine, had been enough to make Tommy let go of the steering wheel. For Miles, it was the perfect way to keep order within the Nearly Dearly Departed Club. It was a means to control the uncontrollable.

Until now.

'Maybe Lucas has had an accident,' said Miles, thinking out loud. 'A traumatic blow. A punch or kick to the head. Something like that might be enough to dislodge the microchip.'

Agatha latched onto one word in particular. 'Might?'

'I'm just guessing. But that would explain why it isn't working. Has he mentioned anything?'

Agatha shook her head. 'Not to me.'

'Then I'm stumped,' admitted Miles. He closed his laptop and returned it to the drawer in the table. 'What now?'

'Now we get out of this ... shithole and head back to the hospital,' said Agatha, wiping her feet on her way out of the room.

Miles followed her, stopping only to close the door behind them. 'And Lucas?'

'Lucas is a big boy,' said Agatha, as she set off along the corridor. 'There's no reason to think he can't get himself out of his current situation, however precarious it may be.'

CHAPTER TWENTY-FOUR

Lucas looked out into the darkness.

There was nobody there. The door to the room must've opened by itself. But what about the rattling handle? That was harder to explain. The wind perhaps.

Yeah, right. What fucking wind?

Lucas gambled on the only plausible alternative. 'You can come out,' he said. 'I won't bite.'

He waited for some kind of movement, but there was none. What the hell was going on?

And then, right on cue, a scruffy blonde head peeked out from around the door.

Lucas remained completely still. It was a child. A girl. Four. Maybe five. School age, but only just. Her eyes – dark, suspicious – seemed to suggest older, but Lucas figured otherwise. He got a better view when she shuffled out into the open. She was dangerously thin with long, straggly hair and a pale complexion. Dressed inappropriately for the time of year in a stained summer dress and scuffed sandals. That was just first impressions, though. You didn't have to look hard to see the telltale signs of neglect. The dirt under her fingernails. The scabs on her lips. Black palms and bloody knees. The girl needed more than just a hot bath. She needed love and affection.

Lucas forced a smile, but then wondered what it looked like. He had little experience with children. It didn't come naturally. Still, how hard could it be?

'Listen, do me a favour and grab that key—'

The girl ducked out of sight before he could finish his sentence.

Bollocks.

Too much, too soon. Easy does it. Yes, he was in a rush, desperate even, but this was his best chance of escaping. Don't blow it now.

'Sorry,' said Lucas, his voice oddly high-pitched. 'I didn't mean to scare you. Silly me. I'm such a massive ... erm ... poo-poo.'

The girl peeked back around the door. 'Poo-poo.'

'Yeah, that's me,' nodded Lucas. 'Mister Poo-Poo ... um ... the poo-poo man.' He felt his heart flutter as the girl giggled. 'So, what else is funny? Let me think. If I'm Mister Poo-Poo, then you must be ... Little Miss Wee-Wee, right?'

The girl fiercely shook her head. 'No. My name's Ellie.'

'Ah, Ellie,' smiled Lucas. 'That's one of my favourite names. Better than Mister Poo-Poo.'

Ellie giggled again. Each burst gave Lucas a little boost.

'My real name's Lucas,' he said. 'I mean, it's a bit boring

really, but that's me all over. I'm a boring, snoring man.' Lucas closed his eyes and pretended to fall asleep. He could hear Ellie laughing. When he opened them again, he saw that she had edged closer.

The key to the handcuffs, however, had vanished.

Lucas scanned the floorboards, but it was nowhere to be seen. Ellie, reading his mind, hopped backwards. The key wasn't under her feet.

No, it was in her hand. Sat fair and square in the centre of her filthy palm.

'Ah, there it is,' said Lucas with a sigh of relief. 'Can I have it, please?'

Ellie clenched her fist and put her hand behind her back.

Lucas didn't show his frustration. He had come this far. Don't throw it all away now. 'What are you doing here?' he asked softly. 'In this house? Did you sneak in?'

Ellie took a moment. 'My house. I live here.'

'You live here?' Lucas looked beyond the room onto the darkened landing. 'You live ... here?'

Ellie pointed at the floorboards. 'Down there. With my mummy.'

'Your mummy?' Lucas sat up. 'I didn't know ... I thought ... can you get her for me?'

Ellie shook her head.

'Please. You'd be doing me a massive favour.'

'Can't. She's asleep.'

'Okay.' Lucas resisted the urge to keep pushing. What time

was it, though? Early evening? Six or seven? Maybe her mum worked nights. Caught up on sleep during the day. Lucas wracked his brain for a different approach. If he pressured Ellie too hard to give him the key, she was sure to refuse. Either that or run off. It was a balancing act and he had no idea what would tip the scales.

He was still none the wiser when a loud *bang* disturbed the silence of the empty room. A late firework or mis-firing car, it was coming from outside. Maybe several streets away. Nothing to worry about.

Not that Ellie knew that. Clearly spooked, she peered over her shoulder. Lucas, fearful of her next move, was all set to call out to her, beg her not to leave, when something unexpected happened.

Ellie skipped forward, stopping when she reached his feet.

'For you, Mister Poo-Poo,' she said, passing him the key. 'Boring, snoring man.'

CHAPTER TWENTY-FIVE

Of the three men, Frank DeMayo led the way into the lift.

At first glance, he thought it was empty. Then he saw her. Pressed against one corner. Head down, awkwardly stiff. A wallflower. Mid-twenties. Maybe more. It was so hard to tell these days. Nobody looked their age. Smartly turned out, though. Sweater, skirt and tights. All black. None of that casual shit. Maybe she worked at the hospital. Admin probably. She looked like she could find her way around a computer. Or maybe she was one of those religious types who drifted from corridor to corridor. Who offered moral support in times of crisis. A shoulder to cry on. One breakdown later and you were running with some satanic cult or another. Ripping a bat's head off with your bare teeth and howling at the new moon.

Fuck that for a game of soldiers.

Frank stared at the woman for longer than was socially acceptable. Satisfied that she wasn't a threat – she was barely awake – he turned away from her so he could switch his full attention to the control panel. The girl had pressed *3*, so he added *1* and *2* before the doors closed and the lift shuddered into action.

'We take a floor each,' he said, urging his companions to gather around so he didn't have to raise his voice above a gruff whisper. 'Sandy, you do the first. Maurice, the second. I'll start on the third. Check every room. Whatever happens, we're not leaving this hospital until we've found the Imp.'

No argument there. Just nods. A murmur of agreement.

The lift ground to a halt, the door slid open, and Sandy stepped out onto the first floor.

The same scenario was replicated on the next floor up. Maurice, however, hurried out into the corridor like a man possessed. He wouldn't knock on doors; he would pound. Didn't know how to speak politely; rather bark out demands. He was a different breed, thought Frank, but for all the wrong reasons. A ticking time bomb. And ticking time bombs had a tendency to go off when you least expected it.

Surely not now, though. In a hospital, of all places. Have a bit of respect.

The lift stopped at the third floor.

'After you,' said Frank, as the door rolled to one side.

The woman lifted her head for the first time. Smiled slightly as she pushed herself off the wall and shuffled out onto the corridor.

Yeah, definitely one of those religious types. Best avoided at all costs.

Rose refused to slow down as she exited the lift.

Without breaking stride, she turned to her right and kept on moving. A simple glance over her shoulder was enough to reassure her. The man – the big man from the lift – had gone the other way. She breathed for the first time in ages. Tried to focus as she looked along the length of the corridor. The door nearest to her was number *32*. She took several paces forward and stopped at *33*. Knocked once. The softest of taps. Knocked again. Harder, but not by anyone else's standards.

There was still no reply.

Rose knew what she had to do. Resting on the handle, she slowly pushed the door open and peered inside. She wasn't sure what she expected to find in there.

Tommy fast asleep with his legs up on a bed, however, would have been some way down the list.

Rose entered the room and closed the door behind her. She should've slammed it. Made him jump. Scared the life out of him.

She should've ... but she didn't. That wasn't her style. Not that she had a style. Nothing that anyone would recognise, anyway.

'Tommy.' Rose took him by the arm and shook him gently. Then slightly harder. A *lot* harder. 'Tommy.'

Tommy stirred. Grunted and groaned before his noises turned to words. 'Steady, Agatha ... not so fast ... let me get my trousers off first.'

Rose let go of him. 'Agatha? No ... um ... it's me. Rose.'

'Shit.' Tommy refused to open his eyes as he stretched his

arms above his head. Yawned and farted in sync. 'Sorry. Bad dream. Well, not that bad. What's up?'

Rose ignored the question. 'Where's Lucas?' she asked instead.

'I don't know … can't remember … he'll be back soon,' mumbled Tommy. 'Panic over nothing, most probably. What time is it? Feels like I've been here for ages.'

'And why *are* you here?' pressed Rose.

Tommy let his chair legs crash to the ground before he sat up straight. Rubbed his eyes with as much ferocity as he could muster. 'Why do you think? I'm keeping an eye on the runaway corpse, aren't I?'

Rose looked around the room. 'What are you talking about?'

'Oh, try and keep up. The walking dead who played chicken with the traffic. Our comatose friend here. Sleeping not-so-beautiful.' Tommy rested a hand on the bed. 'Say hello to Impetus Stokes.'

Rose shook her head, confused. 'Tommy …'

'Yeah, I know what you're thinking—'

'Tommy.'

'But that's his real name. God's honest truth. Pleasant Agatha told me—'

'Tommy.' There was a severity to Rose's voice that even she didn't recognise. A tone that demanded attention. 'Tommy, look,' she said firmly. 'The bed. It's empty. There's no one there.'

CHAPTER TWENTY-SIX

Mercy couldn't tell if Solomon was listening or not.

He was in shock. He was no longer thinking straight. That was natural enough. Perfectly normal behaviour under the circumstances. His life had changed forever with a single punch.

That didn't mean it had to be over, though.

Mercy pulled out a chair. Took a seat at the table next to Solomon. His head was resting on the wooden surface, his hands pulling desperately at whichever of his tight dreads got caught between his fingers.

'Did you hear what I said?' asked Mercy. Firm, not angry. 'I know it's a lot to take in, but we've not got much time. One of your neighbours could easily have called the police by now. If so, they'll be here before we know it. They can't find us like this, Solomon. You and me ... with the body ... Errol ...' Mercy took a breath. Readied herself to run through her plan for what seemed like the umpteenth time in just a few minutes. 'I'll leave by the back door. The second I do, you call the emergency services. Ask for both an ambulance and the police. Tell them there's been an intruder in your house.

There was a scuffle and your step-father's in a bad way. *I'm* the intruder. I'll make some noise out the back to get the curtain twitchers up off the sofa. One or two witnesses should do the trick. They'll see me hanging about in the dark, and that'll be enough to back up your story. You'll be in the clear. There'll be a murder enquiry, but their only lead will be this so-called intruder.' Mercy swallowed. 'And they won't find me. Not ever,' she said, trying to convince herself as much as the broken boy sat opposite her.

The same boy who stood up without warning, almost as if an electric current had jolted him into life. Staggering slightly, he walked clumsily around the table. Stopped at the body. Stared at it in disbelief. 'But I did that.'

Mercy moved into position, ready to catch him if need be.

'I did that,' echoed Solomon. 'Me. Not you. I ... did ... that!'

Mercy put a hand on his arm. Tried to steer him back towards the table.

Solomon, however, wasn't having any of it. 'I killed him. And now I deserve everything that's coming my way.'

'Please ...' Mercy tried again. Leaning in close, she put her hands around his waist. This time, Solomon didn't shrug her off or push her away.

But he did lash out.

Turning sharply, he clenched his fist and threw a wild punch at Mercy's head. Mercy swerved it at the last moment, relieved when it bounced harmlessly off her shoulder. Solomon was facing her now, though, the guilt and confusion of earlier having been swallowed up by an all-encompassing rage that demanded an instant release.

Solomon swung again. Mercy blocked it with her left arm, leant in with her right. The red mist may have overwhelmed the boy, but Mercy knew how to control her emotions. A counter punch was out of the question. She didn't want to hurt him or, worse still, knock him out. No, something lighter would do the trick. Simple shock treatment.

Opening her hand, palm flat, Mercy slapped him firmly across the face with just enough force to stun him.

'Whoa!' Mercy held out her arms as the boy fell forward. The rage had deserted him. He was empty. 'You need to get a grip. I mean it, Solomon. You don't want to go to prison. Murder ... manslaughter ... whatever it is ... it'll destroy you. Ten ... fifteen years gone. Just like that.' Mercy looked him in the eye. Held his gaze. 'Did you listen to my plan? You can trust me, Solomon. Can I trust you?'

This time, Solomon didn't miss a beat. 'Yes. You can trust me. And thank you. I mean that.'

'It's okay.' Mercy touched his arm. Tried to smile. 'There are people who can help you. Good people. Nimble for one. And me. I'll be in touch soon. I promise.'

Without another word, she pulled her hood over her head, opened the back door and made her way outside. She had wasted so much time; she had to move quickly.

First, though, it was best to get the lie of the land.

Using the light from the kitchen, Mercy took in as much

as she could as fast as possible. The backyard of number seven Bartholomew Street comprised a small patch of grass surrounded by a random pattern of assorted paving slabs. There was a shed in the far corner and a gate beside it. The gate led to a back passage that would eventually lead out onto the street itself.

Hopefully.

Mercy was guessing now, but it was all she had to go on. Her wits. Her instincts. It was either that or stand around, staring into space. She turned back towards the house. Solomon had picked up his phone. Had it pressed against his ear. He was making the call.

Time to move.

Racing across the grass, Mercy scrambled up on top of the shed, using it as a springboard to leap into next door's garden. It was identical in every way. Same size, same layout, same shed. She landed smoothly. Too smoothly perhaps. How was she ever going to alert the neighbours to an intruder if she made so little noise? Only one way to change that.

Mercy kicked over a plant pot. Not loud enough. Picking up the same pot, she threw it against the house, avoiding the windows as she did so. The pot smashed upon impact and then dropped onto the patio. That was better. She climbed onto the roof of the shed and waited.

Come on. There's not one person alive who wouldn't hear that. Don't just sit there and ...

Right on cue, the curtains opened and a bald head appeared

in their place. There was another head right behind it. Curly hair and glasses. Perfect. Two witnesses for the price of one.

Turning her back on the couple, Mercy jumped off the roof of the shed into the passageway at the back of the houses. It was a heavier landing, but she was back on her feet in no time. She ducked down behind the fence and moved swiftly in what she hoped was the right direction. Sure enough, the passageway opened up to reveal a row of parked cars under streetlights.

Mercy veered towards one car in particular.

Without slowing her step, she rushed across the road and climbed into the Mini Clubman. She pulled on her seat belt and started the engine. Turning the car around would've meant heading deeper into Bartholomew Street, but that wasn't ideal. Instead, she reversed all the way out, wary of any incoming traffic before she finally got the chance to straighten up. Seconds later, she was heading in the right direction. Away from the house. Away from the body.

Lowering her hood, she tried to focus on the road ahead and ignore everything else that was happening. Where to now?

The hospital. It was her only option. She had deserted Rose, after all. Left her in the lurch. She'd be okay, though. She was with Lucas and Tommy.

What could possibly go wrong?

CHAPTER TWENTY-SEVEN

Tommy stared at the dishevelled sheets.

The flattened pillows.

The empty bed.

'He's gone,' he muttered. 'He's ... not here.'

Rose resisted the urge to say anything sarcastic. Besides, by the look on Tommy's face, he was agitated enough already. He didn't need winding up any more.

'Bollocks.' Jumping up off the chair, Tommy dropped to his knees so he could search underneath the bed. Also known as the best hiding place in a room of very few hiding places. 'I was supposed to be keeping an eye on him. I *was* keeping an eye on him. Most of the time.'

Except when you were asleep, thought Rose. 'Do you know who he is? Who he ... *was*?'

'Fuck knows,' shrugged Tommy, practically spinning on the spot as his eyes darted into every nook and cranny. 'All I've got is a name. Impetus Stokes. The Imp. He was supposed to be dead. Then he was unconscious. And now he's vanished. Agatha's gonna' do her nut.'

Rose shook her head, trying to convince herself as much as Tommy. 'He might have woken up and then wandered off to explore,' she said, turning towards the exit. 'He could be out in the corridor even as we—'

She was about to pull down on the handle when a knock on the door beat her to it. Three firm raps that were loud enough to make her step back in shock.

'You're right,' said Tommy, perking up a little. 'That might be him now.'

Rose doubted that very much. Why would you leave a room without a word and then knock on the door to re-enter? You wouldn't. Fact. The way Tommy was staring at her, though, left her with only one option.

She opened the door.

It wasn't Impetus Stokes.

Not unless Impetus Stokes was the big man from the lift.

'My apologies,' said Frank DeMayo, exuding a certain kind of bonhomie that clearly didn't come naturally. 'I'm looking for a friend of mine. He's somewhere in the hospital. I just don't know where. Not here, though. Sorry for any ...'

Frank let his sentence fade away as he leant forward and took one last look inside the room. He had spotted something. Not Impetus Stokes because Impetus Stokes wasn't there. But the empty bed. The dishevelled sheets. The flattened pillows.

He was about to take a step inside the room when Tommy appeared from nowhere, blocking his path.

'You got a problem, pal?' He puffed out his chest. Stood on tip-toes. Made himself as big as possible.

'Perhaps.' Frank gestured towards the bed. 'Who's room is this?'

'Mine,' replied Tommy, trying to close the door on their uninvited guest. 'I'm in a bad way. Chronic diarrhoea. I could do without the interruptions if I'm being honest.'

Frank was too large a presence to be moved that easily, though. 'Where is he?' he snarled. The transformation came without warning. From calm and amicable to wild beast mode in the time it takes to draw breath. 'Where ... is ... he?'

'What you talking about?' Tommy raised his hands, but Frank swatted him away with ease, pushing him back into the room. He followed that up by closing the door behind him. Trapping them all inside.

'I won't ask you again,' spat Frank, pointing at his two captives in quick succession. 'Where is he?'

Tommy sprang forward, only to be greeted with a punch on the nose. Not hard enough to break it, but with enough force to send him sprawling backwards for a second time.

Rose squeezed herself into the corner. 'Stop it!' she shouted.

'No, *you* stop it!' shot back Frank. 'Stop fucking about. I'm looking for the man who was in this room. Impetus Stokes. You know where he is. I know you do.'

Tommy, blood trickling out of both nostrils, tried to confront the man for a third time. He got a slap across the side of his head for his troubles. It left his ear drum reverberating with the sound of stampeding buffalo. At least, what he imagined that would sound like.

'This is getting tedious,' sighed Frank. 'There's something you might like to know. I've got Lucas. He's one of your lot, isn't he? Whoever you are. Well, he's safe. For now. That could change quickly, though.'

Rose held her breath as the man turned towards her.

'You're not from round these parts, are you?' he began, fixing her with the kind of steely glare that could instantly bring on a panic attack. 'If you were, you'd know who you were dealing with. The name's Frank. Frank DeMayo.' A pause. 'For crying out loud, what's wrong with the youth of today? No education. No respect. No clue. Listen, for the last forty years I've been the most feared villain in Stainmouth—'

'Forty years?' Tommy wobbled from side to side, his balance a little off. 'Time moves on. Now you're just a big shot in the bingo halls and knitting circles.'

Frank's reply was a furious chop to Tommy's neck. It was his firmest blow to date, leaving Tommy momentarily paralysed as he gasped for breath.

Rose's response, in contrast, was a little more audible. A shriek of disbelief. Coupled with the realisation that it was now down to her to do something. Something to end this before Frank could dish out any more punishment.

'We can take you to him,' she blurted out. 'Impetus Stokes. We know where he is. Just stop hurting him.'

'At last.' Frank walked towards the door. Yanked it open.

'What are you waiting for?' he said, ushering Rose out of the room. 'Lead the way, sweetheart.'

CHAPTER TWENTY-EIGHT

Lucas snatched the key from Ellie and unlocked the handcuffs.

He let them crash against the radiator as he released them from his wrist. The resulting *clang* was enough to send the girl scurrying back towards the door.

'Wait!' said Lucas hastily. 'I didn't mean to scare you. Turns out I'm clumsy as well as boring. Who would've thought it? Silly Mister Poo-Poo.'

A smiling Ellie stopped in the doorway, much to Lucas's relief.

'Thank you,' he said, trying desperately to ignore the aches and pains in his body as he clambered to his feet. He needed to get out of there, as far away as was humanly possible, but he couldn't rush. The last thing he wanted was to spook her again.

That particular ship, however, may have already sailed.

Lowering her head, Ellie fiddled nervously with the dirty frills on her dress. 'I want my mummy,' she mumbled.

Lucas nodded. He couldn't argue with that. 'Do you know where she is?'

Ellie tapped the floorboards with her bare foot. 'Downstairs.'

'Okay. Let's go.' Lucas held out his hand, surprised when the young girl took it. 'You'll have to show me the way, though,' he said, hunching over. 'Can you do that?'

Ellie didn't reply. Instead, she shot off out of the room, practically dragging Lucas along with her. He found himself on a landing with a closed door on either side. It was dark out there, but he could still make out the same exposed floorboards, scratched and untreated, alongside badly plastered walls and an empty light fitting. Ellie pressed on until she reached the stairs. Took them at a much slower pace, before hopping off at the bottom step. Lucas was there at all times. They were in the hallway. More darkness with little to see except for three closed doors.

'Mummy,' said Ellie, pointing at the furthest one away.

She stopped dragging and shifted behind Lucas instead. Started to push. In hindsight, he should've wondered why. Not just ignored the warning signs as he strolled straight up to the door. Knocked twice. Entered without permission.

The smell hit him immediately.

It was the sour stench of faeces, trapped in a worryingly small space.

He flicked on the light, regretting it instantly. There were five people in the room, all of them sprawled out on filthy mattresses. Surrounded by bottles and takeaway cartons. Packets and wrappers. And worse. Much, much worse. Syringes. Used, by the look of things. Foil. Spoons. Pipes.

Your basic heroin paraphernalia.

Lucas knew what he had walked into. The Shooting Gallery, Sandy had called it. Not shooting guns, but shooting up. A meeting place for addicts. Smackhead city central. As for Frank, well, it was the perfect place to keep a prisoner, wasn't it? Nobody downstairs would ever ask questions or even know what was going on. And why would the police care about a bunch of zonked out druggies? Surely it was better to keep them congregated together, indoors, out of sight, then roaming the streets. A win-win for everybody.

What nobody had bargained on, however, was Ellie.

Lucas looked on in disgust as she sat on the edge of one of the stained mattresses. 'Mummy,' she said, resting a hand on the ankle of a washed-out, limp-limbed woman. The woman recoiled at her touch, pulling her knees into her chest, curling up into a ball.

Ellie turned to Lucas, held his stare. The rejection had hit a nerve. She looked as if she was about to cry.

She wasn't the only one.

Lucas hovered by the door. He was wasting time. Forget about Frank and the rest of his goons; this was still the last place he wanted to be.

Scrambling up the mattress, Ellie started to shake the woman in a bid to rouse her from her drug-induced slumber. Predictably, it was all to no avail.

'Mummy doesn't like me,' she said sadly.

Lucas shook his head. A strained reaction. If anything, he

wanted to blurt out the truth. *No, damn right she doesn't like you. She doesn't like anyone or anything. Not even herself.* 'Of course she likes you,' he muttered through gritted teeth. 'She's just ... tired.'

'She's always tired,' said Ellie.

Lucas felt his heart sink. This was a pitifully desperate scene. Nothing out of the ordinary, though. He had witnessed it time and time again when he was in the force. Back then, social services would've been contacted and the child would've been taken away.

But this was now and he wasn't a police officer. He wasn't even officially alive. He shouldn't have been there.

'Where do you sleep?' asked Lucas, studying the room a little closer.

Ellie laid down on the same mattress as her mother and pretended to close her eyes.

'And what do you eat?'

She jabbed a finger in different directions. An empty crisp packet tucked under one of the mattresses. A half-eaten apple on the floor. Lucas's blood ran cold as she lingered on a used syringe. Thankfully, she changed her mind and pointed at a packet of biscuits on a side table.

'I don't like it in here,' she said, out of the blue.

'No, me neither,' sighed Lucas.

Ellie grabbed her nose. 'It smells.'

'Yeah, it fucking stinks. Sorry,' added Lucas hastily. Thankfully, Ellie didn't seem to notice. She was gazing at her mother. Wondering when she was going to wake up and give her some attention.

She'd be in for a long wait, thought Lucas.

Whatever had happened to him, whatever he was now, he still had morals. Deep down, he was a good man. An honest man. A caring man.

Mother or not, he couldn't leave Ellie with a strung-out druggie and her motley crew of addicts. No way. Not in a million years.

So he didn't.

'Come on.' He held out his hand and, to his relief, Ellie took it as she leapt up off the bed. As an afterthought, she grabbed a pair of shoes from the corner of the room and pulled them on. Lucas took that as their cue.

Their cue to leave.

CHAPTER TWENTY-NINE

Rose did as Frank suggested.

She led the way. Out of the private room and along the third-floor corridor. Slow, shuffling footsteps. Eyes down as she crept towards the lift.

What was she doing?

No, seriously.

She had no idea where the man from the coffin – the curiously named Impetus Stokes – had vanished to. He could be anywhere in a hospital this size. Anywhere and nowhere. On the run or out cold. For all she knew, he could be dead.

And that was half the problem. Frank wouldn't let them go until he had found Stokes. What he wanted with him was still unclear, but Rose doubted it was anything positive.

The other half of the problem was Lucas. Frank had him held captive and wouldn't give him up easily. Escape Frank, and how would they ever find Lucas? They wouldn't. Not tonight, anyway. Maybe that was the point. Live to fight another day and start again tomorrow. They would have Mercy to help then.

And Agatha and Miles with any luck. The whole gang back together again. Minus one, of course. Their missing member. Still, at least Rose could take a back seat with so many voices fighting for attention. Shrink into the background. Best of all, she wouldn't have to lead the way.

Not like now.

As the first to enter the lift, Rose prodded the button on the control panel. *G* for Ground Floor.

'Where are we going?' asked Frank suspiciously. He had a tight grip of Tommy's arm. Like a short leash on a wayward dog.

'Down,' replied Rose, straight-faced.

Frank glared at her. 'Is that supposed to be funny?'

'No,' said Rose meekly. 'I wouldn't ... I'm not ... I was being serious. The man you're looking for ... the man who was in the bed—'

'Spit it out!'

'He's in the car park,' spluttered Rose, the words rolling off her tongue before she had chance to consider them. 'In a ... car.'

Frank weighed it up. 'This better not be a trick—'

'I wouldn't dare,' said Rose, barely able to speak.

'No, you wouldn't, would you? As long as we both know that. Just take me to him, okay?'

Rose nodded. Why? She was only prolonging the inevitable. The horrible moment when Frank realised she was lying.

The lift *pinged*, the doors creaked open, and Tommy awoke from his relative calm. Freeing himself from Frank's grasp, he rushed out into the hustle and bustle of Stainmouth A and E. Rose feared that he might be planning some kind of great escape, but she needn't have worried. All he did was stagger about in supposed agony, his every step intertwined with his own unique chorus of groans and grumbles. Ever the performer, thought Rose.

'Cut that out,' warned Frank under his breath. 'People are staring.'

'Let them,' muttered Tommy. 'I think you've busted my nose. And snapped my windpipe.'

'Well, you're wrong,' Frank insisted. 'I haven't ... but I can do. And I'll break some other bodily parts whilst I'm at it if you don't keep quiet. If the two of you want this to end well, then I suggest you don't draw attention to us. Give me Impetus Stokes and you might even get out of this in one piece.'

Tommy rolled his eyes, careful not to do it in full view of Frank. The last thing he wanted was another beating. He was sore enough already. No, for once in his life he would leave it in Rose's trembling hands. It was about time she got involved. He just hoped she had some kind of plan up her sleeve. Anything would do.

Because if she didn't ...

She didn't.

There was nothing up Rose's sleeve. Nor in her pocket. Not even in her head. It was all just a blur.

Keep moving. Don't look back. Try not to think about what was around the corner.

The corner being, in this instance, the hospital car park.

Rose and Tommy were out in front, Frank close behind, well within touching distance, ready to strike if need be. The sight of so many cars in one small space seemed to trigger something in Tommy's brain. A distant memory that he had almost casually disregarded.

'You were in that black Ford Focus, weren't you?'

'Not me,' muttered Frank. That much was true. His car, yes. One of many. But only Sandy and Maurice had been driving it earlier on.

'Lucas saw you out here,' continued Tommy regardless. 'Knew you were dodgy from the start. That'll be the copper in him. His inner piglet. He can sniff out a wrong 'un with a blocked nose—'

Frank stopped suddenly in the road. Grabbed Tommy's forearm. 'Copper?'

'Lucas is Old Bill,' smirked Tommy. 'Oh, I thought you would've known that, having him trapped inside your knicker drawer.'

Frank scowled. 'And what about you? Are you police, too?'

'Me? Nah, If anything, I'm more like you.'

'You're nothing like me!' Frank pushed Tommy away in anger. 'Let's cut the crap, shall we? Where's Impetus Stokes?'

'Behind you,' said Rose. At the same time, she took hold of Tommy, pulling him towards her.

Frank didn't see the car until it was too late. It only clipped him, but it was enough to send him rolling over the bonnet. If it was going any faster, he would've been in serious trouble. As it was, he landed heavily after several awkward bounces.

The car – a Mini Clubman – ground to a halt close to the scene of the accident.

Tommy recognised the driver. 'Where you been?' he cried, throwing open the back door.

'You wouldn't believe me if I told you,' said Mercy. She glanced in her rear-view mirror. The man she had hit was climbing slowly to his feet with the aid of several concerned citizens. 'Who the hell was that?'

'Just a doctor,' replied Tommy. 'They'll do anything to free up the beds.'

'Ignore him,' said Rose, fastening her seat belt. 'He's called Frank DeMayo. He's got Lucas. We need to tell Agatha.'

Mercy stamped down on the accelerator. 'Shit. How did that happen?'

'Long story,' said Tommy. He tentatively touched his nose. It was throbbing, but not broken. Just like Frank had predicted.

'And the man in the coffin?' asked Mercy.

'Jeez, that's an even longer story,' moaned Tommy. He tried to swallow, but it still hurt. 'You're lucky I can speak at all after what I've just been through.'

'Yeah, lucky us,' sighed Mercy. She took a sharp left turn and exited the hospital car park. One look in her rear view mirror told her that they weren't being followed. 'Tell me one thing, though. Is this the start of something bad?'

'No, not bad,' replied Rose, her heart refusing to settle. 'Terrible would be a more accurate description.'

CHAPTER THIRTY

Lucas opened the front door and peeked outside.

This was crazy. What the hell was he doing? Kidnapping a kid? Or saving a vulnerable child from a lifetime of neglect and abuse?

It was a fine line, make no mistake. Try explaining that away to a judge and jury. Chances are they wouldn't buy the guardian angel angle, either. Paedophile ex-police officer was a better headline. Proper click bait. No, wait. *Dead* paedophile ex-police officer. Yeah, that was more like it. The press would have a field day. He'd be hung, drawn and quartered before the words had even appeared on the screen. Since when did the truth ever matter? Since never.

Say it again. Loud and clear. Because fuck knows if he had the answers.

What the hell was he doing?

Satisfied that the coast was clear, Lucas opened the door fully and stepped outside. He gestured for Ellie to follow. She shook her head. Held her ground.

'Coat,' she demanded.

Lucas moved back inside the house. Looked around the hallway. There was nothing within sight that resembled a child's coat, nor hooks or a stand to hang it from. Only a carpet of junk mail and a well-worn trail that led all the way to the Shooting Gallery.

'Do you know where your coat is?' Lucas tried to hide the irritation in his voice. The brewing impatience. Time was ticking by. The race had begun, but he was still on the starter's block.

Ellie pretended to think. Because that's what she was doing. Pretending. Lucas could see it in her eyes. Maybe she didn't understand. Maybe she didn't even have a coat.

'Here it is.' Ellie grabbed a blanket from under a pile of old newspapers. Wrapped it around her shoulders. Looked up at Lucas. 'Ready to go now.'

He took her hand and hurried out the door. There were houses on either side and straight ahead. The road was clear, but he could hear traffic in the distance. They needed to get out of there, but which way? Ellie decided for them, dragging Lucas to her left.

'My hiding place,' she said happily. She was pointing at a bus shelter at the end of the street. Brick build. Enclosed. That was good enough for Lucas.

A car turned into view as they disappeared inside. Lucas pulled Ellie into a corner. Crouched down so he was at her level. Resisted the temptation to put a hand over her mouth.

Was it Frank? Had he seen them? It was impossible to tell.

Lucas didn't dare risk a look either. Not yet. Instead, he tried to catch his breath. The exertions of the day had taken their toll on mind, body and soul. The run from the house to the shelter – twenty seconds at most – had completely wiped him out.

So that was that. They were trapped.

No. Not *they*.

He.

'I need you to do something for me.' Lucas regretted his words before they had even left his lips. This was wrong. So, so wrong. But was it any worse than the alternative? Lucas was probably in for some kind of beating, but what would Frank and his goons do to Ellie? Something unthinkable? Something that would scar her for life? Who knows? Maybe not. But could he take the risk?

'I've got to go,' he began, 'but we'll see each other again soon. I've got a mission for you, though. A little adventure. Do you think you can do that?'

Ellie looked puzzled.

Lucas could hear a car in the distance. The engine as it cut out. The sound of slamming doors. He didn't have long.

'What number can you count to?' he asked.

Ellie took a moment to think. 'Twenty.'

'That's good,' said Lucas, trying to smile. 'After I've gone, I want you to count to twenty and then count to twenty again. Can you do that?'

Ellie nodded.

'After that, I want you to go to any of these houses, I don't mind which one, and knock on the door,' continued Lucas. 'Keep on asking for the police. Don't stop until they arrive.' Because you would do that, wouldn't you? Call the police if a small child rocked up at your door repeating that one word over and over again? Unless you were a weirdo. Lucas gently shook his head, answering his own thoughts. People were good. *Most* people were good.

Weren't they?

'The police will take you to their station,' said Lucas. 'That's a nice place. Then I want you to ask for Agatha Pleasant. She's a friend of mine. She'll be able to help us. Can you say that? Agatha Pleasant.'

'Agatha ... Pleasant,' said Ellie slowly. 'It's a funny name.'

'She's a funny woman,' said Lucas. He could hear hushed voices. Footsteps. 'Right, would you like me to repeat myself? Count to twenty and then count to twenty again. Knock on a door and ask for the police. At the station, ask for Agatha Pleasant. Tell her all about me.'

'Mister Poo-Poo,' laughed Ellie.

Lucas felt his heart sink like a stone. The plan had been sketchy enough already. Now it was a plan without a punchline. He didn't have time to tell Ellie anything else. He had to go.

'You're Lucas,' said Ellie.

His heart fluttered. 'That's right; tell Agatha Pleasant about Lucas. Okay, I'll see you soon.' Lucas ran a hand through her hair as he stood up. 'Start counting ... now!'

He stepped out of the shelter without another word. *Don't*

follow me. Please don't follow me. He glanced back. Ellie was stood in the same corner, counting her fingers. She hadn't moved an inch.

Lucas sped up the best he could. A trip. A stumble. A staggering shadow in the darkness. He had to put some distance between himself and the little girl, though. The little girl he was relying on. No, it was more than that. His life was in her hands. Her tiny, filthy hands.

Frank DeMayo was coming out of the house. He looked furious. Sandy and Maurice were closer. On the pavement. Their backs turned. Lucas focussed his attention on Maurice. The goon had struck him too often to mention. Time for a little payback.

Revenge was sweet but short-lived. Lucas crashed straight into Maurice and took him down. Hit him with a flurry of body shots before Frank hauled him to his feet.

'Nice try, sunshine,' he hissed in Lucas's ear. 'Better luck next time. If you live that long, of course.'

CHAPTER THIRTY-ONE
TUESDAY

Agatha's phone began to vibrate at precisely one minute past six.

Ante meridiem. She had been in bed for roughly four hours. Slept for three of those. A ragged sleep, tossing and turning with every passing minute. There were extenuating circumstances, of course. Her brain, for one. It was wide awake whilst the rest of her body had shut down long ago. There were too many thoughts and fears spinning around for it to settle. Nagging away. Feeding the negative voice that always appeared day in, day out whenever she was alone.

Yesterday had been a complete disaster. A categorical nightmare. A fuck up of astronomical proportions. Not only had they lost Impetus Stokes – the man in the coffin – a dead man, no less – but they had also lost Lucas. The former had vanished without a trace, whilst the latter had … what? Been kidnapped by a villain called Frank DeMayo? Perhaps. It was all a little fuzzy. A lot like her head after only three hours sleep.

Reaching over, Agatha snatched at her phone before it could

vibrate straight off the bedside table. It wasn't her alarm; someone was calling her. 'Hello.'

'Am I your only friend?' The question was barked out by a gruff voice that was unnaturally blunt. 'Am I? I mean, I must be. What other explanation can there be?'

Agatha cleared her throat. 'Good morning, Clifford.'

Clifford as in Clifford Goose. The Chief Constable. The top dog of Stainmouth Police Force. He who shall be obeyed. At least to his face. Behind his back, you could do and say what you liked.

Sitting up in bed, Agatha cradled her phone between her neck and her shoulder so she could rub her eyes. 'It's early.'

'Early?' hollered Goose, louder than ever. 'Damn right it's early. That's how you catch the worm. You should count yourself lucky, though. I was woken up about twenty minutes ago. The worm hadn't even poked its head out of the earth by then.'

'Is this about Lucas?' wondered Agatha.

Apparently not. 'Who the fuck's Lucas?' growled Goose.

'It's not important. So, how can I help you?'

Goose took a moment. 'How many children do you know in Stainmouth?'

'Children?'

'Small people,' said Goose, as if it genuinely needed explaining. 'Not the spotty variety. Younger than that. Proper little ones.'

Agatha tutted, frustrated. 'You've lost me, Clifford.'

'Let me set the scene,' he began. 'Last night, about ten-ish, a young girl, four or five years old, somewhere in that ballpark, got taken into Stainmouth Police station and asked for you by name.'

'By name? Agatha Pleasant?'

'Yeah, that's your bloody name, woman!' roared Goose. 'Chuffin' hell, I know it's early, but try to keep up. This young 'un then proceeded to sit in the station waiting room and refused to budge. She says she's got something to tell you. Nobody else.'

'How strange. Who is she?'

'God knows. She's refusing to tell us anything, stubborn little mite. My desk sergeant didn't know what to do, so he called his inspector. The calls went higher and higher up the chain until it finally dropped on my doorstep. Which leads me to you. The mysterious Agatha Pleasant. Who doesn't know a single child in Stainmouth.'

'Clifford, I'm as confused as you. Honestly. At a guess, it's a case of mistaken identity. I'll sort it out, though. Where's the girl now?' asked Agatha.

'She's still at the station. In a cell,' added Goose matter-of-factly.

'A cell? For pity's sake, Clifford. She's not a criminal—'

'Isn't she? We don't know that. Besides, she's got to stay somewhere. Don't worry; she's got a blanket. She'll be fine. Just sort her out for me. I'm no good with small people. Can't stand all the sniffling. If you need to blow your nose, then bloody blow it. Don't just let it run down your face.' Goose paused. 'Talking of small people, where are we at with Impetus Stokes?'

The question caught Agatha on the hop. 'He's ... um ... what do you want to know about him?'

'Where he is for a start? Still in the hospital?'

'No.' At least that was true. 'He's ... safe.'

'Safe?'

'Safe ... and sound,' replied Agatha, stumbling slightly over her words.

Goose took a moment to let that stew. 'You sound funny. You've either got something stuffed in your mouth or you're lying. You do know where he is, don't you?'

'Of course I do,' laughed Agatha. 'It's the early wake up call, Clifford. I've not quite clicked into gear yet.'

'Yeah, well, whatever. I'm pleased you've got things under control, though, because there's been a change of plan. The Imp's premature resurrection has muddied the waters. We'll be collecting him a little earlier than I first suggested—'

'How much earlier?' asked Agatha, snatching at her words a little too eagerly.

'Keep your wig on,' snorted Goose. 'I'm not waiting outside your door. I don't want to see you in your friggin' nightie. Not without a bit of slap on at least. No, I'll send some boys round later on today. Whenever you're free.'

'I'm not,' replied Agatha quickly. *Too* quickly, in fact. Suspiciously fast. 'I mean, I've a busy day ahead of me. We all have. My team and I. We're going to be occupied until late tonight.'

'And yet that's the same team who are currently sat on Stokes, right?' said Goose. As Agatha expected, she had aroused his suspicions. 'I want them by his side at all times. And I mean all times. If he's taking a dump, I want them sat beside him, holding the bog roll. Do you catch my drift?'

'How could I not?' sighed Agatha. She had things to say, but decided against it. Better to keep Goose on side, at least for the time being. Especially when, unknown to him, she was the one in the wrong. 'Tomorrow,' said Agatha. 'I'll keep Mr Stokes under wraps until then. Please don't argue, Clifford. I'm really not in the—'

'Fine,' muttered Goose. 'Who am I to disagree with Stainmouth's secret squirrel? I want the Imp first thing, though. Six on the dot. No excuses. Then we can all wipe our hands of this sorry shit show once and for all.'

'And are you going to tell me what this sorry shit show is actually about?' pressed Agatha. Or why a gang of villains were desperate to get their hairy hands on a temporarily dead convict, even going as far as to take Lucas as a bargaining tool? She left that as a thought, though. No words necessary.

'All will be revealed in due course,' chuckled Goose. 'I'll probably stick it in my memoirs. Let you read it when I'm six feet under.'

'Or just tell me on the phone like a normal person,' suggested Agatha.

'Where's the fun in that?' Goose ended the call without

another word. No long goodbyes or see you laters.

Pompous git.

Slamming her phone down on the bedside table, Agatha climbed out of bed and hurried towards the bathroom. She was awake now; no point trying to get back to sleep. No, a cold shower followed by a strong coffee would do the trick. Two strong coffees. Get the heart pumping. The brain ticking.

She had twenty-four hours.

Twenty-four hours to find Impetus Stokes and rescue Lucas.

Both would have to wait, though. Top of her list was a trip to Stainmouth Police station.

There was a small person there who knew more than she should have.

CHAPTER THIRTY-TWO

Cockleshell Farm was slowly waking to another grim and grisly morning.

Proud Mary was always first up. It was one of nature's laws. Thou shalt not rise before the landlady. Without making a sound, she went about her business. Like a ghost in the dark. Or just someone who knew where all the creaks were in the floorboards.

Next up was Rose. Truth is, she had barely slept. With her nerves on end, she had just laid there, staring up at the ceiling. Thinking. Thinking. Thinking. A lot had happened that previous evening, not much of which made sense. The vanishing Impetus Stokes. The violently insistent Frank DeMayo. The disappearing Lucas. So many different threads woven together with them, the four of them, currently three, Agatha Pleasant's Nearly Dearly Departed Club, stuck in the middle.

There was one particular thread, however, that kept eating away at Rose, tapping at her brain like a woodpecker, demanding her attention.

Where had Mercy gone?

The missing hour. From when they had arrived at the hospital to when they left. If it hadn't been for Frank and the horror that ensued, Rose could easily have disregarded it. But Frank had happened. And Mercy hadn't been there. Not until the last moment. The final act. When she had appeared from nowhere like some kind of movie heroine and saved the day. Lucky. Not just for Rose and Tommy, but for Mercy herself. Because if anything had happened to the two of them, she would've had a lot of explaining to do. She *still* had a lot of explaining to do. Not about Tommy's cuts and scratches and bruised ego; about her whereabouts.

Taking her cue from Proud Mary, Rose slipped out of bed and dressed quickly but quietly. She left the room soon after. It was dark outside on the landing, but she was familiar with the layout now. Shuffling across the carpet, she came to an abrupt halt when she reached Lucas's room. The door was wide open, so she peeked inside. It was spotlessly tidy in there. And empty. So very empty. Yes, she expected that, but something still stirred. That sickening rumble in the pit of her stomach. Her old friend the fear.

Why?

What did Lucas mean to her?

She had only known him a few weeks, ever since he had been forced upon her and vice-versa. That was Agatha's fault. She had bound the four of them together. Through thick and thin. 'Til death do us part. Happily ever after.

Rose was back on the move. Tommy's room was next. Door closed, she could hear a slight *whistle* coming from inside. He was snoring. Fast asleep. Just how she liked him best. No, that was harsh. He wasn't that bad. Admittedly, he wasn't that good either, but she had known worse. Tommy was just a mouth with legs. A cocky kid in an adult's scrawny body. He wasn't malicious or vindictive; he was immature, irritating, irresponsible. And occasionally ... *very* occasionally ... he was something else entirely. Scratch away and you'd find it. Keep looking. It was there. Not far beneath the surface. A softness. A kindness. A vulnerability.

Rose was on the move again. The third door. Mercy's room. Don't wait. Don't hesitate. Get straight to the point.

Where did you go last night?

It was a perfectly acceptable question under the circumstances.

Rose was about to knock when the door swung open and Mercy stepped outside. It was hardly a surprise when the two women collided.

'Jesus, Rose!' moaned Mercy, jumping back. 'What the hell are you doing lurking about outside my door?'

'I wasn't lurking,' insisted Rose. 'It was just a coincidence.'

'Weird coincidence.' Mercy snatched a breath. 'You're lucky I didn't knock your head off.'

Yes, that *was* lucky, thought Rose.

An awkward silence lingered between the two women.

Mercy was first to snap. 'What do you want, anyway?'

Rose felt the anxiety weave its way around her body. 'There's no need to be rude.'

'Okay, what do you want anyway ... please?'

'It's nothing ... I was just wondering ... not that it matters ...' Rose put a hand on the banister behind her, partly to steady herself, partly in case Mercy reacted badly and tried to push her down the stairs. 'Where did you go last night?' she asked eventually.

'What?'

'Last night,' repeated Rose. 'You dropped me off at the hospital and didn't come back until you hit Frank. Where did you go?'

'Nowhere.'

'That's not possible. You must've gone somewhere.'

'I was nowhere, Rose,' said Mercy firmly. 'And that's the end of it.'

Rose nodded. The more she thought about it, though, the more it switched from a nod to a shake of her head. 'That's not true. I needed you, Mercy. We both did. And you weren't there.'

'And I'm sorry. But it's over now and it won't happen again. I promise.'

'What's over now?'

Mercy grabbed her by the hand. 'Nothing important. Not to you. Please, Rose. Just keep your nose out. Some things are best kept secret.'

'We'll have no secrets in Cockleshell Farm, ladies.'

The barking interruption was coming from downstairs.

When Mercy and Rose looked over the banister they saw Proud Mary stood at the foot of the staircase with a frown troubling her forehead and a shot gun clenched tightly in both hands.

'What are you doing with that?' asked Mercy. Swerving around Rose, she made her way down the stairs. 'You only have to ask if you want us to do some housework.'

'I do my own housework,' insisted Proud Mary. 'Others don't tend to reach my standards. As for this ...' The landlady turned the shotgun over in her hands. 'I was just about to clean it when I heard the pair of you whispering. That's why I came to investigate. This little secret you mentioned anything to do with my car.'

Mercy stopped mid-step. 'Your car?'

'There's a dent in the Mini,' said Proud Mary. 'A huge dent. A huge dent that wasn't there when I leant it to you two last night. Any idea how it came to be?'

Mercy opened her mouth. And then left it open when the words refused to come. 'I ... um ... didn't ... is there, really?'

'Yes, really,' frowned Proud Mary. 'That'd be a peculiar thing to joke about, don't you think?'

Mercy looked away. And then looked back when she realised looking away only made her seem as guilty as hell.

'A headlight has been smashed as well,' Proud Mary added. 'These things don't just happen without you realising. So ...'

'We hit something,' said Mercy quickly. She glanced at Rose as she spoke, but the other woman gave nothing away. 'A deer.'

'A deer?'

'Yeah, a deer,' insisted Mercy. 'It was in the road, close to here, when we hit it. I mean, *I* hit it. Sorry. I'll pay for repairs. I'll get the money somehow.'

Proud Mary waved it away. 'There's no need. I know a man who'll fix it for a few eggs. You should have told me, though. Last night. Trust is everything if we're all going to live in the same house. *My* house.'

'Yeah, I know ... I'm sorry ... honestly,' mumbled Mercy. 'This is on me.'

'Well, I'm not one to hold grudges.' Proud Mary hesitated. There was something else. 'Where's Lucas?'

'He's not here,' replied Mercy. 'But then ... you know that otherwise you wouldn't be asking, would you? We don't know where he is. I'm sure he's okay, though. He'll turn up before long.'

'Let's hope so.' Proud Mary made to leave. No, there was still something bugging her. Something she couldn't let go. 'You hit ... a deer?'

'Yeah, a deer,' said Mercy. 'What's wrong with that? You get deer in Croplington. I've seen them before.' She looked at Rose for support. 'That's right, isn't it?'

Rose nodded, all the while avoiding eye contact of any kind.

'It was definitely a deer?' pressed Proud Mary.

'We hit ...something,' mumbled Rose, still nodding, still shifting her gaze anywhere but at the elderly landlady.

'Fine. At least we know where we all stand now.' With that, Proud Mary marched back through the farmhouse.

Mercy waited until the back door had slammed shut before she spoke. 'Ever feel like you've just been interrogated? I thought she was going to tie us up and stick pins in our eyeballs—'

'You should've told her the truth,' said Rose. 'And me. You should tell me the truth about ... you know ... the other thing.'

'Leave it.' Mercy snatched her trainers off the shoe rack by the door, her fingers fumbling as she struggled to tie the laces. More haste, less speed. It wasn't her fault. She was desperate to get out of there.

'Where are you going now?' asked Rose.

Mercy opened the front door. 'For a run.'

'Where to?'

'I don't know,' snapped Mercy. 'Anywhere. Just stop pestering me. So many questions, Rose. You're dragging me down.'

With that, she was gone. Out the door. Along the driveway. Destination unknown.

Rose closed the door behind her. She waited a moment, soaking up the silence, before heading back up the stairs and along the corridor until she reached her room. She laid out on her bed, eyes wide open as she stared up at the ceiling. The thoughts came quickly, but then they always did. Dark thoughts. Negative entries probing a fractured mind.

Like Mercy, she was running away. That was where any similarities ended, though, because for Rose, there was no escape. Not from yourself. From the person you had become.

The person you had always been.

There was only one way to truly rest in peace ...

CHAPTER THIRTY-THREE

Agatha met Miles by the entrance to the Stainmouth Police station.

'Lovely morning,' she said, turning the collar up on her coat to keep out the steady drizzle. 'Hope I didn't wake you.'

'You have to be asleep first.' Miles rubbed his eyes as if to emphasise his grumble. 'I've never known a bed like it in my life. One half of it is rock hard, whilst the other half is like jelly. I've tried sleeping on the floor, but the carpet stinks. I can hear noises coming from the room below as well. A strange whinnying sound. As if one of the other guests is bumming a goat.' Miles checked himself. 'Sorry. That's what a lack of sleep does to you.'

Agatha let it pass without comment. She did, however, make another mental note to find Miles a better hotel as she shuffled through a set of revolving doors. The station was deathly quiet and, barring a single officer, completely empty. The officer in question was a middle-aged, slightly plump, drastically receding male desk sergeant. Stood behind the front counter, he lifted his head when they entered and mustered something that almost qualified as a smile if you were unsure what one looked like to begin with.

'Good morning.' It was just a short sentence – two words – but it still exerted enough effort for him to follow it up with a drawn out yawn. 'Apologies. Monday nights aren't usually so busy. Still, new day, new start and all that. Right, how can Stainmouth's finest be of assistance?'

Chatty, thought Agatha. Slightly cocksure. Worryingly, that was usually a front for gross incompetence.

'We're here to see the child,' she said.

'Ah, yes.' The desk sergeant tapped at a keyboard, his eyes glued to the monitor. 'I got word from above that you were on your way. I just need you to sign in. Oh ...' He pulled a face. 'That's odd. I'm not sure how that's ... must be some kind of glitch ... gremlins in the system—'

'In your own time,' muttered Miles, trying to stifle a yawn of his own.

The desk sergeant threw up his hands in apology. 'Don't shoot the messenger, but it says here that a Hagatha Unpleasant will be coming to interview the girl.' He glanced at Agatha. 'I mean ... I don't suppose that's you, is it?'

'Apparently so.' She could picture Clifford Goose now, chuckling to himself, revelling in his little joke. 'I won't hold it against you though ...' Agatha leant over so she could read the officer's name badge ... 'Sergeant Biggerstaff. Not if you let us in.'

Biggerstaff nodded. 'Certainly, ma'am. Happy to oblige.'

He buzzed them both through and then met them on the other side. 'The child arrived just before midnight,' he began, leading them along a corridor. 'A young couple brought her in. Apparently, she turned up at their house demanding to see the police. She's lucky she didn't get snatched at that time of night. Plenty of weirdos wandering around. We've ... erm ... got the girl in one of the holding cells at the moment. Not locked up or anything. Just for ... you know ... safety reasons.'

'Yes, Goose told me,' remarked Agatha, still struggling to comprehend such ridiculous decision making.

Biggerstaff grinned at her over his shoulder. 'Oh, I didn't realise you were on speaking terms with the Chief Constable.'

'Not through choice,' said Agatha.

'Wish I was. Wouldn't have to work nights if me and him were pals.' Biggerstaff stopped at the last cell in a line of four. He stuck the key in the lock and was about to turn it when Agatha rested a hand on his arm.

'I don't suppose a spot of breakfast would be too much to ask for, would it? An almond croissant would certainly hit the spot.'

'Almond croissant?' Biggerstaff repeated her request as if it was the first time he had heard of such a thing.

'They're readily available in every supermarket across the land,' insisted Agatha.

'And yet, funnily enough, they've never penetrated the walls of this station,' said Biggerstaff drily. 'We're not quite so cosmopolitan in our tastes, I'm afraid. I can get you something else if you like. The canteen's not open yet, but I might be able to rustle up a bread roll if I look hard enough. I'll even butter it if you give us a good review on TripAdvisor.'

Yes, far too chatty, thought Agatha. 'Thank you. That would be ... satisfactory. Miles, would you care for anything?'

'Just a banana.' Miles couldn't fail to notice the shock on Agatha's face. 'I'm on a health kick,' he insisted. 'I've not been eating great recently. It's a tricky balance when you're staying in a shitty hotel and there's about half a dozen takeaways on your doorstep.'

Agatha nodded. Make that three mental notes. Same message. Get Miles a better hotel. 'Two bananas,' she said to the desk sergeant. 'Keep his strength up.'

Biggerstaff gave a little bow before he turned the key to the cell. 'Your order has been processed, ma'am. I'm sure the chef will be preparing your food even as we speak.'

The door opened. Standing up straight, Biggerstaff stepped to one side and allowed them to enter. 'Wakey-wakey,' he said, far too loudly. 'Your audience awaits.'

CHAPTER THIRTY-FOUR

Mercy was blowing hard by the time she reached Bartholomew Avenue.

She had run there. From Cockleshell Farm to the centre of Stainmouth. Looking back now, it was all a blur. Muscle memory leading the way.

What was she doing?

Never return to the scene of the crime. It made sense, really. Why risk it? And yet she wasn't the criminal. That was just a poor teenage boy that she barely knew. A teenage boy who had flipped out after days … weeks … months of torrid abuse. Nobody can bend forever. At some point, they snap. The red mist had clearly descended on Solomon the previous evening. One good punch, one unlucky stumble. That's the way it is sometimes.

Life is cruel. And then you kill your step-father.

Even in the cold light of day, there was nothing special about Bartholomew Street. That wasn't a dig. Just an observation. Mercy wondered if it had been a hive of activity a little over twelve hours ago. Flashing lights and wailing sirens. Neighbours gathered together in their dressing gowns, talking in hushed tones, praying for something to brighten up their evening's entertainment.

Another thought slipped into Mercy's conscience. What if Solomon had just ignored her plan completely? Called the police and taken the blame? Her brain ticked over. The thoughts became more twisted. What if he had tried to dispose of Errol himself? Or the alternative. What if the guilt had overwhelmed him? One life down. How about another?

Without thinking, without dwelling on the consequences, Mercy's hands opened the gate whilst her feet wandered slowly up the path towards the front door. She knocked hard, fast. Then she took a step back.

Who was she expecting to answer? As far as she was aware, only two people lived there and one of them – Errol – was hardly in a position to greet visitors. Unless ... no. Mercy had to remind herself that the dead don't rise again. Well, not usually anyway. There were always exceptions to the rule. She lived with three of them. Not forgetting herself. The last quarter.

Thirty seconds had passed since she had knocked. There was nobody home ... so she knocked again. Force of habit. At the same time, she shuffled to her right, moving from the path to the front garden. There was a slight gap in the sitting room curtains, perfect for peeking through. Mercy leant forward until her nose was touching the glass. If she couldn't see anything now, she never would.

A voice from above was enough to send her stumbling

backwards before she could even focus.

'There's no one home, duck.'

Duck. That was a new one on Mercy. She guessed it was a term of endearment. Better than darling or sweetheart.

She lifted her head. Scanned the upstairs windows. Not Solomon's house, but next door. And there he was. Practically hanging out of one of the bedrooms. Bare arms exposed all the way to the armpit courtesy of an ill-fitting vest that you rarely saw these days. Less muscle and more string, it did little to hide a hairy chest that refused to be tamed, and a potbelly that hadn't just popped up unexpectedly overnight. No, this had been worked on for years. A full-time occupation. Eat, sleep, repeat. With the emphasis on repeat.

'I'm looking for Solomon,' said Mercy, smiling as she spoke.

'The boy?' frowned String Vest. Mercy nodded. 'He's definitely not home. The police took him late last night and he ain't come back since.'

'The police?' Mercy feigned the kind of shock that you only ever see in cartoons. Open mouth, eyes wide. A momentary stunned silence. 'That sounds bad.'

'Worse than bad,' insisted String Vest. 'It was bloody mayhem round here. Now, I can't be certain, but I reckon there might have been a murder.'

'Really?' Mercy put a hand to her mouth. Bit over-dramatic in hindsight. Too much damsel in distress. Still, String Vest didn't know her. Maybe he thought all women were frail and gentle. He looked the sort. 'What makes you think there was a murder?'

'I've got a nose for this sort of thing,' remarked String Vest proudly. 'And a pair of eyes. And those eyes saw a body being carried out of the house. Covered up it was. And they only do that with those that have passed away.' String Vest hesitated as he glanced up and down the street. 'I've not seen the dad since yesterday afternoon,' he said, confident that nobody was listening. 'Now, I'm no genius, but two and two makes four—'

'Or just twenty-two,' muttered Mercy under her breath. 'So, you think the dad's been murdered? Who would possibly do such a thing?'

Don't say Solomon.

'There was an intruder,' String Vest revealed. 'Saw him, I did. He was in our garden, bloody cheek. Good job I didn't have my golf club to hand. I'd have knocked his block off.'

Mercy nodded, distracted. String Vest may have been rambling on, but three words stood out in particular. *Him. He. His.* String Vest had seen Mercy, just like she had hoped. He had seen her ... and thought it was a man. 'Did you ring the police?' she asked.

'Too right,' he grinned. 'Got them on speed dial these days. Not that it made much difference. It was ages before they showed. I stayed up, naturally, but they didn't tell me much. Bloody typical. Don't know what I pay my taxes for ...'

Mercy may have still been nodding, but she had switched off a long time ago. She could even pinpoint the exact moment. When he confessed to ringing the police. Her plan – if you could call it a plan. If anything, it was more like a series of desperate measures in a terrible situation – had seemingly worked. The police would have identified their suspect by now. The mystery intruder. The *male* mystery intruder. And, apart from Mercy, only one other person knew the truth. Solomon. The real murderer. Harsh. He was just a kid, acting in self-defence. His step-dad had got everything he had deserved.

Yeah, keep telling yourself that. If it helps you to sleep at night.

'Are you going to answer me, or just stand there looking gormless?'

Mercy snapped out of her trance. Glanced up at the window. 'Pardon?'

'I asked you a question,' said String Vest gruffly. 'How do you know the boy? Solomon, you said he was called. Never spoken to him myself.'

'We train at the same boxing club,' said Mercy, sticking to the facts. 'We're friends.'

'I used to do a spot of boxing myself.' String Vest clenched his fists and waved them about as if that was all the confirmation anyone would ever need. 'I was decent. Lot thinner back in those days, of course. Faster on my feet. I once went ten rounds with—'

'I've got to go,' said Mercy, backing away. 'Thanks for the chat. If you see Solomon, tell him I called, won't you?'

Mercy slipped through the gate before String Vest could stop reinventing his past and maybe ask an obvious question or two. Like, who are you? What's your name? And, worse still, do you want any boxing tips? Mercy could hear him now. *Let me give you some advice. Don't get in the ring. I mean, it's not normal, is it? Girls fighting. Knocking seven shades out of one another. Not very lady-like. Pretty little thing like you could ruin your looks.*

When he spoke, however, it was more of a revelation than a rant.

'There was a car. A Mini. One of the new kind. Parked up out the front, under the streetlight. I saw the intruder get in and drive away.'

Mercy gripped hold of the gate, her knuckles white. 'Did you report that to the police as well?'

'What do you think?' said String Vest smugly. 'I even got the number plate.'

Of course you did.

Mercy waved. Nodded. Smiled. In no particular order. And then she was gone. Running back along Bartholomew Street. Away from the scene of the crime. She had wanted a witness. What she didn't want was the neighbourhood nosey bastard. The neighbourhood nosey bastard who had given the police details about Proud Mary's car.

Mercy was heading for home. Her temporary home of Cockleshell Farm.

What she didn't know, however, was if she was heading into trouble.

CHAPTER THIRTY-FIVE

A memory struck Agatha as she entered the cell.

She had been there once before. With Rose, of all people. The layout was still the same – empty except for one long bench that acted as both a seat and a bed – but the occupant was different. Female, yes, but this one was much younger. Tragically thin. A walking, talking human, but barely out of nappies.

The moment the door had opened and Biggerstaff had spoken, the girl had practically jumped out of her skin. Now she was sat bolt upright, not scared, more intrigued by the new arrivals. She was wearing a pink sleeveless dress, although a flurry of grubby brown stains had largely camouflaged the colour. An unfortunate combination of being overused and under washed. If her hands were black, then her bare feet were a shade that had yet to be invented. Blacker than black. Layer upon layer of dirt pressed together over time.

Agatha cleared her throat. Locked the emotion away. Kept it professional. 'You wanted to see me,' she said stiffly.

The girl pulled the blanket tight around her shoulders.

'Tone it down a bit,' said Miles under his breath. He received a hard stare in return. 'I mean, that's probably not the way to speak to a child, is it? I'm not criticising. I know you've not had much experience.'

'I've got grandchildren,' said Agatha. She regretted it instantly. It was nothing against Miles, but she didn't like to give much away. Remove too many layers and you left yourself exposed.

'I didn't know,' said Miles, taken aback. 'Good for you.' He held out a hand. Gestured towards the child. 'Show me how it's done.'

Agatha shook her head. 'No, *you* show *me* how it's done.'

Miles shuffled forward until he reached the bed. Crouching down, he kept any sudden movements to a minimum. 'I'm Miles. What's your name?'

The girl put a hand over her mouth.

'Okay. It's like that, is it?' His eyes darting around the cell, Miles pondered his next move. Unfortunately, he didn't have one. 'Well, if you won't tell me your name, maybe you'll tell me what you want.'

The hand dropped, the mouth opened and the girl whispered two words. 'Agatha Pleasant.'

Agatha moved forward, deciding at the last moment not to join Miles in a crouch. 'That's me. I'm Agatha Pleasant.'

'Silly name,' laughed the girl.

'Yes, I suppose it is,' shrugged Agatha. 'So, how do you know my silly name?'

There was a knock on the cell door before the girl could reply.

'One bread roll and two bananas,' announced Biggerstaff, barging his way in. 'The breakfast of kings.' He glanced at Agatha. 'And queens. Hope you enjoy.'

The sergeant distributed the food accordingly and then shuffled out of the cell before he could bear the brunt of any complaints.

Agatha studied the bread roll. It was hard and dry. By the look of things, it had been ripped apart by desperate fingers, before a small block of butter had been dumped in the middle and then left to spread itself. Hungry or not, she wasn't going to eat it.

But that didn't mean it had to go to waste.

'Would you like this?' asked Agatha, offering the roll to the girl. She nodded repeatedly whilst swiping out a hand.

Agatha moved it out of her reach before she could snatch it. 'Shall we play a game? You tell us your name and I'll give you my breakfast? What do you say?'

'Ellie,' said the girl, without missing a beat.

'Ellie.' Agatha passed her the bread roll and then watched in amazement as she furiously chomped on it, devouring it like a ravenous beast. 'Wow! You really are hungry, aren't you?'

'What's wrong with these people?' moaned Miles, jabbing an accusing finger at the cell door and all those who lingered beyond it. 'It's verging on child cruelty.'

'I'll fill in a complaints form on the way out,' remarked Agatha. Okay, maybe not a form, but she'd tell Goose. And he'd bloody well listen. Agatha would make sure of it. Things had gotten sloppy in Stainmouth, and sloppiness tended to start at the top.

'Was that nice?' she asked Ellie. The girl nodded as she swallowed the last of the roll. Wiped her mouth on the back of her hand and smiled. Agatha smiled back. That was one way to win a child's trust. Feed them. And why stop now? 'Would you like my friend's bananas?' she asked, much to Miles's dismay.

Ellie, to nobody's surprise, held out her hand.

'Well, you can,' said Agatha. 'You can have them both. That's a promise. There's just one thing I need to know. Only a little thing. How do you know my name?'

'Mister Poo-Poo told me,' said Ellie, between fits of giggles.

Agatha side-eyed Miles. 'Did she just say ...?'

'Yes, she did.' Miles shifted his attention to the girl. 'Who's Mr Poo-Poo? Is he your friend?'

'Yes, he's my friend. My best friend. He's been to my house and then we ran away.' Ellie leant forward. She had something to say. Something secret. 'Mister Poo-Poo isn't his real name though,' she whispered. 'He's called Lucas.'

CHAPTER THIRTY-SIX

Tommy heard it before he saw it.

A car.

No, scratch that. This was no ordinary car. This was a Skoda Octavia VRS. Plastered in blue and yellow checks. Flashing lights if and when required. It even had a siren, for pity's sake.

Until then, Tommy had been perfectly content. Alone in the sitting room, laid out on the sofa, he had the TV switched on to some pointlessly banal morning show presented by a vision of loveliness in a ridiculously tight top. There was no man alive who wouldn't appreciate that. Except for the gays, of course. But then they had the male presenter, and he was a fine-looking chap, make no mistake. Ex-boy band, most probably, fallen on hard times. All stubble and smiles. Fair play to the lad. Whatever takes your fancy.

Breakfast had been and gone in the form of a bowl of muesli. A little dry for Tommy's tastes admittedly, but cover it in enough sugar and he could just about get it down. Throw in three cups of coffee and he was practically buzzing his tits off. The day had just begun. The world was his oyster. Nobody had told him what to do or who to do it with. He was young, free, and single. Well, young and single, at least.

The *free* part slipped even further from his grasp when he heard the grinding *crunch* of tyres rolling over gravel.

The car had come to a complete halt by the time Tommy had dragged himself up and peered through the window. Seconds later, he was face down on the carpet, scrambling towards the door on his hands and knees.

Fuck.

Two questions sprang immediately to mind. What the hell were the police doing here? And what had he done?

He started with the latter. Nothing. Well, not much anyway. He had always done *something*. Nothing to bring the police, though. He had kept his nose clean recently, in more ways than one. Drugs of any kind had been strictly off limits ever since he had first arrived at Cockleshell Farm. Okay, so that was largely due to a lack of funds, but the facts remained the same. He was no longer a dealer. He was no longer a user. He was no longer a person of interest.

Tommy was out in the hallway when he heard the knock at the door.

Double fuck.

Five firm raps in quick-fire succession. Seriously serious. No messing about.

Not that it made much difference. You could put your fist through the door for all Tommy cared; he had no intention of answering. All he had to do was lie low for a few minutes and they would soon jog on. Nobody enjoyed hanging about on someone else's doorstep. Especially when there was no one at home. Or just someone pretending not to be at home. Same difference, really.

Tommy was halfway up the stairs when Rose appeared on the landing. 'What are you doing?'

'Keep your voice down,' he said, hushing her. 'They'll hear you.'

'They?' Rose looked beyond him. Towards the door. 'Who are *they*?'

'The police.' Tommy tried to squeeze past her, but only succeeded in tripping on a step and stumbling forward. He swore loudly before clamping a hand over his mouth in case they heard him outside.

'Why are the police here?' asked Rose, confused.

Tommy pulled a face. 'How am I supposed to know?'

'Sorry,' muttered Rose, taken aback. 'But if you don't know why they're here, why are you running away?'

Tommy spluttered something completely unintelligible. If he was being honest, Rose had a point. Why was he so keen to scarper? Was it the past sneaking up on him? Or just a guilt complex? Probably a bit of both.

Another five knocks interrupted Tommy's thoughts. Footsteps followed them on the gravel. The low hum of muted conversation. The police were moving around the house. Peering through the windows. Searching for the occupant. Or occupants. Plural. The wizened old landlady and her four curious lodgers.

'You'll have to answer,' said Tommy, gesturing over his shoulder at the door. 'Smile sweetly and tell them to ever-so politely bugger off.'

Rose tried to turn away from the stairs. 'I can't—'

'You can,' insisted Tommy, grabbing her by the ankle. 'You've got an innocent face. They'll lap up every word you say.'

Tommy stopped, listened. He could hear more footsteps. The last thing he wanted was them snooping around the back of the farmhouse. Proud Mary was out there at a guess. In one of the barns, mucking out the pigs. She would hit the roof if she found the police wandering around her yard. Then she'd hit Tommy when he inevitably got the blame.

'Go on, Rose,' he demanded. 'Stop dicking about.' He pulled harder, leaving her little choice but to do as he asked.

Against her better judgement, Rose shuffled past Tommy and made her way down the steps towards the door. She slowly lowered the handle ...

And didn't say a word. Instead, she took in the scene on the doorstep. Two police officers. One male, one female. Both uniformed. Both smiling. That was a good start.

The female officer was the first to speak. 'Good morning, madam. I'm PC Burrell and this is PC Tuffers. Are you the owner of this property?'

Rose shook her head.

'Who is then?' asked Burrell.

'I am, officer. Is there a problem?'

A relieved Rose shifted to one side so Proud Mary could join her on the doorstep.

'Perhaps.' PC Burrell pointed towards the Mini Clubman. 'Is that your car, madam?'

Proud Mary nodded.

'Last night, it was spotted at the scene of a crime,' began Burrell. 'A murder. We traced the number plate and it's brought us to your door. Do you think we could come in and discuss it further?'

'Of course.' Proud Mary stepped to one side so they could enter the property. She glanced at Rose as she did so. What was that? A scowl? A grimace?

And Rose ... well, she would've shrunk into her shell if she had noticed. But she hadn't.

No, Rose was in her own head.

Burdened with a secret that she hadn't been told yet.

A secret that led all the way to the scene of a murder.

Oh, Mercy, what have you done?

CHAPTER THIRTY-SEVEN

Problem.

Ellie didn't know her address.

Solution. Take her back to the beginning. When the girl had first appeared on their radar. The moment she had knocked on a door and begged to see the police.

The Critchleys were a young couple in their twenties. A nurse and a post-woman. Long-term dating to recently married. Forty-seven Malcolm Street was their first home together. Okay, so it was hardly the most salubrious of localities that Stainmouth had to offer, but in a world of rising house prices and chronic inflation, it was as good as it got. You have to start somewhere, after all. And Malcolm Street was definitely *somewhere.* They had been there three months now and things had gone smoothly. Yes, you still got the odd late night reveller stumbling about in the front garden, or screeching car ripping up the tarmac, but that was nothing out of the ordinary in any street in any town.

Unlike the moment the little girl had wandered up to their

door.

They had both hesitated at first, unsure whether to invite her in or leave her where she was. Fair enough. Things were different these days. You could be accused of all sorts if you weren't careful. All the girl would say is that she wanted to see the police. Nothing else. Not her name or age or address. In the end, the Critchleys had relented. They had strapped her into their car and driven her all the way to the station. They felt relieved when the desk sergeant had accepted their story before taking the girl off their hands. He had promised to take care of her. At least she would be safe now.

Safe in a cell. Alone but for a scratchy blanket. Left to starve whilst the inebriated and idiotic wasted everybody's time.

No, the Critchleys had done the right thing. Agatha was sure of that. Though it did make you wonder. Wonder how bad the wrong thing could've been ...

At that very moment, Agatha was speeding through Stainmouth in her own car. An Audi A8. A luxuriously spacious interior with particularly comfortable seating in the rear. Agatha had read that in the brochure. Snapped it up immediately. Her driver, Olaf, practically mute yet irrefutably reliable, was at the wheel. Miles joined him in the front passenger seat, whilst Agatha and a young female police officer were enjoying the *particularly comfortable seating in the rear*, either side of a restless Ellie. To Agatha's surprise, the girl had perked up a little. Maybe it was the car journey, especially the way she swayed from side to side as Olaf swung the Audi around the tight Stainmouth bends.

Or maybe it was just the bread roll and two bananas that were currently resting in the pit of her stomach. Food equals energy equals one highly strung child stuck in a small space with four attentively nervous adults.

Olaf eased the Audi to a halt right outside the Critchley's humble abode. Agatha climbed out first, keen to extract herself from the bombardment of sticky fingers. She looked around, quickly deciding that there wasn't much to look at. The street was largely deserted. Not unusual for a Tuesday morning. Make that early morning. Before rush hour.

Agatha waited for Miles to join her on the pavement. 'What do we do now? Let Ellie off her leash and play follow the leader?'

'Bit risky,' he muttered. 'We could be walking around in circles all day.'

Agatha glanced at the girl. She was out of the car now, hopping up and down on the spot as she clung on tightly to the female police officer's hand. Without warning, she pointed at a brick bus shelter only a stone's throw from where they were standing.

'Mr Poo-Poo in there,' she said cheerfully.

That was easier than any of them had expected.

Agatha nodded at Miles, who shot off across the road. He slowed down the closer he got. The shelter wasn't the biggest. If Lucas had been in there all night, hiding out, it would be one hell of a stroke of luck.

It wasn't.

Miles peeked inside. A second later he turned back to Agatha and shook his head. Barring the odd bottle and scrunched-up chip wrapper, the shelter was empty.

'Lucas isn't in there anymore,' said Agatha, crouching down beside Ellie.

'I know,' said Ellie. 'The men took him. I watched them.'

'What men?'

'Don't know.' Ellie bit her lip. 'Mummy knows.'

'Where did they take him?' pressed Agatha. She tried to keep her cool. Not too desperate.

'Didn't see.' Ellie paused. Looked along the length of the street and smiled. 'Would you like to come to my house?'

'Yes, I would,' said Agatha, smiling back at her. 'I would like that very much.'

And I'd also like to meet your mother.

Agatha stood up as Ellie rushed past her. Without another word, the little girl set off along the pavement, skipping as she went. She had a spring in her step that Agatha couldn't fathom. She was still absolutely filthy. Under-nourished. Scarred inside and out. Everything about her shouted neglect and yet she knew no better.

Ellie stopped outside number twenty-nine. 'My house,' she said, itching to get inside.

Agatha rested a hand on her shoulder. Firm enough to stop the girl in her tracks. She waited for Olaf to draw up beside them before she spoke to the police officer. 'Can you take Ellie and wait in the car please?'

The police officer took the girl's hand and ushered her onto the back seat.

'Something troubling you?' asked Miles, moving towards the front door.

'Perhaps,' Agatha admitted. 'You just get a feeling, don't you? If we believe Ellie, then Lucas was in this house. He might still be, for all we know. Alive *or* dead. And he might not be alone. Frank DeMayo could be in there, too.'

Miles nodded in agreement. 'Should we call for back-up?'

'There's no time,' said Agatha, dismissing it with a shake of her head. 'I'm sure we'll be fine.'

'You hope.'

'Hope and good fortune have got me this far. Why change the habit of a lifetime?' Agatha took a moment to study the inside of Miles's jacket. Not in an admiring way, either. 'You are armed, aren't you?'

Miles removed his trusty Sig Sauer P365 without another word. Grabbed the door handle. Drew breath.

He didn't bother to knock.

CHAPTER THIRTY-EIGHT

Mercy skidded to a halt when she saw the police car.

It was parked on the gravel driveway at Cockleshell Farm. Within touching distance of Proud Mary's Mini Clubman.

The mystery intruder's ... no, the *murderer's* getaway vehicle.

Mercy started to walk, edging closer with every wary step. The police car was empty, which meant whoever had driven it was now inside the farmhouse. Talking to Rose. Talking to Proud Mary. And ... shit. Talking to Tommy.

Oh, please don't be talking to Tommy. You'd get more sense from the pigs in the barn.

Mercy's mind had spiralled out of control. The police were here because they knew. They knew everything. That it was her inside seven Bartholomew Street. That it was her leaving in the Mini Clubman. That it was her who had killed Errol. She hadn't, of course, but all the signs pointed to it. The second she entered the farm they would cuff her and take her away. No point begging for justice. Save it for the judge and jury.

Mercy looked back along the driveway. She could always beat

a hasty retreat. Head somewhere else. Somewhere nobody knew her. Somewhere she could lie low and then start again.

And how easy would that be without a change of clothes and barely any money?

Rhetorical question. No need to shout out *practically impossible*.

Mercy was still debating her next move when the door opened. A smiling Proud Mary was stood in the entrance.

'Oh, here she is,' she cooed, ushering Mercy into the farmhouse. 'Nice run, dear?'

'Yeah, it was ... erm ... okay,' mumbled Mercy, more than a little confused as she passed through the door and carried on into the sitting room. The sight that greeted her was a colossal head-fuck. Yes, the police were there, a woman and a man, both dressed in standard uniform with added stab-proof vests, but it's what they were doing that really messed with Mercy's brain.

Being sat on the sofa, nursing both a cup of tea and a slice of Proud Mary's fruit cake, was one thing.

Doing all that with Tommy in between you, however, was something else entirely.

He was talking, and they were listening. No, that wasn't it at all. He wasn't just talking; he was holding court. And they weren't just listening; they were also laughing their heads off. Barely able to breathe. Tears trickling down their faces.

'And then I said, well, if that's a tortoise, what's it doing poking out of your trousers?' Tommy waited for the laughter to fade before he rested a hand on PC Burrell's knee. 'What do you reckon to that, Sarah? It's all true. Happened about a year ago.'

'If you say so,' grinned the police officer. 'Listen, as enjoyable as this has been, we've really got to go.'

'Don't be like that,' said Tommy. 'Have a word, Alan. Proud Mary will cut you another slice of cake and I'll tell you all about the time I got my peeping Thomas trapped in a gym locker.'

'Mate, I'd ... *we'd* love to stay, but we can't.' PC Tuffers stood up to prove his point. Placed his empty cup and plate down on the coffee table. 'We've got work to do. The boss will string us up if we don't get back out there.'

'Have it your way,' shrugged Tommy. 'You should come back when you're not working, though. Proud Mary keeps her drugs in her bedside table. We could get proper spangled sometime between breakfast and lunch. Just look at Rose. She's been completely off her head since sunrise.'

Predictably, everybody looked at Rose. And then they laughed. Sat bolt upright in the armchair, she was staring vacantly at the wall whilst rubbing her hands together. It took a moment, but she finally realised she was the centre of attention. 'What?'

'I heard that, Thomas.' Proud Mary appeared at Mercy's shoulder. 'This is my other lodger, by the way. The one I was telling you about. Mercy. She's been out all morning.'

'Nice to meet you,' smiled PC Burrell. She kept on moving. Straight past Mercy on her way towards the door. As an afterthought, she turned back to Proud Mary. 'Thanks for your hospitality—'

'And the cake,' chipped-in PC Tuffers.

'Yes, and the cake,' PC Burrell added. 'There's nothing to worry about concerning your car. From what you've told us, it must've been kids. You were lucky to get it back. Joyriding is on the rise in Stainmouth at the moment. It always seems to come and go in cycles.'

'I blame the parents,' called out Tommy from the sofa.

Both police officers nodded in agreement before they finally left the farmhouse. Closing the door behind them, Proud Mary walked over to the sitting room window. As soon as the gravel had crunched and the Skoda had set off along the driveway, she turned back into the room. The smile, like the police, had gone.

'Sit down,' she ordered. When Mercy didn't jump to it, she barked it out again. 'Sit down!'

She had their attention now. No need to fetch her gun.

'You've brought the police to my doorstep,' Proud Mary began, shaking her head at Mercy. 'You've kept me in the dark and I've been forced to lie for you. All three of us have. That's unacceptable.'

'I'm sorry—' said Mercy.

Proud Mary cut her down with an icy glare. 'I don't want your apologies – I want the truth. From all of you. Why didn't anybody tell me we had a murderer here at Cockleshell Farm?'

CHAPTER THIRTY-NINE

Miles was about to close the door behind him when he realised there was something blocking it.

A foot. And not one of his own.

'What are you doing?' he whispered.

'Coming with you,' insisted Agatha, moving swiftly into the house.

'Do you think that's safe?'

'Thanks for your concern, but there's really no need. I can take care of myself.'

Miles closed the door behind them. There was no point arguing. Instead, he focussed on the job in hand. The silence that surrounded him was a worry. If Lucas was being held there, then he would've hoped to have heard something by now. Footsteps perhaps, coming from upstairs or down. The low grumble of voices from another room.

He edged forward. Followed his nose. There was a closed door in front of him, only partially concealing a particularly rancid stench.

You don't just stand there, waiting for things to happen ...

Striding across the hallway, Miles threw open the door and burst inside. Body low, gun raised. The curtains were pulled to, plunging the room into darkness. Seconds passed before his eyes adjusted. Seconds that could've been fatal.

Not this time.

The room consisted of five mattresses. Side by side, they took up virtually all of the floor space.

Five mattresses and five bodies.

More dead than alive, but definitely the latter. Curled up or spread-eagled. Shuffling about. Moans and mumbles as each one drifted in and out of a fitful sleep.

Miles had been in enough drug dens to know one when he saw one.

A flash of movement caught him momentarily off guard. A body, from out of the shadows, was up and off their mattress. Snarling through gritted teeth. Hands flailing like claws.

Miles shifted to one side and met him halfway. His instincts kicked in immediately. Muscle memory through years of training. Leaning in, he kneed the man between the legs. The target may have been small, but his aim was accurate. Hard enough to hurt, but with nowhere near enough force to cause any serious damage. The man cried out and the other zombies stirred. Seconds passed before their brains processed the information.

Two strangers. Not on their wavelength. Not riddled from the toes up with narcotics.

Another man climbed clumsily to his feet, hands waving

about in exaggerated annoyance. A greasy ponytail and straggly beard dressed in stained tracksuit bottoms and a ripped t-shirt. Nine stone wet through. Barely a threat, thought Miles, but a threat nonetheless. He could always knock Beardy back down again, a simple jab, maybe even a slap, but then he would have to do that to all of them if they decided to confront him.

No, there was an easier option. Neater. Tidier. Less exhausting.

Miles raised his gun and pressed it against the man's temple. 'Don't.'

Beardy rocked back on his heels. Struggled to keep his balance. 'Get the fuck out of here!'

Miles increased the pressure, sending the druggie stumbling backwards. 'Where is he? Lucas? The black man?'

'What you talkin' about?' Beardy covered his face. What you can't see, can't hurt you. 'We ain't done nothin'.'

'You don't say,' frowned Miles. 'Has nobody ever told you lot about personal hygiene? It stinks in here. Try opening a window from time to time. And who decided that shitting yourself was socially acceptable—?'

'Leave him alone!'

Miles pushed Beardy back onto the mattress before he spun around. This time it was a woman. Creeping out of view, she had grabbed the closest thing to her.

The second stranger.

She used one hand to grip Agatha by the arm, whilst the other was holding a syringe, its tip hovering dangerously close to the older woman's neck.

'Sneaky,' said Miles, silently cursing himself. 'Not the smartest move you've ever made, though—'

'What you doin' here?' spat the woman. 'And where's my girl? What the hell you done with her?'

'Your girl?' piped up Agatha, one eye trained on the syringe. 'Ellie?'

The woman stiffened. 'Yeah, my Ellie. Where is she?'

'She's safe,' said Agatha. 'I promise. I wouldn't lie about that. What's your name?'

The woman hesitated. 'Mandy.'

'Okay, Mandy. I'm Agatha. And that's Miles. Despite what you may think, we're not the enemy. Yes, we may have burst in a little heavy-handed, but there's no reason that this has to end badly. Now, if you'll just let me go, we can—'

'Shut it!' The woman tightened her grip. 'You're not going anywhere. Not until I see my girl.'

'You weren't that bothered about her last night when she was wandering around in the dark,' muttered Miles.

'Don't you dare judge me,' spat Mandy. 'You know nothin' ... what I've been through ... all the shit that's happened. If anyone's the victim here, it's me.'

'Ah, I'm welling up,' said Miles. 'Someone pass me a tissue.'

'Shut your fuckin' mouth!' growled Mandy.

'Yes, that might be for the best,' said Agatha, glaring at him.

'Okay, okay.' Miles tucked his gun back inside his jacket. 'I'm sorry. This is tense, right? I don't want anyone to get hurt.' He locked eyes with Agatha. 'I don't want *you* to get hurt.'

'Miles, will you please stop fretting?' scowled Agatha. 'I'm not in any danger. I've *never* been in any danger—'

'Shut it, you old bitch!' shrieked Mandy.

Old bitch. Agatha exhaled slowly. The bitch she could handle, but old? It wasn't even an insult, not really, but something about it struck a nerve. Old implied weak and feeble. Incapable. That's what irritated Agatha. No, it was more than that. It angered her.

Lifting her foot, Agatha scraped the heel of her shoe down Mandy's ankle, before finishing it off with a fierce stamp on her bare toes. A satisfying *crunch* of broken bones was followed by a piercing squeal. The pain was so sudden, so intense, that Mandy had little choice but to drop the syringe, release her grip on Agatha and fall back onto the nearest mattress.

'You brought that on yourself,' said Agatha, wagging a disapproving finger at the sobbing addict.

'Nice,' said Miles, trying not to smile. 'Where did you learn that? Spy school?'

'I think I saw it in a film,' admitted Agatha, brushing herself down. 'You know the kind. One man against four hundred. Oddly enjoyable when you can't sleep.' Agatha snatched a breath. Waited a moment for the adrenaline to subside. 'We don't want to be here any longer than we have to,' she said, addressing the room, 'so let's cut straight to the chase. Is there anybody else in the house?'

Sat with her knees up to her chin, hands rubbing frantically at her battered toes, Mandy somehow spluttered out an answer. 'Not that I know of.'

'And the man we're looking for. Lucas. Has he been here?'

'I don't know. Maybe. A friend of ours ... Frank ... he's got a room upstairs. He brings people ... does shit to them ... we try to ignore the screams.'

Agatha nodded at Miles, who raced out of the room. She could hear him stomping around upstairs. Twenty seconds later, he had returned.

'All clear,' he said, trying to catch his breath without showing it. 'There were handcuffs attached to a radiator, though. Someone's been held prisoner up there.'

Agatha turned back to Mandy. She was chewing on her knuckle, rocking back and forth. What was that? Fear? Or just the body demanding its morning hit? 'Tell me about Frank.'

Mandy shrugged. 'Frank's just Frank. Everyone knows him. I met him in a pub one day. He's a nice guy. Not pervy. He's too old for that sort of thing. He asked if he could use a room ... you know ... for business. Said he'd pay. He sorts us out from time to time.'

'What kind of ... *shit* does he do to people?' pressed Agatha.

Mandy blew out. 'Horrible shit.'

'We think Frank might have a colleague of ours.'

'Yeah, well, good fuckin' luck with that. Like I said, Frank's a nice guy. Get on his wrong side, though, and he'll tear you limb from limb. Now, where's my girl?'

Agatha ignored her. Turned to Miles instead. 'Call this in.

Get the locals to shut the place down. Forensics can pull any prints from upstairs.'

'I asked you a question,' shouted Mandy, rearing up.

'A question I've already answered,' said Agatha bluntly. 'For once in her young life, Ellie is safe. It's the least she deserves.'

'Can I see her?'

Agatha made her way towards the exit. Muttered under her breath. 'What do you think?'

'I've got rights,' shrieked Mandy. 'She's my daughter.'

'She *was* your daughter,' said Agatha. With that, she swept along the hallway, straight out the door, all the way to Olaf and the Audi. Fresh air had never tasted so good. Now all she needed was something to wipe her hands on. Followed by an intense body scrub, although that would probably have to wait until this was all over.

This being the safe return of Lucas Thorne.

Everybody knew Frank DeMayo, Mandy had insisted. Agatha didn't need everybody, though. Just one person.

Why scrape around at the bottom when you can demand answers from those at the very top?

CHAPTER FORTY

Mercy stopped pacing the sitting room floor.

'That's it. The truth. The way I see it, anyway. There's nothing more to say.'

Silence. Open-mouthed, unblinking, gormless silence.

'Bloody hell, Mercy,' blurted out Tommy eventually. 'And I thought *we* were having fun with furious Frank back at the hospital.'

'Language, please, Thomas,' warned Proud Mary.

Tommy screwed up his face. 'Apologies. I have sinned and for that I am truly sorry. Wash my mouth out with soap and water and send me to bed with no supper.'

Proud Mary rolled her eyes at him whilst trying not to smile.

'Poor boy,' said Rose. 'Solomon, you said his name was. And you know him from the boxing club?'

Mercy nodded. 'Not that well, though.'

'But you gave him your number. You wouldn't have done that for no reason.'

'Nimble told me he was having a bad time of it. I was trying to help. It's no big deal.'

'Yeah, leave it out, Rose,' said Tommy. 'Mercy probably fancied grabbing herself a toy-boy. He's black, isn't he? He's probably got a massive—'

Mercy sighed. 'Casual racism at its very best.'

'Massive *personality*,' said Tommy, emphasising the word. 'Get your mind out of the gutter, Mercy. You're better than that.'

'Well, I for one think we've heard enough,' said Proud Mary. 'Mercy went to visit a friend in need and got there shortly after a horrific incident. A man was murdered in his own home by an intruder, for goodness' sake. It was enough to make Mercy leave in a fluster and then lie to the police. I'm not condoning it, but it's perfectly understandable. Getting caught in a compromising situation is hardly to be advised. No, unless the police decide to call again, we'll draw a line under the whole sorry ... no, sad ... tragically sad affair. Agreed?'

Mercy nodded, Tommy yawned, and Rose ... hesitated. Not everything seemed to add up. She was about to raise her concerns when a ringtone beat her to it.

'It's Miles,' said Mercy, removing her phone. 'I should probably take it.'

Rose waited until the other woman had left the room before she spoke up. 'Do you think she'll tell him what happened?'

'I doubt it,' replied Proud Mary.

'Maybe we should.'

'No.'

'Agatha?'

'Certainly not,' Proud Mary barked. 'She'll react badly. Worst-case scenario, she'll take you all away. It's been nice having a full house again. If I'm being honest, I'll miss the company.'

Tommy put his arm around the landlady's shoulder. 'You'll miss my handsome face and sparkling charisma more like.'

'If you say so,' smiled Proud Mary, pushing him away. 'Right, I've got work to do. No more secrets, though.'

There was one out, one in as Proud Mary headed towards the back door and Mercy returned from the hallway.

'Miles wants us out on the street,' she said, tucking her phone back into her pocket. 'We're to look for Impetus Stokes.'

'I'd rather look for Lucas,' said Rose.

'Yeah, me too. Miles seems to think that him and Agatha have got a better chance of finding him, though. I suppose that's a good thing. At least they haven't just washed their hands of him.'

'So, what do we know about old stumpy Stokes?' wondered Tommy. 'We've got to start somewhere. Maybe he's gone back to the rest of the Oompa Loompas at the Chocolate Factory.'

Mercy ignored that. 'According to Miles, he's got a mother in Stainmouth. Seems like Stokes has lived with her all his life before he went inside.'

'You got an address?' asked Tommy. Mercy nodded. 'Well, what we waiting for? Let's go visit mummy dearest.'

Mercy held up a hand. 'You two can. There's somewhere I need to go first. You can drop me off on the way ...'

Rose waited for her to fill in the gaps. She didn't. 'Proud

Mary said no more secrets.'

'This isn't a secret,' snapped Mercy. 'I'm going to the boxing club. To see Solomon.'

'And that's where you think he'll be?'

Probably not. 'Got to start somewhere,' shrugged Mercy. 'You said that yourself. Listen, his step-dad's just been murdered in the family home. He's gonna' be a right mess. Give the kid a break, eh? And, whilst you're at it, give me one, too!'

The severity of Mercy's tongue was enough to stun the other two into silence. Rose peered down at the floor, the carpet suddenly the most fascinating thing in the sitting room, whilst Tommy skipped off to find Proud Mary so he could get her car keys. Mercy moved as well. Out the front door as fast as possible, never slowing for fear of more questions.

Yes, she had told them everything that had happened the previous evening.

Everything ... with one glaring omission.

They didn't need to know how Errol had been murdered. How he had died at the hands of his stepson. No, like everybody else that had been dragged into this unfortunate event, they now believed there had been an intruder. And that's how it would always be remembered. Logged and recorded. Mercy had rewritten history, and the more she repeated it, the more she told herself it was true.

Stay strong, Solomon. Don't crack. Because Mercy knew that she wouldn't. Not now, not ever.

There were some secrets she was prepared to take to the grave.

CHAPTER FORTY-ONE

Agatha couldn't believe an establishment like this still existed.

Not in this day and age. The twenty-first century. Where everyone was equal, regardless of sex or colour or religion or anything else that distinguished one individual from another. Where it no longer mattered whether you spoke in clipped tones. Could recite Latin. Played croquet to a professional level. Stamped all over the weak and flailing with the finest leather brogues.

Who was she trying to kid? Agatha wasn't naive. The old way would always be the *way,* at least in her lifetime. Why change what had worked so well for so few? Fuck the rest of them. The unassuming masses. Joe and Josephine Bloggs. Especially Josephine. Know your place, woman.

And that place was certainly not The Wild Boar Private Members' Club.

The private members being men. And not just any men, either. Men of a certain standing. Of dignity and repute. Men born into money. Into class. Agatha could've howled with laughter. There were probably more paedophiles and rapists in here than Stainmouth prison. Cynical perhaps, a little judgmental, but so what? They had judged her first. Judged her to be inferior. Inadequate.

In hindsight, she should have sent Miles. He had the look, after all. The voice. The mannerisms. More importantly, he had a penis, and yet, oddly enough, he wasn't a grade A prick like the rest of them.

Agatha shuffled her feet in the lobby. From where she was stood, she could see the dining room. She could also see a gangly man with a thin face and oily hair swept back over his scalp marching towards her.

'This is a members only club I'm afraid, madam.'

Agatha studied the man's name badge. *Godfrey. Head waiter.* He spoke with a lisp, which was probably encouraged.

'Members only?' Agatha put a hand to her mouth in mock horror. 'How silly of me! I didn't realise. Maybe I could sign up.'

'Not possible.'

'Because ...'

Godfrey looked her up and down. 'Just ... because.'

Agatha nodded. Appeared to take it in her stride. 'Would you like me to leave?'

'Yes, please, madam,' said Godfrey, clearly relieved.

'Not possible,' said Agatha. 'And, before you ask, it's just ... because. Now, I know it's against club policy, but I'm going to walk into your dining room and talk to one of your distinguished clientele. If that offends you so much, then I suggest you fetch the manager. Although that would probably create a scene. And nobody likes a scene. Really, Godfrey, there's no need to look so worried. This shouldn't take long. Just turn the other way and pretend it's not happening.'

With that, she swept past the head waiter before he could protest. She wondered if he might try to stop her, but he didn't even raise a bony finger. Wise man.

With nothing or no one stood in her way, Agatha strode confidently towards a particular table. The dining room was half full, but all eyes shifted in her direction.

One pair of which belonged to Clifford Goose.

His face dropped when he realised it wasn't just a woman; it was Agatha bloody Pleasant.

'What now?' he groaned.

'Nice to see you too, Clifford.' Agatha turned towards the other man at the table. He had a bloated face and small, piggy eyes. 'Sorry for the interruption.'

'No need to apologise.' The man smiled, revealing a mouthful of crooked teeth. His next move was to raise a bushy eyebrow at the Chief Constable. 'I didn't know you'd got married for a third time, you old dog—'

'I bloody haven't!' shot back Goose. 'Two dragons in one lifetime is enough for any poor sod.'

'Oh, where are my manners?' The other man at the table stood up. Offered his hand. 'I'm Councillor Martin. And you are ...'

'Not in the slightest bit interested in who you are or what you have to say.' Agatha stared at the dirty plates and used cutlery. 'Nice breakfast on taxpayer's money, was it?'

Councillor Martin mumbled a reply as he sat back down again. 'Everybody's got to eat.'

'True,' nodded Agatha. 'Keep it in perspective, though. Coco pops instead of foie-gras. Coffee instead of Champagne—'

'It's brunch, not breakfast,' argued Goose. 'You struggling to keep up, Agatha? I mean, you do look pretty rough this morning. Early wake-up call, was it?'

Agatha nodded. 'Indeed. It was more of a cock than a cockerel, though. And, funnily enough, it's the same cock I'd like a chat with now.' She paused for effect. 'That's you, Chief Constable. Shall we talk in private, or would you rather I pull up a chair?'

Goose answered the question by removing his napkin from inside his collar and standing up. 'If you'll excuse me, Councillor, I'm just going to use the facilities. I won't be long.'

'And neither will I,' chipped-in Agatha. Without another word being passed between them, she followed Goose all the way across the length of the dining room and into the lobby, practically snapping at his heels. They had almost made it to the restroom when Goose turned sharply.

'Where do you think you're going?' he barked.

'Wherever you're going,' said Agatha matter-of-factly.

'Well, I'm going for a piss.'

'Then so am I.'

'There are no women's toilets.'

'Then I'll just have to follow you into the only ones available, won't I?'

'Fuck's sake.' Goose set off again, huffing and puffing, with Agatha close behind. His momentary delay had given Godfrey the chance to block his path, creating a barrier between Goose and the relief of emptying his bladder.

'Chief Constable, whatever your relationship with this woman, I'm afraid that, under no circumstances, is she permitted on the premises. It is against club policy. Members will complain. You'll be cautioned—'

'Listen, you spindly prick ...' Lunging forward, Goose grabbed Godfrey by his cheeks, squeezing them so tight that the head waiter's teeth poked out of his mouth. 'Talk to me like that again and I'll have you arrested for abusive language. This woman is nothing to do with me. I have no relationship with her. She is not my friend ... sister ... mother ... and she's certainly not my wife. Stop wetting yourself, though. I'll deal with her accordingly and she'll be gone before your pants have dried. Now, run along and never speak to me again. Not unless I give you permission. Which I won't. Understand?'

Godfrey understood alright. Freeing himself from Goose's grip, he scampered away in the opposite direction.

Rant over, Goose marched purposefully into the restroom. Agatha stayed one step behind. Pushing open the door, the first thing she saw was a vast, luxurious space, all glass and marble, flattering lighting and a smattering of spider plants.

And a man. He was looking in the mirror, rearranging any

loose strands of hair in a vain attempt to cover an increasingly noticeable bald spot.

'Get out,' said Agatha firmly.

The man's mouth fell open in stunned disbelief. 'You ... you can't say that.'

'I just have,' remarked Agatha. 'I could always repeat myself if it'll help. Get out. Now.'

'Clifford, are you going to let this ... *female* talk to me like that?'

Goose swayed awkwardly from side to side. 'Sometimes it's easier just to do as they ask,' he mumbled. 'Easier on the ear drums.'

The man half-chuckled, half-frowned as he exited the restroom, all the while giving Agatha the widest berth imaginable.

'You really are a sexist pig, Clifford,' said Agatha, shaking her head at him.

'Got rid of him, didn't I?' shrugged Goose. 'Thought you'd prefer it if it was just the two of us.' Without warning, he wandered over to one of the urinals and unzipped his trousers. Side-eyed Agatha and tutted. 'Bit of privacy wouldn't go amiss.'

'Don't worry yourself,' said Agatha, perching on the corner of a row of sinks. 'If I wanted to look at willies, I'd find one attached to a better body. Younger. Firmer. Not quite so flabby.'

'Now who's being sexist?' Goose returned his gaze to the urinal. Sighed as the liquid started to flow. 'Ah, that's better. Champers always seems to pass straight through me. Right, if it's not my body you're after, then what is it? And don't dick around, no pun intended. I've got a lunch date at the tennis club in a few hours. Wouldn't want to be late now, would I?'

CHAPTER FORTY-TWO

Tommy wasn't the easiest person to be stuck in a room with.

It wasn't exactly plain-sailing if you had the run of the entire house. If he was upstairs and you were down. Or on a different street. Village. Town. Country. And so on and so forth …

In a car, however, a Mini Clubman, he was practically unbearable.

Uncharacteristically, he sat in silence until they had dropped Mercy off at the Come Fight With Me boxing club. Then, the second she had hopped out of the car and they were all alone, his brain vibrated, his mouth quivered and the words began to flow.

'She's hiding something. I can see it in her eyes. It's as clear as day. You don't think it was her who copped for that Errol geezer, do you? She's got a fierce temper, our Mercy. It doesn't take much for her to blow her top. What do you reckon, Rose? Go on. Tell me. You must think something.'

'I do,' said Rose defensively. 'I'm just … concentrating on the road.'

'Why? We're not even moving,' muttered Tommy.

Good point, thought Rose, as she started the car. A good point that all but ended her argument.

'You know what you are,' Tommy began, banging the back of his head against the headrest. 'An NPC. Non-playable character. You get them on video games. They don't do anything. They're just screen fillers. Like extras in a film. Nobody remembers them. Nobody cares about them. Nobody notices them. They just ... exist.'

Rose took a breath as she pulled away from the kerb. 'And can these NPC's drive?'

'I don't know. Probably not.'

'Exactly,' said Rose, oddly smug. The smugness vanished in a flash when her phone unexpectedly *pinged*.

Tommy waited. 'Are you going to check that?'

'I'm driving.'

'Yeah, but driving where? It's probably Miles with the address for Stokes's mother.'

Another good point. Damn you, Tommy O'Strife.

'Let me get it ...' Tommy had barely leant over, his hand hovering over Rose's leg, when she jerked to one side, spinning the steering wheel as she did so. It was enough to send the Mini into a momentary swerve before she thankfully regained control.

'Whoa!' Tommy, both hands on his seat belt, had gone a deathly shade of pale. 'I was only trying to help. No need to scare the shit out of me.'

Rose avoided eye contact as she carefully removed her own

phone from her own pocket. '*Ada Stokes. Fourteen Peartree Court*,' she read out loud.

'I'll get the original sat-nav,' grumbled Tommy, reaching onto the back seat so he could grab the map of Stainmouth. 'Try not to crash into anything whilst I'm not looking.'

Ten minutes later, they arrived.

Driving under a narrow archway, Rose steered the Mini Clubman into a concrete courtyard. She parked up in the first space she came to. There was a semi-circle of bungalows straight in front of them. Rough estimate twenty.

'What is this place?' frowned Tommy, gazing out the window at an array of benches, ramps and potted shrubs. 'It's like an old folk's wet dream. One step from heaven.'

'It's sheltered housing,' said Rose. 'Warden controlled, most probably. For people who might need assistance from time to time.'

'I could do with a bit of that,' grinned Tommy. 'Some fit nurse to scrub my back whilst I'm in the bath.'

'Ask nicely and I'm sure Proud Mary would lend a hand.'

'It's what she'd do with those hands that worries me,' said Tommy, eyebrow raised in mock horror. 'Believe it or not, Rose, but women find me irresistible.'

'Not. But then you did give me the choice.' Rose looked out over the courtyard, keen to steer the conversation away from Tommy's sheer animal magnetism. 'Over there,' she said, pointing towards one particular bungalow, albeit one that was identical to all the others in shape and size. Even the colour of the door. A majestic blue. Peeling in all the wrong places to reveal its original wooden surface lurking beneath. 'Number fourteen.'

'It's tiny,' said Tommy, climbing out of the car. He slammed the door shut with unnecessary force. 'There's barely room to swing a Stokes in there. He'd crack his head on the lampshade.'

Rose locked up. Walked over to Tommy, before dropping slightly behind him.

'It's only fair that you go first,' she said, urging him on with a nod of her head. 'Women do find you irresistible, after all. I'm sure you'll be able to win Ada over.'

'She's only human,' said Tommy, bounding up the short path. 'You shouldn't try to fight it either, Rose. Ask nicely and I'll put you on the waiting list. You might even get special perks seeing as we already live together. Early access.' Tommy swivelled around. Pointed at himself. 'Early access to *this*.'

Rose stopped. Panicked. 'I'd rather not jump the queue,' she said hastily. 'It wouldn't be fair to all the other women who have been waiting so patiently.'

'True.' Tommy turned back towards the door. Rang a bell that played a jolly little tune with a hint of Christmas. 'No one home.'

'Give her a chance,' said Rose. 'She might not be that quick on her feet.'

'She wouldn't have to be,' moaned Tommy. 'You could crawl backwards with your eyes closed and still make it to the door in seconds.'

He rang the bell again. And again. And again.

Rose eventually removed his finger. 'Stop it. She'll be a nervous wreck.'

'Except she's not in, is she?' Tommy slammed his hand down on the door handle. To his surprise, it dropped, and the door flew open. 'Oh, maybe she is ...'

Rose reached out to grab him, but she was too late. Tommy had already stepped inside, stopping only to wipe his feet on the rug whilst he checked out the decor.

'I don't think—' began Rose.

'No, you wouldn't, would you?' Tommy moved forward, leaving a Rose-sized gap in his wake. 'Close the door behind you. Any old riff-raff could just wander in if you're not careful.'

Tommy stared at Rose until she did as he asked. With one stipulation. Tommy was all set to head deeper into the house when she pulled him back. Mouthed a single word.

Wait.

'Hello,' she called out softly. 'Ada. Are you home?'

Tommy rolled his eyes. 'Give it a bit more oomph, why don't you? Wakey-wakey, granny,' he hollered. 'We've come to clean your false teeth.'

Rose winced. Her embarrassment was short-lived, though. Largely because nobody answered.

'Told you she was out,' said Tommy, reaffirming the obvious. 'We might as well hang around now we're here, though. Wait until she returns.'

Rose watched as he continued along the narrow hallway. The house comprised four rooms. Two bedrooms directly in front of them, a bathroom to their left and, at a guess, a sitting room to their right. They would find out soon enough, thought Rose, as Tommy turned into the room.

Without warning, he staggered back out until he crashed into the wall behind him. 'Sweet Jesus! What the fuck is that?'

Rose hesitated. Once upon a time, she would've turned and run. Maybe she should've now. And yet something urged her on.

She took several shuffling footsteps until she reached the entrance to the room. Peeking inside, she took it all in the best she could.

A square room. Low ceiling. Old-fashioned in both design and decoration. A swirly carpet of every shade of brown clashing with garish flock wall paper. Limited furniture. A sofa. A coffee table. And a rocking chair. Rose let her gaze linger on the last of those.

There was an elderly lady moving gently back and forth. White hair, slightly balding on top. Eyes freakily wide behind thick horn-rimmed spectacles. A shawl draped over her shoulders and a blanket on her lap.

'Sorry ... we didn't ... we shouldn't have just walked in uninvited,' stammered Rose, eager to get her excuses out.

The lady blinked. It was a start. At least she was still alive.

Pushing himself off the wall, Tommy rejoined Rose in the doorway. He was back. Composure restored. Confidence set to max. It was just an old granny, after all. Creepy, yes, in a wrinkly kind of way, but nothing to have nightmares about. 'You must be Ada,' he said, flashing her his best smile. 'We're looking for your son.'

'Impetus?' Ada Stokes lifted her rug. There was something there, balanced in her lap, pointing straight at them. 'Well, you're too late,' she remarked, her mouth barely moving as she spoke. 'He's gone. Now it's your turn.'

Tommy stared at what she was holding. He tried to edge away, but he had barely shifted before the old lady's body jerked and she was thrown back into her rocking chair.

What followed was a *crack*.

A *flash*.

And a cloud of smoke.

One down. One to go.

CHAPTER FORTY-THREE

'What did you say his name was again? I couldn't hear you over all the splashing.'

Clifford Goose zipped up his trousers and turned away from the urinal, thankfully in that order.

'Frank DeMayo,' repeated Agatha, her eyes fixed in the opposite direction for fear of seeing something she'd rather not.

'Yeah, I know him,' nodded Goose. 'A career criminal, he's been running gangs out of Stainmouth for over forty years now. What would that make him? Early ... mid-sixties. Practically a pensioner.' He looked Agatha dead in the eye and smiled. 'Okay, not a pensioner. Just seasoned. Maturing like a fine wine in a dusty cellar. DeMayo is proper old school in his ways, though. You know the kind. Respects his elders. Loves his mum. Loves everyone's mum, most probably. Tough but fair, you'd call him back in the day. Well, fair-ish. He's put more people in hospital than you've had facials. Killed a fair few, too. And yet nothing ever seems to stick. Nothing solid. Yeah, he's done time, but only a few years here and there, and that's mostly for something petty. Right, can I go now?'

The Chief Constable marched past Agatha before she had time to answer. He was heading towards the exit. Towards freedom.

'Aren't you going to wash your hands?' asked Agatha.

'What for?' shrugged Goose.

'It's hygienic.'

'I'll wipe them on my trousers. No one will ever know.'

'*I'll* know.' Agatha fixed him with an icy glare.

It seemed to do the trick.

'Chuffin' hell,' muttered Goose, heading back towards the sink. 'You're not married, are you? I can't imagine why not.'

Agatha ignored that. 'What links Frank DeMayo and Impetus Stokes?'

Goose spun around, flicking water down his front in the process. 'What's any of this got to do with Impetus Stokes?'

'Calm down, Clifford. You'll give yourself a heart attack.' Agatha drew a breath to buy herself some time. Goose didn't know everything. He didn't *have* to know everything. And she had no intention of telling him. 'This has got nothing to do with Stokes. Not really. But DeMayo has been sniffing around, asking questions we'd rather not answer. So, I'll repeat myself. How do they know each other? What's the link?'

Goose finished washing his hands. And then ruined it all by picking his nose with an unacceptable level of intensity. Like Agatha, he seemed to be delaying things. The information was there to be drip fed; not blurted out in one long sentence. And yet lunch was calling and Goose was growing more and more impatient by the second.

'Stokes was part of Frank's gang for a while,' he began. 'They did a few jobs together. The jobs were sophisticated for a blunt tool like DeMayo. Not just theft by fear. Threaten the general public until their arses go and they hand over their life savings. No, these were planned to perfection. A bank raid. Museum robbery. Some online stuff. Identity fraud and all that. Things went wrong when they targeted a top end jewellers. This guy had all the gear. Alarms in every room. Security cameras. Lasers. Proper hi-tech. And yet Frank and his boys beat it all. They walked away with a right stash. They were home and dry until one of the gang, a right mad-head by the name of Maurice Maddison, slipped up. Mad Mo they call him behind his back. He was beating some poor sucker to a pulp when he spilled the beans. Every criminal's got that bragging reflux. The guy wanted revenge when his wounds had healed and came running to the police. Threw Frank and his boys under the bus. And this is where things get weird. Impetus Stokes took the rap for the whole caboodle. The planning. The execution. Even the getaway vehicle. We knew different, but it's hard to argue with a confession. Stokes was sent down for a seven-year stretch. He was two years in and then ... well, you know the rest. He died—'

'And yet he didn't, did he?' Agatha's eyes narrowed. 'Is there something else you're not telling me, Clifford?'

'Probably, but we'll save that for another day, shall we?' said Goose, eager to get out of the restroom before any other members decided to use the facilities.

Too late.

'Oh my, is that a lady I see before my eyes?' The door swung open to reveal an overweight man with flushed cheeks and coiffured hair. 'I say, Clifford, don't be a greedy goose. I'll have a bit of what you're having, thank you very much.'

'Not now, Mervyn,' replied Goose, edging past the new arrival.

'Don't be like that.' A beaming Mervyn rubbed his hands together excitedly. 'Share and share alike. She looks delightful. A little older than most of the ladies I partake in, but with age comes a certain grey glamour.'

'Don't go there,' said Goose, desperate to get outside. 'She's not what you think. Nothing like the other women we invite here.'

'Oh, I see,' said Mervyn, tapping his nose. 'No need to explain. We all have that special friend we like to keep under wraps. Is she expensive?'

Agatha glared at the Chief Constable. 'I think your friend here is under the impression that I'm a prostitute.'

'Certainly not,' shot back Goose. 'I mean, he might be. Perhaps. It's a possibility.'

'I'm going to leave now,' frowned Agatha, squeezing between the two men. 'Before I do something I regret.'

'Oh, you wouldn't regret it,' said Mervyn, practically salivating at the prospect. 'I'm an honourable man. I'll make sure you're suitably reimbursed for your time and efforts.'

'He *does* think I'm a prostitute,' blurted out Agatha. 'Unbelievable.'

'Yes, you are.' Mervyn reached out and rested a hand on Agatha's shoulder. Without warning, she took hold of his forefinger and bent it backwards. Mervyn yelped, more in shock than pain. Agatha increased the pressure, and the yelp turned to a fully formed squeal. Yes, that was definitely pain-related. Quite satisfying, actually.

'Touch me again and I'll snap your finger,' she said matter-of-factly. With that, she let go.

'Little bit over the top, don't you think?' sighed Goose.

'Not at all,' said Agatha, pushing open the door. 'Over the top would've been smashing his head against the wall. That was my next move. Goodbye, Clifford. I'm sure we'll speak again soon.'

Agatha walked out of the restroom and into the lobby. Without breaking stride, she carried on moving until she had left the building. The Audi, as expected, was already waiting for her.

'You were a long time.' A pensive-looking Miles was leaning against the door. 'All sorted?'

Agatha nodded. 'As good as. Frank DeMayo is well known to our beloved Chief Constable. He's also got a strong link to Impetus Stokes, but it doesn't quite seem to fit. Not convincingly, anyway.'

'We can make it fit,' said Miles. 'Piece it together. I'll get a home address for DeMayo. We can pay him a visit.'

'No, pass it on to the others,' said Agatha, fastening her seatbelt. 'There's somewhere else we need to be. Olaf, will you take us to Stainmouth Prison, please?'

Olaf grunted. Just the once. That was the code. One grunt for yes. Two for no. To grunt twice was rare, though. Maybe that was a good thing. Maybe Agatha's driver was happy with what was being asked of him.

Unlike Miles. 'The prison?'

'It's time to rewind,' said Agatha. 'Let's take this back to the beginning. To the day that Impetus Stokes failed to die properly.'

CHAPTER FORTY-FOUR

Lucas was still alive.

That was what he kept telling himself. Over and over again. On repeat. He was still alive. Not dead.

That was about as good as it got, though.

They had worked him over. Taking turns. One at a time. Frank, Sandy and Maurice. Particularly Maurice. He punched harder, kicked in all the wrong places. He had even stamped on Lucas's head at one point, crushing his ear, until Frank had warned him off.

'What's wrong with you? We're teaching him a lesson – not trying to kill him! Calm it down, okay?'

But Maurice couldn't calm down. Any excuse to let rip and he always went one step too far. In the end, both Frank and Sandy had had to drag him away. Out of sight, out of mind. You can't punch someone when you're in a different room, however hard you try.

All alone, Lucas tried to shift his weight in an attempt to get comfortable. Laid on his side, he took in his surroundings through dry eyes. Best guess he was in a stable. A single stall.

There was sawdust on a concrete floor, whilst the stench of horse shit lingered relentlessly in the air. His wrists were bound with a metal chain, which had then been secured to a railing that ran along the back wall. Lucas hadn't tried to break free and probably never would. What was the point? He was already defeated. A series of steady beatings had seen to that. His mind wandered to Ellie. His last hope. Had she done everything he asked? And, if so, what good would that actually do? Frank had moved him out of the Shooting Gallery after his failed escape and brought him here.

Here.

Where the hell was here?

Even if Agatha knew he was missing, how could she ever find him?

Frank would've taken him to the middle of nowhere. A secret hideaway lost in time. Lucas rested his face on the sawdust and let his eyes close. There was no coming back from this. No use pretending otherwise. He was right royally screwed, make no mistake.

And it was all because he had left the hospital to check on a suspicious car. Tommy had even warned him not to. Yeah, say it again. Really rub it in. Tommy. Of all people ...

The door to the stable swung open, forcing Lucas to lift his head.

His body breathed a sigh of relief when he realised it wasn't Maurice.

'Only me, sunshine.' Frank placed a small wooden stool in

the centre of the stable. 'I'm back for one of our little chats. I've been looking forward to it if I'm being honest.'

'Yeah, me too,' sighed Lucas. The effort that came with speaking was enough to make him cough. He could taste blood in his mouth. Never a good sign. 'If you wanted to take me out on a date, you only had to ask.'

'You're not my type,' smiled Frank. 'Don't take it personally. In fact, don't take any of this personally. I don't know you from Adam, and you don't know me. Our paths have crossed by accident and here we are. You chained up in one corner, battered and bruised, and me sat here, freezing my nuts off in this shabby old barn. There are no winners as far as I'm concerned.'

Frank stopped to remove something from the pocket of his overcoat.

It wasn't a weapon. Not unless he usually attacked people with a mobile phone.

Lucas's mobile phone.

'The boys reckon this is yours,' he began. 'It looks a little old-fashioned if you ask me, but then what do I know? Truth is, I'd rather go back to simpler times. All this tech stuff leaves me cold—'

'Am I going to die?' Lucas blurted out. He couldn't explain where the words had come from. Too late to retract them now, though. He only hoped that the answer didn't chill him to the bone.

Frank leant forward. 'Now, why would you think that? Killing another man is way more hassle than it looks in the films. Not so much the act itself, but the aftermath. The whole getting rid of the body and then hoping that the law don't come sniffing around. It's a ball ache of massive proportions. No, I'm prepared to forgive and forget, but we have to work together. Let's try to find a solution to our little predicament, eh? There are four numbers on this piece of shit,' he said, studying Lucas's mobile. 'Again, that's odd, but we'll shelve it for now. Maybe there's an innocent explanation. Whatever, it doesn't matter. All I want to know is which one I should call.' Frank scrolled down the contact list. 'Mercy ... Miles ... Rose ... Tommy. Funnily enough, they've all been trying to call you. Repeatedly. You're a popular man, even if it is only four people. Better than none, I suppose. Right, take your pick and we can get the ball rolling.'

Lucas strained his neck, tried to focus, but the strength was slowly deserting him.

'You understand what I'm trying to say, don't you?' pressed Frank. 'One of these is the thread. The thread by which your life is hanging by. Choose wisely. Who knows more than you about Impetus Stokes? Where he might be? Who's got him? Where and when he was last seen?'

Lucas pretended to think. The answer was obvious, though. Only one of the four would read between the lines. See the situation for what it was and adapt. Lie for him. Fight for him. And still manage to do all of that without cocking it up spectacularly.

'Mercy,' he said eventually. 'Call Mercy. She'll tell you what you need to know.'

Frank stood up. Nodded his appreciation. 'Mercy it is then. Wasn't so hard, was it? I'll give her a bell. Hopefully, she can shed some light on what's going on. Because if she can't ...' Frank mimed running a finger across his throat before he turned and walked away. 'I keep telling you, son,' he called back. 'It's nothing personal. It's just the way of the world. *My* world. Only the strongest will survive and all that nonsense.'

CHAPTER FORTY-FIVE

The atmosphere in the Come Fight With Me boxing club could be best described as flat.

At worst, it was deathly sombre.

Solomon was nowhere to be seen, not that unexpected really, so Mercy had sought out Nimble, the owner. She found him in the locker room. He was mopping the floor. Head down, shoulders hunched, grunting with every push and pull.

He stopped when he saw her, his usual smile absent from his face. 'You hear what happened last night?'

Mercy nodded. 'Bits. Don't know all the details, though.'

'Better make yourself comfy then,' said Nimble, pointing towards the long wooden bench.

So Mercy had sat and she had listened. Gasped and sighed and shook her head in all the right places. Or wrong places. The places where bad things had happened. Her worries had eased by the time Nimble had finished. His story seemed to mirror the one she had created. Errol had confronted an intruder in his kitchen. They had tussled, a tussle that ultimately resulted in his death. Solomon had found the body. No mention of anybody else. Anybody else being Mercy, of course.

She wasn't there. She had never been there. No reason why she would ever have been there.

'Poor Solomon,' she said, shaking her head for what seemed like the umpteenth time. 'Where is he now?'

'At the police station,' replied Nimble.

Mercy tensed up. 'How come? Surely they don't suspect him of anything.'

'Nah,' said Nimble, much to Mercy's relief. 'It's just ... he's at an awkward age, isn't he? Neither a kid nor an adult. He's got no other family either. The police don't want to leave him at home on his own, which is fair enough, but I doubt he'd want to go and live with another family. Doesn't leave many options, does it? Only one.' Nimble shrugged his shoulders. 'Me.'

'You?' Mercy regretted that instantly. 'Sorry. That came out wrong.'

Nimble waved it away. 'I'm the best of a bad bunch. I'm off to pick him up in a bit. You can tag along if you want—'

'I can't,' said Mercy hastily. 'I've got things to do. Work.'

'I didn't know you had a job,' said Nimble.

A job. Mercy tried not to smile. Is that what this was? Running around with Agatha's Nearly Dearly Departed Club? Getting into scraps and scrapes for the privilege of staying alive? 'It's voluntary,' she said.

'Ah, should've guessed,' nodded Nimble. 'You've got a kind soul. Always willing to help others.'

'Something like that,' muttered Mercy. 'Tell Solomon I'm

sorry, won't you? About what happened. I'll come and see him soon.'

And then she was gone. She was in no mood for Nimble's casual flirting, although in fairness, neither was he. Instead, he grabbed the mop and got back to work. Anything to keep the mind busy. Block out the thoughts. She hoped Solomon could do the same.

Mercy kept on moving, passing through the boxing club until she stepped outside. She removed her phone and flicked through her contacts. Tommy or Rose? One talked bollocks, whilst the other barely talked at all. There was a good chance that Rose would be driving, so she settled on Tommy. Was about to hit the button when her phone beat her to it. An incoming call.

Lucas.

Mercy stopped dead in her tracks. Pressed the phone to her ear. 'Where the hell have you been?'

There was a stifled silence. She could hear breathing, though. And then a voice. Deep. Gruff. 'Is that Mercy?'

Not Lucas.

'Yeah, it is. What have you done with—?'

'Don't worry about your pal. He's fine. *Mostly* fine. A little sore in places, but nothing that won't heal with a tender touch. You his girlfriend?'

'No.'

'Wife?'

'What is this? Some kind of dating service?'

'No, this is me trying to find out what part you're playing in all of this. Lucas told me to call you, but you're not his wife or girlfriend. Suggests you're something else. Something hush-hush. What I can't quite figure out, though, is if you're top end, MI5 perhaps, MI6, or just a ragtag bunch of nobodies, in way over your head?'

'I could say the same about you.' Mercy's thoughts rolled back to the previous evening when she had collected ... no, *rescued* Tommy and Rose from the hospital. She put two and two together and landed on the caller. 'It's Frank, isn't it? How you feeling this morning? A little birdie told me you got hit by a car.'

Frank laughed. A hoarse rasp, it vibrated the speaker. 'Ah, that was you, was it? I owe you one.'

'Any time, any place.'

'Yeah, well, that's why I'm calling. We need to talk.'

'We're talking now.'

'In person. Face to face. We need to find a resolution. I'm too old to be running around Stainmouth with my tail between my legs. I'd rather be relaxing by a log fire, warming my bones, preferably in the company of my good friend Impetus Stokes.'

And there it was. The crux of the conversation. The knockout blow after a volley of verbal sparring.

'The dead guy in the coffin?'

'The not-so-dead guy in the coffin,' said Frank, correcting her. 'But, yeah, they're one and the same. The Imp and me are close. We go back years. That's why I'd like to see him again.'

'And you think I know where he is?'

Frank paused. Most probably for dramatic effect. 'I *hope* you know where he is. And so does Lucas. He really hopes you know. His life depends on it.'

'Okay, I get it. You can keep the threats to yourself. So, where do you want to meet?'

'I know a lovely little café. The Ugly Mug, just up from Stainmouth town centre. It's by the church. You can't miss it. One o'clock suit you?'

'Make it two,' said Mercy. No reason. If anything, just to be awkward. 'Will you be alone?'

'I don't need any big boys to hold my hand if that's what you mean,' insisted Frank. 'Anyone would think you don't trust me. It'll be broad daylight in a public place, for pity's sake. I'm not going to try to jump you. But I don't want you bringing any back-up either. We can sort this out between ourselves. Man to woman.'

'Fine. Two o'clock it is,' said Mercy. She ended the call without another word. A second later and the phone rang again. Surely it wasn't Frank ...

It wasn't.

'Most people tend to say hello when they answer a call,' moaned Miles.

'Hello,' said Mercy. 'Better late than never. What's up?'

'The sky. Sorry. Dad joke. You with the other two?'

Mercy took a moment. 'Pretty much.'

'Well, you either are or you're not ...'

'I am,' lied Mercy. They kept on coming. 'We're just finishing up with Impetus Stokes's mother. Nothing going there. It's a dead end.'

'Okay. I've got another address for you. The last known residence of one Frank DeMayo. Go there together, but don't do anything stupid. If you think there's any kind of threat, then hang back. Don't jump in and regret it later. If you need me, call. I'll get there as soon as I can. Right, I'll send you the address.'

Miles ended the call before Mercy could say another word. The message came through soon after. *Wild Wood Hall, Chambers Lane.* Very grandiose. Alright for some.

If Miles had waited just a moment or two longer, Mercy would've told him about her meeting with Frank. Maybe she still could. All she had to do was ring him back. She thought about it for less than a second. And then put her phone back in her pocket. Frank had demanded that she come alone. And if Lucas's life depended on it, then that's what she would do. Whether she liked it or not. And she didn't. Not in the slightest.

Only time would tell if she had made the wrong decision.

'You still here?'

Mercy snapped out of her trance and spun around. She was surprised to find that it was Nimble who had disturbed her thoughts. Even more surprising was the fact he had pulled up beside her in a white Vauxhall Corsa, practically mounting the pavement in the process. 'I didn't have you down as a boy-racer.'

'Just young at heart,' grinned Nimble. 'You changed your mind? Do you want to come and pick up Solomon, after all?'

Mercy shook her head. 'I would if I could, but I can't. There is one thing ...' With that, she pulled open the passenger side door and dived inside. 'A lift. Please. I've got an address,' she said, fumbling for her phone.

'Your wish is my command,' laughed Nimble. He revved the engine whilst Mercy strapped on her seat belt. 'You'd better hold on tight, though. This baby flies like the wind!'

CHAPTER FORTY-SIX

The *one down* was Tommy.

He had thrown himself at Rose when the gun had fired.

And missed.

Instead, he landed heavily in the hallway. Shit. He tried to jump back up again, but stumbled over his own feet. Third time lucky and he was upright. Rose was exactly where he had missed her. Stood in the doorway. Frozen solid. Shock. Horror. Fear. You name it.

Tommy squeezed past her, all the while shielding his face in case the old lady fired off another shot.

'We come in peace,' he said hastily. 'Just put that bloody thing down and we can talk.' A pause. 'Please,' he added.

Ada Stokes glanced down at the shotgun she was balancing in her lap. 'Over thirty years I've had this thing,' she said slowly. 'Almost as long as I've lived here in Peartree Court. It's never gone off before. Then again, I've never pulled the trigger before.'

Tommy resisted the urge to say anything sarcastic and peered over his shoulder instead. 'Where did the bullet go?'

'It didn't,' replied Ada. 'The gun's loaded with blanks. Just a lot of smoke and bluster. Like I said, I've never fired it before.'

'First time for everything, I suppose,' muttered Tommy under his breath. He turned back to Rose. To his surprise, she was still yet to move. 'Snap out of it,' he said, waving a hand in front of her face. 'You're still alive. That's about as good as it gets these days.'

A single blink and Rose had broken the trance. The last minute or so had been nothing but a blur. Whether it was true – and it wasn't – she thought she had been shot. Fact. From then on, time had stalled. When nothing happened, her initial reaction was one of disappointment. Not relief. Not joy. And yet that could have been it. A shot to either the head or heart and it would've been the end. Over and out. Rest in peace, Rose Carrington-Finch. A short, unremarkable life cut down in a blaze of inadequacy.

Was that what she wanted? She had tried to end it herself, of course, until she had been rudely interrupted. Why not try again? And this time without the interruption.

'Rose.' Tommy tapped her on the forehead. 'I said, snap out of it.'

'I have ... I'm good,' she mumbled, pushing his hand away. She turned her attention to the old lady. Mustered something resembling a smile when she realised she was being stared at.

'You look troubled,' said Ada. 'I recognise the signs. You've got that distant look behind your eyes—'

'She has that most days,' chipped-in Tommy. 'I don't mean to be rude, but we're not here to talk about Rose.'

'No, I know why you're here.' Ada gestured towards the sofa opposite her rocking chair. 'You'd better take a seat. Both of you. Settle those frayed nerves. The gun was only meant to scare you. I don't feel safe without it. I have so many visitors, you see. In and out. Men mostly. All looking for the same thing.'

'The Imp?' nodded Tommy.

'Impetus,' said Ada, correcting him. 'My lovely boy. The only family I've got.' She paused. 'The only family I *had*. Impetus and I are no longer on speaking terms. We never fell out; we just drifted apart. That was about the time ... the time ...'

'He got banged up,' finished Tommy. 'Listen, I'm not one to judge. I've been in plenty of scrapes myself. I was just smart enough to stay out of prison.'

'Not helpful,' muttered Rose.

'Oh, Impetus was smart,' said Ada. 'Ridiculously so. They called him a genius at school. By the age of eight, he knew more than the teachers. He was quiet with it, though. Never in any trouble. He just put his head down and worked hard. Took all his exams early and passed with top marks. I was so proud of him—'

'*Was?*' chipped-in Tommy.

Rose responded with a sigh. 'Not helpful ... again.'

'I'm *still* proud of him,' insisted Ada. 'Proud of what he was back then. That all changed, though, when he met a man called Frank DeMayo.'

'We've crossed paths,' said Tommy. 'Proper hard nut.'

Ada gently shook her head. 'He's worse than that. He's

an evil swine who'll stop at nothing to get his own way. He manipulated Impetus. Preyed on his insecurities. And that's why he's ended up where he is now. Locked up.'

'Except he's not,' remarked Tommy. Whoops. Still, better out than in. No turning back now. 'It's a long story that we can't quite get our heads around. Impetus died ... and then he didn't ... but he did get hit by a car ... and he was in a coma ... but now he's not ... he's on the run ... and we're looking for him.' Tommy took a breath. 'That sounds like a load of old bollocks, but it's true. Oh, sorry. Did I swear? Sometimes they just roll off the tongue without me noticing—'

'I don't think it's the swearing that's the problem.' Rose jumped up off the sofa. Hurried over to the rocking chair. Ada, to her horror, had turned a deathly white colour, whilst her body had gone oddly limp.

'That must've come as an enormous shock,' began Rose, taking the old lady's hand. 'I take it you didn't know any of that?'

'Not in the slightest,' said Ada, breathing heavily. 'But if Impetus is out of prison – and still alive – then where is he?'

'Exactly.' Tommy stood up and paced the room. Took a look around whilst he did so. 'We were hoping he might be here. You know, just chilling out. Enjoying some mother and son time.'

'I wish he was,' said Ada. 'More than anything. It'd be my last request to see him again. Before I ...' She stopped. 'There's something you need to know. Not about Impetus. About me. I'm not sure you'll believe it, though.'

'Try us,' said Tommy. 'Rose is quite gullible, after all, and I have a tendency to switch off—'

'I'm about to die,' declared Ada matter-of-factly. 'And I don't mean in the future. I mean now. This minute. In all honesty, I think I was well on my way when you burst into the room ...'

CHAPTER FORTY-SEVEN

Agatha wasn't used to waiting.

It wasn't that she was impatient; she was just keen to crack on. Time was of the essence. Nothing new there, but this felt different. More desperate. Hours rather than days. Act now or suffer the consequences.

According to her secretary, Sandra, mid-forties but older than her years in both appearance and mannerisms, the Governor of HM Prison Stainmouth was currently in her office. She had been there all morning. Doing what exactly? Paperwork? Bullshit. Paperwork was just another excuse for browsing the internet for videos of somersaulting cats, thought Agatha. Rather that than get prodded and probed by a persistent pensioner who had turned up insisting that she worked for the government. The secret side. Strictly confidential.

Agatha had done her homework on the journey there. Bridget Moir had been Governor for six years now. She was fifty-one years old. Single. Devoted to her career, at a guess. Nothing wrong with that. Agatha was the same. Had been so for much of her life.

Back in the waiting room and Agatha coughed once ... twice ... three times until Sandra gave in and looked up from her screen.

'I'm sure Miss Moir won't be much longer,' she said in a monotonous tone.

'Why don't we find out for certain?' Agatha gestured towards the intercom. 'Remind her that I'm still here, please. And, whilst you're at it, tell her that I'm not just going to disappear. There's more chance of me dropping down dead than walking out of here without answers.'

Sandra hesitated before she leant forward and pressed the button on the intercom.

The voice that came back at her was abrupt. 'Yes.'

'Sorry for the disturbance, Miss Moir, but Agatha Pleasant is still here.' Sandra dithered. 'She asked me to remind you.'

A deep breath. 'Thank you for the reminder, Sandra. Kindly inform Mrs Pleasant that I'll see her when I'm good and ready.'

Sandra looked up. 'Miss Moir says she'll see you when she's—'

Agatha climbed to her feet. 'She'll see me now,' she said, marching across the waiting room. 'There's no need to get up, Sandra. I can find my own way.'

With that, Agatha took the half dozen steps required to reach the door to the Governor's office. She didn't bother to knock, choosing instead to pull down on the handle and walk in without encouragement. Once inside, she closed the door behind her.

'What the hell do you think you're doing?'

The office was uncomfortably small and thankfully minimalist. A desk. A filing cabinet. A laptop. A potted plant and several framed photographs. And a woman. Stood by the window. Hair scraped back and top button digging into her neck. Serious turned up a notch.

'I asked you a question,' said the Governor sternly. 'You don't just come barging in here. I'm busy.'

'You don't look very busy,' replied Agatha. 'Besides, I'm not planning on staying long. Take a seat and we can begin.'

'You don't ... I won't ... this is my office,' the Governor blurted out.

'Congratulations. Now sit down.' Agatha took her own advice and pulled up a chair. 'What can you tell me about the recently departed Impetus Stokes?' she asked bluntly.

The Governor recoiled. Salvation came in the form of Sandra. Knocking once, she opened the door and poked her head inside. 'Would you like me to call security, Miss Moir?'

The Governor hesitated for far too long. 'That won't be necessary,' she said eventually. 'I'm sure Mrs Pleasant comes in peace.'

'I'm sure Mrs Pleasant would rather be called Agatha,' insisted Agatha. 'As for the other part of your sentence, that largely depends on what you tell me. The truth is always my preferred option.'

Sandra lingered in the doorway until a flick of the wrist from the Governor was enough to send her on her way.

'Please. Call me Bridget.' The Governor offered her hand as she moved behind a sturdy-looking desk. 'You said it was urgent on the phone. Sorry I kept you waiting. Turns out that everything is pretty urgent at the moment.'

'A sign of the times,' said Agatha. She waited for the Governor to sit before she spoke again. 'So, let's not beat around the bush. Impetus Stokes. What can you tell me?'

Bridget clammed up immediately. Agatha could see it in her face. The way her eyes narrowed. Jaw tightened. Nose began to twitch.

'Not much really,' she began tentatively. 'He passed away in his cell. Natural causes—'

Agatha stopped her mid-sentence. 'Is that the official line? Because it's also a crock of shit. Impetus Stokes is alive and kicking. And, funnily enough, I don't think that'll come as a massive surprise to you.'

The Governor took a moment to regain her composure. 'I understand your frustrations, but this is a sensitive issue. It goes way above my head and then some. The Chief Constable—'

'Clifford Goose?' Agatha shook her head. 'You don't need to worry about Goose. I overrule him.'

'Oh.' Bridget avoided eye contact. 'I didn't know—'

'Well, you do now!' said Agatha. 'You can ask him if you like. Give him a call. He'll confirm it. He'll have to. It's impossible to deny.'

Bridget picked up her phone. Pretended to scroll down her contacts. And then placed it back down on the desk. 'I'm sure there's no need,' she said. 'Truth is, I did some digging before you ... erm ... barged in uninvited. It was all a little vague, hidden away in the darkest corners of the internet, but records seemed to suggest that you work for the government. In defence.'

'Defence *and* attack,' remarked Agatha. 'Depends what sort of mood I'm in.'

'And ... how's your mood today?' wondered Bridget.

Agatha didn't hold back. 'Wretched. I've had an exasperating couple of days, but that's largely down to Goose. He really is an infuriating weasel of a man, don't you think? I gave up on him, eventually. And that's where you come in.'

Bridget swallowed. 'I don't understand.'

'You will do,' said Agatha. 'It was my team that picked up the coffin from your prison. They didn't get far, however, before Stokes came back to life. Unsurprisingly, it was quite a traumatic experience for all involved.'

'I see,' said Bridget, nodding slowly.

'Stokes made a run for it,' Agatha continued. 'It was a run that led him straight into the road. And one car, in particular.'

Bridget put a hand to her mouth. 'That's horrible. Is he dead?'

'Not the last time I saw him. If I'm being honest, though, we're a little unsure as to his whereabouts at this current moment in time.'

'You've lost him?'

'Don't turn this onto me,' shot back Agatha. 'The Chief Constable asked us to watch over a dead body, and that's what we did. What escaped, however, was in perfect working order. That's the bit I can't quite get my head around. Did nobody think to check that Stokes was actually dead?'

'Oh, he was definitely dead,' insisted Bridget.

'How can you be so certain?'

'It was me that killed him.' Bridget gestured towards the door. Towards Sandra sat nervously outside. 'Would you like a cup of tea, Agatha? This is going to take some explaining.'

CHAPTER FORTY-EIGHT

Nimble was all mouth.

The Corsa didn't fly at all. If anything, he drove it conservatively. Both hands on the steering wheel. No stamping on the brakes or ignoring the speed limit. A selection of soothing classical music drifting faintly from the speakers at all times.

Mercy had actually relaxed enough to nod off when Nimble eased to a complete halt.

'Bad night, was it?' he asked, tapping her on the shoulder.

'Like you wouldn't believe,' said Mercy. 'I've got a lot on my mind.' That much was true. A hell of a lot, actually. Enough to keep her awake in the darkest hours. Time to change the subject. 'Is this it?'

'This is it,' nodded Nimble. 'Chambers Lane.'

Mercy looked along the length of a rough old dirt track. 'I can't see anything.'

'I would drive down there, but that's not an option.' Nimble gestured towards a *No Entry* sign hanging from a metal chain connected to two wooden posts as if to prove his point. 'It shouldn't be too far on foot.'

'Let's hope not,' sighed Mercy. She pressed down on the door handle, ready to leave, when Nimble spoke up.

'You gonna' be okay?' he asked. He had worry lines on a screwed-up face. A look of genuine concern. That alone was enough to stop Mercy from coming out with a sarcastic reply.

'I'll be fine,' she said, forcing a smile. 'You just worry about Solomon. That's where your focus needs to lie now. Get him back to yours and take good care of him. Give him my love, won't you?'

'Can I keep a little bit of that love for myself?' Nimble closed his eyes, puckered his lips.

Leaning over, Mercy kissed him softly on the cheek. 'That's all you're getting. Thanks for the lift. I'll be in touch. I promise.'

Mercy climbed out of the Corsa without another word. Started to walk. She turned back once and waved. Squint hard enough and she could just about make out Nimble waving back at her. By the time she had returned her gaze to the winding lane, he had started the engine, easing the car back into the road.

She was on her own.

Mercy, more determined than ever, stepped over the *No Entry* sign and kept on going. It was a long track. Mostly straight, it dipped in the distance. She thought about running, but then decided against it. The last thing she wanted was to arrive at Wild Wood Hall out of breath. Better to keep her cool. Her composure.

Just in case she needed to get the hell out of there at short notice.

Further along Chambers Lane, at the foot of a slight slope, there was a man and his dog.

Leant against a wooden gate, the man had a pair of binoculars pressed to his eyes. There was a figure approaching. A woman. Young. Not a walker or rambler, although first impressions can be deceptive. Who was she then? And, more importantly perhaps, what did she want?

The man lowered his binoculars. Turned to his four-legged companion. 'Looks like we've got company, Benton. I say we prepare ourselves for their imminent arrival.'

Benton, a black Labrador, didn't offer a reply. Not even a bark. Instead, the two of them turned away from the gate and headed back towards the hall.

Thou shalt not pass ...

CHAPTER FORTY-NINE

'You're about to die?'

Tommy stopped pacing the room and stared at the old lady in the rocking chair.

'That's right,' said Ada, nodding gently. 'It can't be that much of a shock. It happens to us all. And, in case you haven't noticed, I am well into my advancing years.'

'I get that,' nodded Tommy. 'You're old ... no offence. What I don't understand is why you think you're going to die soon?'

'Not soon,' said Ada, correcting him. 'Now. My time is up. I can sense it. I knew the end was creeping up and now it has arrived.'

Tommy turned to Rose and shrugged. If he was searching for answers then he was looking in the wrong place. She knew no more than him. Which probably explained why her immediate response was nothing more than a confused frown. She didn't know what to say. And, even if she did, she doubted she could find the words.

Thankfully, Tommy was there to fill in the gaps. 'Are you like a fortune teller or something? Predicting the future in your tea leaves?'

Ada shook her head. 'Not at all. But I've lived a long life. I'm weary now. At some point, my body will just give up on me. My brain will follow soon after. And that will be it.' She paused. 'That day is today.'

'Would you like us to stay with you?' asked Rose, finding her voice. 'So we're ... you know ... here when it happens.'

'Not particularly,' replied a brutally honest Ada. 'You seem perfectly pleasant, but I barely know you. I don't think it would be much comfort having two complete strangers waiting for me to stop breathing and drift away.'

'It wouldn't be like that,' insisted Rose.

'It probably would,' muttered Tommy. 'I get bored very easily. I'm guessing there's another reason you don't want us hanging around, though. You think Impetus is coming here, right?'

Ada half-smiled. 'I *did*. Once. With all my heart. Not anymore, though. He would've been here by now. He was always a stickler for good time-keeping. Being late for anything was never an option.'

'We haven't seen him since last night,' said Rose. 'In the hospital. He vanished when we weren't looking.' She side-eyed Tommy. 'When *one* of us wasn't looking.'

Tommy ignored that. 'Hey, you don't think he's lying in a ditch somewhere, do you?'

'Tommy.' Rose turned the side-eye into a fully blown glare. 'Think before you speak.'

'I'm just trying to get to the bottom of things,' said Tommy. 'Surely Impetus wouldn't just disappear. Not without a damn good reason.'

'That's true,' nodded Ada. 'But I don't think Impetus has disappeared at all. He's close. I can feel it. His spirit is with me, even if his body is elsewhere. That's enough for me.' Ada blinked slowly. 'I think ... yes, I'm ready to go. Now, if you wouldn't mind, I'd like to say goodbye to the life that surrounds me.'

Nobody moved an inch.

'Oh, you want us to leave?' said Rose eventually. 'Yes, of course. It's the least we can do.' She turned towards the exit. Stopped. Shuffled awkwardly on the spot. 'Would it be possible for me to use the lavatory before I go?' she asked.

'Be my guest,' smiled Ada. 'You can't miss it.'

'It's the room with the toilet in,' muttered Tommy under his breath.

With that, Rose swept out of the room and along the hallway. Ada was right; she couldn't miss it. The smallest room in the house, she wandered in and was about to shut the door when she realised she wasn't alone.

'What are you doing?' she blurted out.

'Keep your voice down.' Tommy gently closed the door, trapping them both inside the bathroom. 'Don't look so nervous; I'm not going to watch you do your business. I just want to talk. Something doesn't quite add up. I reckon Ada's having us on.'

'Really?' Rose crossed her legs. She wasn't desperate before. Things had changed, though. 'Can't we have this conversation outside?'

Tommy shook his head. 'It'll be too late by then. Listen, I'm not buying the whole Impetus hasn't turned up thing. It wouldn't take him long to get here from the hospital. Even by foot. Besides, this is his home. He's lived here all his life. He's got nowhere else to go.'

'You're just speculating,' said Rose, ushering him towards the door.

'Perhaps,' said Tommy. 'But I'm willing to find out for sure.'

'What does that mean?'

Tommy tapped the side of his head. 'I'm a man with a plan, Rose. Hear me out. You're gonna' love it.'

Rose finished up in the bathroom before making her way back towards the sitting room.

She didn't go all the way in. Just poked her head around the door frame. 'We'll be off now, Mrs Stokes. Thank you for your time. I'm sorry about the circumstances. Well, about everything really. I ... um ... don't know what to say.'

'Then say nothing,' smiled Ada. 'The story of my life might have reached its final chapter, but that's not to say this is the end. Not really. Lost souls live on forever. I'm sure we'll meet again sometime in the future.'

With that, Rose left the old lady to it. She closed the door on her way out and set off for the Mini Clubman. It was hard to believe, but Ada had rapidly deteriorated in the short time she had been in the house. Her words were beginning to slur, her actions slow and hesitant. Maybe she was telling the truth. Maybe she really was about to die. And, if so, Rose would rather be anywhere but there. Stuck inside the house. Trapped in a tight space with a dead body.

No, she had a better idea. She'd sit in the car and wait for Mercy to call her. Pick her up from wherever she wanted. Pretend to be busy.

Tommy could deal with the consequences. It was his plan, after all. He had nobody to blame but himself.

Tommy blamed Mercy.

If she hadn't gone running off to the boxing club, then she could've done this. She was smaller than him. Probably. There wasn't much in it. Shorter height-wise, but then she had bigger muscles, so maybe that balanced things out. Whatever. It didn't matter now. Mercy was elsewhere, Rose had walked out on him, and Tommy ... well, he was here.

Here being nose to the carpet, flat on his stomach, hidden under Ada's bed.

That was his plan. Well, the first bit at least. For Rose to leave the premises with Ada none the wiser as to the actual whereabouts of her handsome companion.

The rest all hinged on a feeling. A feeling that refused to go away. That prickled and poked.

The Imp was out there somewhere. In the big, bad world.

Also known as Stainmouth and its surrounding area. So, if that was the case, why wasn't he here?

Tommy shifted from side to side, unable to get comfortable. He had dust up his nose, and springs from the mattress digging into the back of his head. He had already wondered how long he could hide there for. One? Two hours? That was a hell of a long time. Five minutes and he was starting to get irritable. No, not starting. He was irritable already.

How would Ada know if he rolled out and just sat on the bed? She wouldn't. By the look of things, she barely ever left that rocking chair.

Tommy had another thought. What if she had died in the last few minutes? She kept banging on about it, after all. Almost as if there was some kind of geriatric grim reaper lurking at her shoulder. Maybe he should go take a look. Tiptoe along the hallway and peek into the sitting room. Or maybe not. Five short minutes had only just turned to six. Patience, dear boy.

Yeah, right. What patience?

Tommy was still weighing up his next move when the decision was taken out of his hands. First, he heard a loud *clunk* from somewhere else within the house. Followed by voices. Plural. Not whispered, but natural. A two-way conversation.

Crawling out from under the bed, Tommy climbed silently to his feet. Nice and easy does it. Don't stumble and fall in your haste to get out there. Pushing the bedroom door to one side, he held his breath as he shuffled along the hallway.

The voices were louder now.

Tommy stopped at the sitting room door. He chose not to peek inside. Too subtle. Nowhere near dramatic enough. Instead, he stepped out into the open with the confident air of a man who knew he was about to be proven right.

Ada was still in her rocking chair. Now, however, there was a man knelt down by her side.

A man who had started all this by bursting out of his coffin.

Tommy smiled. 'Well, well, well. Ain't this a turn-up for the books? Look who's just been outsmarted by yours truly.'

CHAPTER FIFTY

Bridget Moir waited for her secretary to bring the drinks in and then swiftly depart before she started to speak.

'Milk? Sugar?' she asked, pouring from the teapot.

'Just milk, please,' replied Agatha.

'Don't tell me; you're sweet enough already,' said Bridget, trying to force a smile.

Agatha gently shook her head. 'No, that'd be a downright lie.'

Bridget lifted the cup and saucer and placed it in front of her guest. She took a sip of her own drink before she drew breath. 'Impetus Stokes came to see me about a week ago. He wanted me to arrange a meeting with the Chief Constable. He had a proposition for the two of us.'

'And you duly obliged him?'

Bridget considered her answer. 'It's hard to explain. Impetus isn't like the other prisoners. He has a way about him. A charisma. When he speaks, you listen. He demands your attention.'

Agatha nodded. Fair enough. Who was she to argue?

'Impetus told us that he was willing to dish the dirt on Frank

DeMayo,' continued Bridget. 'Every last detail about him and his little gang of thugs. A chronology of crime. Dates and times and all those involved. As you can imagine, that was like music to the Chief Constable's ears. The police have never been able to pin anything big on DeMayo for his entire criminal career. Stokes had one stipulation, though.'

'You had to ... *kill* him?' guessed Agatha, filling in the gaps.

'Yes and no,' said Bridget. 'Impetus wanted a pass out of prison. Not forever. Just a few days. He had received a letter from his mother telling him that she was about to die. Don't ask me how she knew; we didn't go into that. The Chief Constable was too busy frothing at the mouth about Frank DeMayo to worry about the finer details. From that point onwards, I was pretty much in the background. They concocted the plan between them.'

'How did they fake his death?'

'The Chief Constable sorted it. He provided a pill and I distributed it accordingly. I don't know exactly what it was, but it was supposed to put Impetus into a coma-like state for at least forty-eight hours. Something must've gone wrong because, from what you told me, he woke up less than twenty-four hours later.'

Agatha's mind wandered back to her meeting with Clifford Goose at the bottom of his garden yesterday morning. He had told her to look after the coffin for two days. If things had gone to plan, Stokes would've awoken after that. 'What were you going to do once he had seen his mother?'

'Take him back to prison,' revealed Bridget. 'Not this one. No, somewhere else entirely. Give him a different name, a different identity. The Chief Constable had it all arranged. Impetus didn't object. It was part of the agreement. The wheels would be set in motion as soon as he had confessed all.'

'About Frank DeMayo?'

'About Frank DeMayo,' nodded Bridget. 'He's one of the biggest fish in Stainmouth. In comparison, Impetus Stokes can barely swim. I don't care what anyone says. Stokes isn't a criminal. Not in the real sense of the word.'

'So, all this was about his mother,' muttered Agatha under her breath. 'Quite sweet, really. I've sent a team to her house to check it out.'

'That's probably the best place for them,' said Bridget. 'If Stokes is going to turn up anywhere, it'll be there.'

Agatha pushed her chair back and stood up. She hadn't touched her tea. 'Thank you for your time,' she said, holding out her hand for the Governor to shake. 'And thank you for telling me the truth. We got there in the end, didn't we?' She paused. 'Who else knew about this arrangement? Someone must've leaked it to Frank DeMayo because he was following us from the moment we left the prison.'

Bridget pulled at her top button. 'Nobody from my end. I'm sure of it. I mean ... there's always Sandra, I suppose—'

'You might want to have a word with her,' suggested Agatha. 'Just in case.'

'I will.' Bridget hesitated. 'Can I ask a favour? Don't tell the

Chief Constable that you heard any of this from me. I'd rather he didn't know where it came from if that's okay.'

'Of course,' said Agatha, turning towards the exit. 'It can be our little secret. And when the right moment arises, I'll confront Goose with the truth.'

Bridget pulled a face. 'He won't like that.'

'Yes, that's what I'm hoping,' said Agatha, slipping through the door as she left the office. 'A grumpy Goose is enough to brighten up even the dullest of days.'

CHAPTER FIFTY-ONE

Mercy could see the house.

It had taken her over five minutes to get to the point where Chambers Lane dipped, but it was clearly worth the wait. Quite simply, Wild Wood Hall was stunning. A mock-Tudor mansion, fashionably half-timbered, you could easily tick off all its distinguishing characteristics without searching too hard. The gable ends. Tall chimneys. Dormers in the roof. Throw in the glorious countryside views that could be observed from every possible angle, and it was a rural paradise.

Mercy passed through a wooden gate. The only way to approach the house was along a poker straight driveway, flanked by a neat lawn. Mercy wondered how much a house like this would cost and quickly motored past eight figures. One-and-a-half million, at a guess. Stainmouth prices. Drop it somewhere in London and you could easily quadruple that. And all paid for from a life of crime. Bloody typical, thought Mercy. She would die for a house like this. Not literally. Been there, done that. Still, dead or alive, no one could argue that Wild Wood Hall was seriously spectacular.

And empty.

That only dawned on Mercy the closer she got. There were no curtains or blinds in the windows. No ornaments on the windowsills or lampshades hanging from the ceiling. Closer still, and all the rooms on the ground floor were free from furniture of any kind. Bare from top to bottom. The final confirmation arrived in the shape of a *For Sale* sign planted firmly in the immaculate grass. Yep, Mercy was in no doubt now.

Wild Wood Hall was no longer inhabited by Frank DeMayo or anyone else for that matter.

Moving around to the side of the house, Mercy spied another much bigger lawn out the back and several stone barns situated beyond it. There was a car parked up beside one of the buildings. It was too far away to make out the make or model, let alone the number plate.

Head down and determined, she was all set to press on when something caught her attention. She heard it first, saw it a moment later. A grumbling engine powering an unnaturally fast vehicle across the grass.

It was a ride on mower … and it was heading towards her.

No, not towards her. *At* her. Big difference.

Mercy threw herself to one side as the mower refused to either slow or change direction. Rolling over, she was back on her feet in a flash, just in time to see the vehicle grind to a halt. A man hopped down from the driver's seat. Old, but certainly not incapable judging by his size and stature. Dressed in a flat cap, wax jacket and wellies. Your bog standard country attire. A dog followed close behind. A black Labrador, it seemed perfectly placid at first glance. Its own first glance was at Mercy, though, and it snapped into life. Suddenly it was barking repeatedly. Interested, yes, excitable, but in no way dangerous. Hopefully not, anyway.

'You could've hit me,' said Mercy, barely disguising her anger.

The man didn't bat an eyelid as he marched towards her. 'You shouldn't be here.'

Mercy drew breath. Calmed her emotions. Changed tack. 'Yes, I know. Sorry. I must've strayed off course whilst out walking. My mistake. Is this your house?'

The man shook his head. His hair was thick and unruly, whilst his forehead wore a constant frown that refused to shift, even when he spoke. 'I'm just the hired help. Forbes is the name. And that's Benton. We look after the property and all that surrounds it. Even put up that *No Entry* sign at the entrance to the lane. Didn't you see it?'

'Sign? What? I mean ... I wasn't really concentrating ... I was looking at my phone,' mumbled Mercy, stumbling over her excuses. 'I came out trying to clear my mind. Shame it hasn't worked. If I take anything from this, it's that I should probably look where I'm going in future.'

'Can't argue with that,' said Forbes, his jaw tight. 'I could say it's normal to get lost around here, but that would be a lie. In all honesty, we don't get many trespassers.'

He placed huge emphasis on the final word in the sentence. Not that it needed emphasising. His whole demeanour practically screamed it from the rooftops.

You are not welcome.

'I suppose I'll just head back the same way I came,' said Mercy, gesturing along the lane. 'Find that *No Entry* sign you mentioned and make a promise never to ignore it again.'

'You do that,' said Forbes frostily.

Mercy took one last look at the old barns. She would've liked to have checked them out, but that wasn't possible. She could always ask Forbes but, for crying out loud, that man was hard work.

'Something keeping you?' he asked, confirming her assumptions.

Mercy turned to him and smiled. Maybe there was still time to win him over. She'd have to work bloody fast, though. 'It's a lovely house,' she purred. 'And the grounds are immaculate. Like something out of a stately home. You should feel very proud.'

'I do,' said Forbes. And there it was. A slight chink in his armour. 'It's not easy, I'll tell you that for nothing. There's a hell of a lot of land to go at. Mr DeMayo always seems happy with the results, though.'

Mercy fought hard not to smile. It didn't matter who you were. Man or woman. Young or old. Massage anybody's ego for long enough and the juices always flowed eventually.

'Mr DeMayo?' repeated Mercy, feigning ignorance. 'Is he ...?'

'The homeowner,' said Forbes. 'Not for much longer, mind. Wild Wood Hall will be sold before the week's out. It's proven very popular on the market.'

'I can see why,' nodded Mercy. 'Can't believe anyone would ever want to leave. So, where's Mr DeMayo moving to?' She winced as the question passed her lips. Too much, too soon.

Forbes, sure enough, seemed to think the same. 'It's about time you were leaving,' he said stiffly. It was less a suggestion and more of an order.

The opportunity had passed. Forbes was no longer so amenable, his guard back in place, his defences up. To question him now would be like banging your head against a brick wall time and time again.

Mercy smiled before setting off back along the lane. She ticked Wild Wood Hall off her imaginary checklist as she walked. It was a no-go zone, largely because the owner had already gone. Frank DeMayo had flown the nest. Moved on to pastures new. Not to worry. Mercy was meeting him soon enough, anyway. At The Ugly Mug café. Now all she needed was a lift.

Behind her, Forbes climbed onto the mower, ready to get back to work. It was what he got paid for, after all. That and keeping his nose out.

See no evil. Hear no evil. Speak no evil.

Good job really because a lot of evil went on at Wild Wood Hall.

Some proper twisted shit.

CHAPTER FIFTY-TWO

The first time Lucas realised there was someone else in the stall was when he felt a sharp kick to his stomach.

Incredibly, considering the circumstances, he must've been asleep. Now he wasn't, of course. Now he was wide awake, feeling the pain as it raced up and down his body.

The kick had come from a leather boot.

'See. He's still alive.' Maurice stepped to one side, revealing Frank and Sandy in the entrance to the stable. 'I can always kick him again, though. Just to be sure.'

'Settle down,' said Frank. 'And don't be getting up to any of that whilst we're away, either.'

Lucas lifted his head the best he could. Looked Frank dead in the eye. 'You're leaving?'

'Afraid so,' he nodded. 'Don't panic. Maurice will stay here and keep you company.'

'I don't need a babysitter,' shot back Lucas.

'Maybe not, but someone needs to watch over you,' Frank replied. 'You can't be trusted. The last thing we want is you making a run for it. *Another* run for it. No, you've seen too much now. Things you could easily let slip if we released you out into the wild. Names. Faces. Locations. Anyway, we'll talk again when I get back. You'll never guess where I'm going.'

No, you're right, thought Lucas. I won't. Largely because I'm not even going to try.

'I've got a meeting with a fiery young lady,' said Frank regardless. 'I think you know her. Mercy. She seemed spiky on the phone. Proper hot head. Just the way I like 'em.'

Lucas felt his blood run cold. What had he done? He hadn't thought it through. Not properly. In his haste to save his own skin, he had dropped Mercy in it. Plunged her into danger. 'If you lay a finger on her—'

'You'll what?' laughed Frank. 'Don't give it all Billy Big Bollocks now.'

Lucas held his tongue. The more he spoke, the worse things could get. Both for him and Mercy. However bad his current situation, he was no good to anybody dead.

'See you soon,' said Frank. He ushered Sandy out of the stable and kept on walking. 'Don't wait up,' he called out. 'You never know. I might get lucky.'

Lucas rested his head on the sawdust. Let his eyes close. Surely Mercy wouldn't meet Frank by herself. She was smarter than that. More savvy. She would tell Agatha. And then Agatha would call in the cavalry. She had contacts, after all. Contacts who could get him out of there.

Lucas stirred at the sound of a strange shuffling close to where he lay. When he looked again, Maurice was looming large.

'They've gone. It's just you and me now,' the man whispered.

'Wow! That didn't sound creepy, did it?' Lucas tensed up, convinced that Maurice would lash out. A kick probably. Maybe a punch.

He did neither.

Instead, he removed his jacket and laid it over the stable door. 'Do you know what they call me behind my back?' He didn't wait for Lucas to reply. 'Mad Mo. Pretty self-explanatory, really. And quite fitting, as it turns out. Because I do get mad. Frequently. I can't help myself. Still, that's not such a bad thing, is it? Not in the heat of battle?'

Lucas was barely listening as he wriggled over to one side of the stall.

'Do you know what I reckon?' asked Maurice, eyes bulging with a wild intent. 'Life's too short to play it safe all the time. I'm a man of action. I've been desperate to get you on your own. And, no, that's not creepy. Not in the slightest. It's natural. Two men. Alone. Together.' Maurice unbuttoned his shirt. 'So, what are we waiting for, big boy? Let's have ourselves a little bit of fun, shall we?'

CHAPTER FIFTY-THREE

If only Rose could see him now.

And Mercy. And Lucas. Oh, yeah, definitely Lucas. He'd try to deny it, but he'd be absolutely devastated. Choke back those tears, pal, because facts are facts.

He, Tommy O'Strife, had come up trumps.

He loved being right. And this was as right as right could be. Right with a cherry on top. The stuff of dreams. He'd had a feeling, an inkling, and he was bang on the money.

At that very moment, the runaway corpse, Impetus Stokes, was in the sitting room of fourteen Peartree Court. He was knelt by his mother's side, one arm around her shoulder, one resting in her lap, the shock all but apparent on his face.

'You're not the biggest, but then neither is this house,' began Tommy, studying the room. 'Where were you hiding when we first got here?'

'Certainly not in the same place as you,' replied Impetus. He had a deeper voice than Tommy had imagined. Well-spoken, too. Refined. 'That was a neat trick, by the way. I wouldn't say you out-smarted me. I was just … out-manoeuvred.'

'Same difference,' shrugged Tommy. 'I was under your mum's bed in case you're wondering. That sounds a bit weird now I've said it out loud.'

'I was in that cabinet,' said Impetus, pointing over at a wooden sideboard in the adjoining dining room. 'The cupboards are quite roomy once you're inside. I could've stayed in there longer if I'm being honest. Maybe I should climb back in and pretend this never happened.'

Impetus moved, not much, just a twitch, but it was enough for Tommy to step back and close the door behind him.

'Sorry, fella, but you're slipperier than a snake in a bubble bath,' he said. 'You've led me a right merry dance these past few days. Well, you both have,' he added, nodding at Ada. 'You told me you didn't know where your darling son was. Liar, liar, pants on fire. I suppose all that dying stuff was a load of old guff as well, wasn't it?'

Ada took a shallow breath. 'Regrettably not.'

'My mother hasn't got long left to live,' said Impetus, stroking the old lady's hand. 'That's what all this is about. This entire escapade. The moment I heard about her forthcoming demise, I had to come and be by her side.'

Tommy pieced it together. 'What? So you pretended to die and then escaped from prison?'

'Not quite.' Impetus gestured towards the sofa. 'I think you should make yourself comfortable. It's a long story.'

Tommy did as he asked and sat down.

'Yes, I faked my death, but that wouldn't have been possible without the aid of another,' Impetus began. 'Well, two others. One was the prison Governor, Bridget Moir. And the other was Clifford Goose, the Chief Constable. I went to them with a proposition. If they let me out of prison for a few days, I would tell them everything I knew about Frank DeMayo.'

'You were in his gang, right?' said Tommy.

'I *was* his gang,' insisted Impetus. 'Not the muscle, but the brains. Frank had plenty of men to do his punching for him, but no one to plan his jobs. Funnily enough, I have very little interest in crime or the rewards it can reap. I never wanted to steal or fight. I do like to impress people, though. Impress them with my intelligence. Frank saw my potential and handpicked me. I could barely refuse, could I? Yes, fear was one overriding factor, but there was more to it than that. I saw it as a challenge. Together, Frank and I were incredibly successful. He took the limelight, of course, as was my wish. Things only turned sour when one of his more volatile gang members, a ridiculously unhinged individual called Maurice, got careless. By then I had had enough, anyway. I wanted to stop, but Frank was never going to let that happen. Not whilst I was making him so much money. And that's why I took the rap for the whole caboodle. It was my way out. My exit plan. And the rest, as they say, is history. I was sent to prison for seven years. Fast forward two of those and I was knocking on the Governor's door with my proposition. The Chief Constable supplied the pill. They call it the 'zombie' drug. Tetrodotoxin and Bufotoxin. A coma inducing ticking time bomb where the victim falls ill, collapses and seemingly dies, before suddenly awakening. I wasn't convinced, but I was desperate. That's why I chose not to take the whole pill. Just half. Which also explains why I woke up a little earlier than expected.'

'In the back of the van,' frowned Tommy. 'You scared the life out of me.'

'And you did much the same to me,' admitted Impetus. 'My mind was befuddled. Beyond confused. I had no idea where I was or what I was doing there. I tried to escape and ... and after that it's all a blur.'

'You got hit by a car,' said Tommy matter-of-factly. 'Crash bang wallop. Up in the air and straight over the bonnet.'

Impetus winced. 'Then I'm a very lucky man. I've barely got a scratch on me and yet, a split-second later, and I may never have made it here. When I woke up in the hospital, I had slightly longer to get my bearings. You were there,' he said, nodding at Tommy. 'Fast asleep.'

'Resting my eyes,' Tommy insisted. 'I don't know how you managed to slip past me.'

'Then I'm a lucky man again,' said Impetus. 'Once I was out of the hospital, I made my way here immediately. I had to keep a low profile, though. You never know who might be watching. Lurking outside.'

'Like Frank DeMayo?' said Tommy. 'He's been on your tail ever since we picked you up at the prison. I don't know how he knew you had faked your death, but you're going to be in a whole heap of shit if he ever gets his hairy hands on you.'

'I disagree,' said Impetus. 'Frank needs me. For the past few years, he's kept a low profile himself, but that's not through choice. No, it was an unavoidable consequence of my imprisonment. I'm not one to brag, but Frank can't operate without me.'

Tommy screwed up his face. 'So, you're not in any danger at all? And here's me thinking you were in for a right pummelling.'

'You almost sound upset,' said Impetus with a wry smile. 'No, Frank won't hurt me. But I don't want to be a criminal anymore. I can't do that to my mother. I've been an immense disappointment to her all my life—'

'You haven't,' said Ada, her voice practically a whisper.

'And it's only right that I finish my sentence accordingly,' Impetus continued. 'That was the plan, after all. Miss Moir agreed that I could see my mother during her dying days, and after that they would transfer me to a new prison with a new identity. Frank would be none the wiser that I was still alive. More importantly, he would be at the mercy of the justice system. A lifetime's worth of crimes laid out before him. He would have to face the consequences.'

Tommy shook his head. 'This is fucked-up on so many levels. The thing is, I ... no, wait. Not me. I'm not really that arsed ... the *others* have got a problem. Frank's got one of our ... *colleagues*. We need to get him back—'

'I hope you're not proposing some kind of swap deal,' said Impetus. 'If so, then I'm not really in favour.'

'No, me neither,' said Tommy. 'I still have to take you in,

though. Back to my boss. It's what I get paid for.' He paused. 'If I got paid. Which I don't. Not really. But she has promised me a pay rise on top of the peanuts I get tossed from time to time.' Another pause. 'You are listening, aren't you?'

Tommy shifted his gaze to the old lady. She had slipped down in her chair, her head slumped forward.

'Time is running away from us,' said Impetus. 'There's nothing more for me to say. It's over. You've caught me. I'm going back to prison. And that's fine. I can deal with that. I deserve to be punished. First, however, I need to ask you a question. Have you got a heart?'

Tommy laughed. 'This isn't the Wizard of Oz. Stop playing games—'

'I'm desperate,' said Impetus. 'My mother is about to depart this mortal coil. You can see it for yourself. All I ask is for us to have some time together so she can pass peacefully with me by her side. It's her dying wish. After that, I'm all yours. Do with me as you please. I don't care anymore—'

Tommy raised a hand. Tried – and failed – to shut him up.

'I'm begging you,' pleaded Impetus. 'Grant my last request and I'll be forever in your debt.'

Tommy hesitated. It was true. The life seemed to be draining out of Ada with every second. If he left it any longer, she might just drop down dead in front of his eyes.

'Rest in peace,' he muttered. With that, he turned towards the door, stopping only to point at the Imp. 'I'll be waiting in the kitchen,' he said. 'Don't go running out on me, will you?'

CHAPTER FIFTY-FOUR

Mercy had called Rose as she walked away from Wild Wood Hall.

By the time she had reached the end of Chambers Lane, the Mini Clubman was already waiting for her. There was only one person inside, though.

'Where's your mate?' asked Mercy, sliding onto the passenger seat.

Rose stared at her, confused. 'Pardon?'

'Tommy. You never told me you were on your own.'

'I didn't want to worry you.' Rose checked herself. 'Not that you'd be worried. You don't really like him, do you? You find him irritating. I bet you're pleased he's not—'

Mercy cut her off. 'Chill out, Rose. You had one too many coffees or something? I don't think you've said that much to me since we first met.'

Rose swallowed. 'Sorry ... I mean ... sorry ...'

'You don't have to apologise.'

'No, of course not. It's just ... all this sneaking about ... confronting people ... it's not me, is it? I don't know what I'm doing. And I'm scared. So scared. And I don't even know why. Yes, things keep on happening ... bad things ... but never to me. Lucas has been kidnapped. Tommy has been beaten up. You found a dead body and crashed a car into a man. And me ... I just wander through life completely unscathed. You must all hate me.'

'Just a bit,' smiled Mercy. She regretted it instantly. 'Joke. You're just lucky, I guess. And long may it stay that way.' Mercy checked the clock on the Mini's dashboard. Twenty-five past one. Little more than half-an-hour before she had to meet Frank. 'Right, let's shift,' she said. 'We can have this conversation later, Rose. I promise. I know you're troubled, but things are moving fast. Lucas is still in danger, but there might be a way out.'

Rose started the engine, slowly steering the car away from the dirt track. 'Where do you want to go?'

'The Ugly Mug cafe,' said Mercy. 'Top end of Stainmouth. Just up from the town centre. I'm not exactly sure where, so we'll have to keep an eye out. I've got a meeting.'

'With?'

'Frank DeMayo,' said Mercy.

'Frank DeMayo?' The Mini Clubman momentarily shuddered as Rose's hands shook. 'Does Agatha know?'

'Not yet.'

'Do you think you should tell her? Or Miles? At least one of them—'

'DeMayo said I should come alone.'

'Well, he would do, wouldn't he?'

'Don't worry. I've got back-up.'

'Good.' Rose took a breath. The same breath caught in her throat when the realisation dawned on her. 'It's me. I'm the backup, aren't I? I've just been telling you how useless I feel … how I'm completely out of my depth … and now you're relying on me when it really matters … putting your life in my hands.'

'Bit over-dramatic,' Mercy frowned. 'I'm going for a chat with a middle-aged man. That's all. We'll talk, try to come to a compromise, and then I'll get the hell out of there. You just have to park up out of view and wait for me. Nothing to get worked up about. I've got faith in you, Rose. You're my right-hand woman.'

'You've been hanging around with Tommy too much. You sound just like him.'

'Don't say that. Besides, Tommy would end his sentence with a wink and then try and stick his dick in your ear.'

'Oh, that's disgusting.' Rose paused. 'Has he … you know … ever tried to …?'

'Ever tried to stick his dick in my ear?' laughed Mercy. 'Trust me, he wouldn't dare! I'd rip it off for a start. Feed it to the pigs for breakfast.'

'There wouldn't be much to go around,' said Rose under her breath.

'Rose!' A grinning Mercy shook her head at the other woman. That was more like it. She was back on side. 'So, talking of maggot boy, you never told me where he is?'

'Fourteen Peartree Court. The home of Ada Stokes. Impetus wasn't there, but Tommy said he had a plan. The last time I saw him, he was climbing under Ada's bed.'

'As you do.' Mercy took out her phone and tapped out a message to Tommy.

I'm with Rose. She said you've stayed behind. Any joy?

The reply came in a matter of seconds.

What do you think?

Mercy sighed. Hit the screen just that little bit harder. *Just answer the question.* She sent the message and looked up at the road. 'Take a right. DeMayo said it's near the church.'

'I think I know where,' said Rose, easing the Mini around the twisted streets.

Mercy's phone pinged again.

Who's rattled your cage, sister? If you've nothing nice to say, then don't say anything at all.'

Mercy breathed through gritted teeth. '*Just answer the question.*' She paused. '*Nobhead,*' she felt obliged to add.

'There's the church,' said Rose, slowing the Mini to a crawl. 'How close did he say the café was?'

'That close.' Mercy pointed across the road. At a bright yellow sign and blue window frames. 'Turn around. I think I saw somewhere to park back there.'

Another ping.

Okay, because it's you, I'll let that slide. This nobhead, however, has saved the day. Impetus Stokes is here with me now. You can thank me later.

Mercy tapped out her reply. Short and sweet. Nowhere near as aggressive. *Fine. I suppose I should say well done.*' Pause. '*You're still a nobhead, though. In case you were wondering.*

She took a moment to process the information. Tommy had Impetus Stokes. And Frank had Lucas. The swap was on.

Would she do that? Hand Stokes over to a violent criminal like Frank DeMayo in exchange for the safe return of Lucas?

Damn right she would.

Every day of the week.

CHAPTER FIFTY-FIVE

Tommy couldn't help but smile as he stuck his phone back in his pocket.

Mercy nibbled every time. She was so uptight. No, what she needed was a good massage. Loosen her up a little. He'd suggest that later. When all this was over. Dim the lights and get the candles out. Proud Mary was bound to have some oils he could use. If not, he'd just have to rely on his bare hands. Dig into all her creases and crevices. Rub her up the right way for a change.

Feeling frustrated, Tommy leapt up off his chair. Paced the kitchen floor. There was a time and a place for everything. And this wasn't it. Not stuck in a granny flat with a fast-fading pensioner and her three-foot-tall son.

He glanced at the clock on the wall. One forty-five. How long had they been in there now? Twenty minutes? Maybe more. In that time, he had made himself a coffee and then rummaged about for food. His search had yielded a loaf of bread and half a pack of ginger nuts. The bread was dry and the biscuits were soggy. Nothing he couldn't force down with the help of the coffee, though. They would only go to waste otherwise.

Impetus was going back to prison and Ada ... well, she was heading somewhere else entirely. Upstairs, at a guess. She looked decent enough. Pure of mind. No need to send her down below to burn with life's scumbags. She could fly with the angels.

What about Tommy? Where would he end up?

Tricky. He'd done some pretty horrible things in his life, but nothing that bad. Illegal, yes, but nothing sick and twisted. Nothing that could scar an innocent.

His mind wandered to Kamil Milick, the gangster who had ultimately ended his life. He had pulled the trigger, shot Tommy in the chest, and for what? To prove a point? As far as he knew, Tommy was dead. Could he live with that? Sleep easy at night? Look his family in the eye?

Maybe. Maybe not ...

Tommy walked out of the kitchen and across the hallway. Pressed his ear to the sitting-room door.

Silence.

He had expected to hear something. Softly spoken words perhaps. Gentle sobbing. A life didn't end with a big crescendo, though. It just petered out. Faded with a whimper.

He turned away, all set to head back towards the kitchen, when he heard a scraping sound coming from the room. Somebody was moving about.

Tommy rested a hand on the door. Did he really want to do this? Maybe he should give them a few more minutes.

Nah, fuck it.

He knocked.

'Are you alright in there?' Tommy waited for a reply that never came. 'Has it happened yet?' he asked. 'You know ... has ... erm ... the horse bolted? I can give you longer if it hasn't.'

The silence lingered.

'Right, I'm coming in.'

He pulled down on the handle before he could talk himself out of it. Entered with his head down, eyes glued to the carpet. He didn't want to look. Didn't want to see Ada slumped over, a lifeless lump with Impetus sat beside her, his arms wrapped around his mother, consumed with grief.

Only half of that was true.

Ada Stokes had died. That was a fact. She wasn't slumped over though, but leant back. Chin up, eyes closed. Perfectly still.

Impetus wasn't by her side. Nor was he fighting back the tears. As far as Tommy could tell, he wasn't even sad. But then, what did Tommy know? It was just guesswork. Pure speculation.

Because Impetus Stokes was nowhere to be seen.

CHAPTER FIFTY-SIX

Lucas looked on in horror as Maurice dropped his trousers.

He folded them and placed them down gently beside his shirt. His boots and socks had already been removed. Now he was stood in the entrance to the stall, completely naked except for a pair of tight, black underpants.

'What are you doing?' spat Lucas, pressing himself into the corner.

'What does it look like?' A grinning Maurice slapped his hands together. 'I'm doing what men have always done. You are, too. Both of us. Right here, right now.'

With that, Maurice pulled down his underpants.

'Whoa! Whoa! Whoa!' The chains cut deep into Lucas's wrists as he tried desperately to free himself. 'Get the fuck away from me!'

'What's wrong with you? You never seen a naked man before?' Maurice walked forward. Big, confident strides. 'Don't resist or I'll fetch my gun. Put a bullet in your brain before this has even begun.'

Go on then, thought Lucas. Kill me now. End this nightmare

once and for all.

Maurice came to a halt. Held up a key that he had concealed in one hand. 'I'm just going to release you from your shackles. I like a challenge. This should make it a fair fight.'

Lucas stopped wriggling about. 'Fight? Is that what we're doing? Fighting? Or ... you know ... something more intimate?'

'Fighting, of course,' frowned Maurice. Grabbing the chains, he slotted the key into the lock and turned it until it *clicked*. 'Man on man as nature intended. No weapons. A fight to the death.'

Lucas laughed as the chains fell free. It started as a snort and then erupted into a cackling howl. He didn't know why. The fear hadn't faded; it had just changed course. Shifted from one punishment to another.

The laughter came to a sudden halt when Maurice punched him in the face. It was a sharp jab, just off centre, less than an inch from his nose. Lucas rocked back on his heels. Collided with the wall behind him.

Now it was Maurice's turn to laugh as he threw the chains through the door. Turning back into the stall, he stretched his arms above his head. Limbering up for what was to come. 'Take your clothes off,' he demanded.

Lucas shook his head. 'No. I mean ... why?'

Maurice held out his arms, revealing himself in all his glory. 'It's how we came into the world and it's how we'll go out.'

Lucas hesitated. 'Fair enough,' he said eventually. Leaning forward, he began to untie his shoelace. He had barely pulled at it, however, before he put all his weight on one leg and lashed out with the other. The kick caught Maurice fair and square between the legs. It was hard enough for him to cry out in agony as a searing pain rippled up and down his body.

For the first time in a long time, Lucas had a slight advantage. He was weak, yes, but the momentum was behind him. He had to keep going.

Without missing a beat, he threw himself at the other man. The two of them landed on the stable floor, Maurice taking much of the strain as Lucas fell on top of him. Maurice was clearly still in shock, but that wouldn't last forever.

Lucas had to act fast.

Using his weight to keep Maurice in place, he lifted the naked man's head and bounced it off the concrete. Once. Twice. Three times. Maurice grunted and groaned, but he was still there. Eyes open. Conscious.

Lucas tried again. He had barely raised Maurice's head, however, before he felt a punch in the ribs. Another in his stomach. A shot to the side of his head.

Three in quick succession.

The punches kept on coming as shock gave way to rage. Maurice was refusing to just lie down. He was fighting back.

The slight advantage had gone. Fading fast, Lucas needed something, anything, to give him the upper hand.

He found what he was looking for in the doorway.

Straightening his arm, extending his fingers, he strained with every fibre of his being. He held his breath in anticipation, but it made no difference. The chains that had been attached to his wrists, that Maurice had voluntarily removed and then tossed to one side, were just beyond his reach. He wanted to inch forward, but didn't dare for fear of Maurice squeezing out from under him.

He needed something else. Something closer to hand.

His gaze fell upon the clothes that Maurice had piled up at the entrance. His first thought was to grab a boot. Think again. Maurice was a next level maniac. A boot was hardly going to stop him, however many times he was hit around the head with it.

Lucas turned his face away as Maurice gnashed his teeth and attempted to bite a chunk out of his cheek. At the same time, he grabbed Maurice's trousers from the pile. Quick as a flash, he removed the belt. It felt soft to touch. Leather. Good quality.

Lucas had seconds at best. If this didn't work, then he was in trouble. The kind of trouble that would wind up with him dead.

Moving onto his knees, he leant forward and wrapped the belt around Maurice's neck. Slipped the strap inside the buckle. And pulled tight.

Maurice finally cottoned on to what was happening. He used both hands to claw frantically at Lucas's face, but it was too little, too late. Now it was Maurice who was fading fast. His eyes bulged and his mouth began to hang open. Lucas pulled tighter still, but he couldn't hold on forever. If Maurice didn't pass out soon, then it would all be for nothing.

Just give in, you stubborn bastard.

Maurice stopped moving.

Lucas waited a few seconds and then let go of the belt. He rolled to one side and caught his breath. His eyes, however, refused to stray from the man laid beside him. Stark bollock naked and completely still. Not dead, but the next best thing. Out cold. Unconscious. For now, if not forever.

Lucas had seen enough. Time to get out of there.

'You said you liked a challenge,' he muttered. 'Happy to oblige.'

CHAPTER FIFTY-SEVEN

Mercy waited for the clock on the dashboard to reach one-fifty before she made her move.

Rose's response was to grip hold of the Mini's steering wheel. 'I thought you were meeting at two.'

'I am,' nodded Mercy, halfway out the door. 'But the early bird catches the worm. And Frank DeMayo's the kind of worm you need to be wary of. If I go in now, I can take a look around. Spot the escape routes. I might even grab myself a spot of lunch.'

'You seem very relaxed,' said Rose. 'Promise me you'll take care.'

Mercy wasn't listening, though. Her eyes were trained on the Ugly Mug café. Her mind focussed on the job in hand.

Rose reached over and pulled on her friend's sleeve. 'I mean it,' she insisted. 'You don't know what you're letting yourself in for. Things could get dangerous.'

'I like a bit of danger,' said Mercy, ducking her head back inside the vehicle. 'Just kidding, Rose. It's a Tuesday afternoon and the café's about two-thirds full. Frank DeMayo may be a criminal, but he's not a madman. It'd be too risky to try anything. No, you just wait here and I'll be out before you know it.'

With that, Mercy slammed the door shut and made her way across the road. She entered the café without breaking stride. No turning back now.

The Ugly Mug was a bright, vibrant establishment with patterned walls and soft furnishings. A variety of clientele occupied the tables. Suits and skirts sat side by side with tracksuits and toddlers. The smart and the not so. No judgment here, though. Just tea and coffee and a wide assortment of sugary treats.

Mercy chose the nearest empty table to the counter, positioning herself in the chair that faced the door. She had barely sat down when a woman crept up beside her. A big smile matched with an equally big voice.

'Can I get you something, love?'

'Tea please,' said Mercy, smiling back.

The woman nodded before moving behind the counter. 'I'm on my lonesome today,' she said, busying herself with Mercy's order. 'I'll get it to you as soon as.'

'No worries,' said Mercy. That much was true. If anything, she wasn't even thirsty. Not now the nerves had kicked in. That was Rose's fault. Always thinking the worst. Spreading bad vibes.

One fifty-eight. Also known as not long now.

'I'm Maggie,' said the woman, placing the mug down on Mercy's table. 'Mags to my friends. This is my place. I don't think I've ever seen you in here before.'

'You haven't,' said Mercy. 'I've not been in Stainmouth that long. I'm meeting someone here, though.'

The woman nodded. Was about to speak again when something outside caught her eye. 'Oh, bugger! Don't tell me it's him ...'

Mercy followed the woman's gaze. The *him* in question was coming through the door. A big bear of a man, she recognised Frank DeMayo from the hospital car park.

And another. His pet gorilla. Same age. Same build. Same demeanour.

Mags scurried back behind the counter as Frank made his way across the length of the café.

'How did you know?' asked Mercy, as he stopped at her table.

'You were the only person in here who didn't flinch when I wandered in. May I?' asked Frank, placing a hand on the empty chair.

'Be my guest,' replied Mercy.

Frank sat down at the table. Straightened his back as he looked over at the counter. 'Coffee when you're ready, please, Maggie. Milk and two sugars.' He returned his gaze to Mercy. Studied her. 'I know you, don't I? You should look where you're going in future.'

Mercy held up her hands. 'What can I say? Female drivers. If you ask me, they shouldn't be on the road.'

Something resembling a smile passed across Frank's face. 'Yeah, funny. Next thing you know, you'll be telling me it was an accident.'

'No, it was definitely deliberate,' said Mercy, deadly serious. 'If anything, I should have hit you harder. Put you in a hospital bed. You wouldn't have had far to travel at least.'

The smile vanished as Frank's jaw tightened. Casually, he peered around the café. 'You alone?'

'It's what you wanted,' said Mercy. She nodded at the other man, who had positioned himself by the door. 'Shame you're not.'

'That's Sandy,' revealed Frank. 'He's the closest thing I've got to a brother. He's also a pussycat. You should be more worried about me.'

'Oh, I don't scare easily,' said Mercy. 'Especially not with all these people about.'

'Ah, yes. All these people ...' Without warning, Frank stood up and cleared his throat. 'Ladies and gentlemen, sorry for the inconvenience, but I'm afraid it's time to leave. I need this café for a private function. Maggie will reimburse you all tomorrow. I'll pay for it out of my own pocket. Again, sorry for the inconvenience.'

Mercy snorted as Frank sat back down again, crossed his arms and smiled. No way. No *fucking* way.

Yes way.

One by one, the customers rose from their chairs and made their way towards the exit. Mercy looked over her shoulder, searching for Mags, but she seemed to have vanished too.

By the time she had turned back, the last customer – a young mum with a pushchair – was about to leave. Sandy smiled at her before high-fiving the child.

The door closed behind them.

'I think we're alone now,' sang Frank, butchering a well-known tune. He gestured towards Sandy. 'Lock up, please. The last thing we want is to be rudely interrupted.'

CHAPTER FIFTY-EIGHT

Tommy couldn't believe what he was seeing.

If Ada had passed away, then Impetus had just pissed off.

Vanished into thin air.

Rushing over to the wooden cabinet, Tommy yanked open every door and peered inside.

Shit. Shit. Shit.

There was no way the Imp could've hidden in there. He was small, of course he was, just not that small.

Standing up straight, Tommy's gaze turned towards the windows. They were all locked from the inside. Similarly, the ceiling was free of any openings.

Shit. Shit. Shit.

Tommy pulled out his phone. Don't panic. Play it cool. With that in mind, he selected Miles from his list of limited contacts. Hit the call button.

Miles answered on the third ring. 'Yes.'

'Afternoon, Millie. Just keeping you in the loop, old boy. There's been a development.'

Miles wasn't in the mood. 'Cut the bull.'

'Someone's grouchy today. Where's Pleasant Agatha? Sat beside you with her hand stuck so far up your arse she can move your lips, right?'

'Not quite. She's sat beside me, but her hands are in her lap. Talk any louder and she'll hear you.'

'Oh, is that so?' A shiver swept over Tommy as he glanced at Ada. 'I've got some good news and some bad news. Take your pick.'

'Give me the bad news.'

Tommy hesitated. 'No, that's not the way this works. There's a natural progression. You start with the good and move onto the bad.'

'I prefer to get the bad news out of the way first,' insisted Miles. 'End on a high.'

'But that'll ruin everything.'

'I don't care. Just tell me the bad news.'

'Have it your way,' sighed Tommy, as he paced the sitting room floor. 'You're not going to like it, though. I've lost Impetus Stokes.'

Miles fell silent. 'What's the good news?' he asked eventually.

'I've found Impetus Stokes,' revealed Tommy. 'And now I've lost him. But you know that, don't you? Because I've already told you. That's what happens when you go bad before good.'

Miles drew an exasperated breath. 'Where's Stokes now?'

'You do understand the meaning of the word lost, don't you?' shot back Tommy. 'And here's me thinking you went to university, Millie. Such a wasted education.'

'Don't be a smart arse,' said Miles. 'Where are you now?'

'At the Imp's mum's house. His *late* mum's house. She passed away whilst I was here—'

'You killed his mum?' blurted out Miles.

'Course not,' cried Tommy. 'She died ... you know ... naturally. And then Impetus vanished. Just like that.' Tommy stopped pacing. Stared at Ada. She had moved. No, not her. The rocking chair. It had shifted to one side. Only slightly, but Tommy could see its old outlines in the grooves on the carpet. 'Hold on a minute. Something's come up.'

Kneeling down, he ran his fingers over the grooves. It didn't take long to find. A square strip, detached from the rest of the carpet. Tommy lifted it up. And there it was. A trapdoor. He pulled it open without missing a beat. Looked down into the darkness. There was no way anybody could fit in there. No man or woman. A child perhaps.

Or somebody small and sneaky with an attention to detail.

'You still there?' asked Miles.

Tommy picked up his phone. 'Impetus has built himself an escape route. A tiny passage in the floor. I'm guessing it leads somewhere. Somewhere that isn't here.'

'Yeah, escape routes tend to do that,' sighed Miles. 'Agatha wants to speak to you.'

Tommy could hear the phone being passed from one to another. Then the voice. The voice of authority.

'Sounds like you've been a busy boy, Mr O'Strife,' began Agatha. 'Now, I've heard bits and bobs, but I think I'd like the full story. From the very beginning, please. Don't miss anything out.'

Tommy responded with a groan. 'Right, I've got some good news and some bad news.'

'Let's start with the bad news, shall we?' said Agatha.

Oh, for fuck's sake …

CHAPTER FIFTY-NINE

Lucas swayed from side to side as he staggered out of the stable.

He was in a wooden barn. Long and narrow with more stalls along the length of both walls. No horses, though. Maybe once, but not now.

Carefully, so not to stumble and fall, he made his way towards the exit. Stopped in the doorway. It was getting dark. Mid-afternoon, at a guess. And when the dark came, the cold was sure to join it.

Lucas, however, had no intention of hanging around long enough for either to disturb him.

Think about it. Frank and Sandy were sure to return soon. And Maurice wouldn't stay unconscious forever. At some point, he would wake up. And when he did, he'd be more enraged than ever.

Stepping outside, Lucas felt a sharp breeze pass his face as he checked out his surroundings for the very first time. There were immaculate green lawns on either side of him, unusual for this time of year, and a path to his left that led all the way to an eye-catching house. Frank's perhaps, although it was hard to imagine he had either the money or the taste for such a spectacular purchase. Beyond the house, the path merged into a lane that appeared to go on and on into the distance.

The view to Lucas's right, meanwhile, couldn't have been more different. A few steps and the lawn gave way to an area of dense woodland. Impenetrable at first glance. Tall enough and thick enough to conceal the house from both prying eyes and thieving fingers.

Lucas was still weighing up his options when he heard a bark.

His instincts led him back inside the barn. He had no idea if he had been spotted, but he had clearly spotted them. *Them* being a man and his dog. Not out walking, but working. The man was pushing a wheelbarrow across the lawn, stopping occasionally to pick up something from the grass, whilst the dog stayed close at all times. A black Labrador, it looked old, even from a distance. As did the man. Not exactly on his last legs, but close to retirement. Friend or foe, it was impossible to tell. But if he worked for Frank then he was more likely to be the latter. Better not to take any risks.

Under normal circumstances, Lucas could've dodged the pair of them, even out run them if need be. Normal circumstances, however, had gone out the window the second he had been snatched at the hospital. For the time being at least, his dodging days were over. He could barely walk, let alone run. And any last ounces of strength he had in reserve had been exhausted during his fight with Maurice.

Lucas felt compelled to take another peek outside. It was

darker still. Dark enough to bring about a premature end to the working day. Setting down his wheelbarrow, the man stretched his arms above his head and took it all in. One glimpse – even another bark from his four-legged companion – and he would be heading Lucas's way. That was enough to make Lucas duck out of sight, regretting it instantly as his eyes glazed over and his legs gave way beneath him. Before he knew it, he was sliding down the barn wall. Broken in every way imaginable. Mind, body and soul.

The threat from outside was nothing compared to the one inside the barn, though.

Lucas let his eyes fall upon Maurice, relieved that the maniac was still yet to stir. That was when he saw it. Resting on top of a pile of straw by the entrance to the stable. By accident perhaps, although not necessarily. Maybe Frank had discarded it on purpose after he had called Mercy. In fairness, he had probably never imagined that this scenario would ever arise. That Lucas would be free from his shackles. That Maurice would be out cold. Oh, and naked. Don't forget about that. No one would ever have foreseen that peculiar occurrence.

Pushing himself off the wall, Lucas crawled over to the pile of straw and picked up the phone. *His* phone. He turned it over in his hands. Studied the screen. It was still in working order.

Scrolling down to the last number called, he pressed the button.

And then crossed his fingers that Mercy would answer.

CHAPTER SIXTY

Frank looked over at the counter.

Pulled a face when he saw that it was empty.

'Maggie never did get me that coffee, did she? I must have scared her off.'

'It's Mags,' said Mercy.

'What is?'

'Her name. Her friends call her Mags.'

'Oh, that's low.' Frank leant forward. Placed his elbows on the table. 'What are you trying to do? Hurt my feelings? You're about fifty years too late if that's your game. I had to toughen up from an early age. We both did, didn't we, Sandy?'

'Yes, mate.' Sandy moved away from the door. 'If you spoke about your feelings on our estate you'd get your tongue ripped out. At some point we decided to start ripping tongues out ourselves.'

Mercy sighed. 'Is that a threat?'

'Just back story,' insisted Sandy. 'We'd hate for you to leave here thinking you were dealing with a pair of nobodies.'

'*If* you leave here,' added Frank.

'Another threat.' Mercy shook her head as she sat back in her chair. 'It's getting boring now. All this macho bullshit.'

'Don't throw cliches at me,' said Frank. 'You came in here and thought you were in control. You were wrong. I've already got one prisoner – your man Lucas – and now I've got you as well. I could kill you both. Just like that. I wouldn't bat an eyelid. There is a way out, though. A simple solution. And his name is Impetus Stokes.' Without warning, Frank crashed his fist down on the table. 'Where the hell is he?'

Rose leant over the steering wheel and tried to make sense of what she was seeing.

The Ugly Mug had been about two-thirds full. Emphasis on *had*. For no apparent reason, the customers had come swarming out in their droves. One after the other. Leaving the café empty.

Virtually empty.

Mercy was still inside. As was Frank DeMayo and the other man that Rose had never seen before. How had that happened?

And, more importantly, why had Mercy put herself in such a dangerous situation?

No. Put them *both* in a dangerous situation. Because Rose was involved now, too. She was no longer just the driver. Safe on the outside.

Like Mercy, she was in it up to her eyeballs.

Rose opened the glove box more in hope than expectation. As luck would have it, there was a thick, knitted hat stuffed into one corner. It was Proud Marys at a guess. Rose removed it and pulled it down over her head. Stopped when it reached her eyes.

Admired herself in the rear view mirror.

As disguises go, it was pretty abysmal.

It was, however, the best she could come up with at short notice.

For Mercy, things had gone disastrously wrong in a short space of time.

She thought she was safe in The Ugly Mug. A public space. Broad daylight. Numerous people passing through. She had imagined she could talk to Frank. Get on his good side, however small that side may be. Make him listen. Persuade him to release Lucas.

She had mis-read the situation, though.

Massively.

A *ping* disturbed her from her thoughts. Casually, she removed her phone from her pocket. Placed it in her lap. Glanced down at the screen.

It was a message from Tommy.

The Imp's done one. I doubt we'll see him again. What you up to?

Mercy read it several times, her face twitching with every pass.

'Bad news?' asked Frank. 'Man trouble?'

'Something like that,' replied Mercy. Her hands shook as she squeezed the phone back into her pocket.

'So, let's keep things simple,' began Frank. 'Tell me where you're keeping Impetus Stokes, and I'll go get him. Don't ... and I can't. That also means that you're no longer of use to me. Neither is Lucas. We've disposed of bodies before in

Stainmouth. It's nothing new, is it, Sandy?'

'Unfortunately not,' said Sandy. 'You get used to it after a while.'

Mercy rolled her eyes. Groaned. Her bravado was all an act, but it was one she wanted to maintain. It was like her boxing days all over again. Scared or not, she couldn't let it show. She had to keep a straight face and an even manner. She was about to say something when her phone sounded again. This time it wasn't a *ping*, but a chiming ringtone. Someone was trying to call her.

'Don't answer it,' said Frank sternly.

'I won't,' muttered Mercy. Not true. Her fingers crept down her side before they reached her pocket. The phone was in her hand a moment later.

'I mean it,' stressed Frank. 'Answer that and your phone will be in bits.'

Mercy lowered her head. Stared at the caller's name lit up on the screen.

Lucas.

She blinked. Tried to focus. Could barely believe what she was seeing.

'You're testing my patience,' warned Frank. 'No more distractions.'

Mercy's phone *pinged* again before she had a chance to reply. This time it was a message.

A message from Lucas.

I'm out. Call me.

Mercy slipped the phone back into her pocket. The meeting was over. Move quickly. Move confidently. Get the hell out of there.

'This has been nice, but I've really got to go,' she said, standing up. 'I'll be in touch soon—'

'Sit down!' ordered Frank.

Mercy held her ground. 'You can't keep me here against my—'

'Sit down and shut up!' shouted Frank. 'I've already told you. You're not calling the shots anymore. You're disposable. An inconvenience. I'd rather have not met you and your interfering pals if I'm being honest.' Frank took a breath. 'You're still standing.'

'I'm still leaving,' insisted Mercy.

Frank stood up, too. He was about to grab her when a sudden movement caught his eye. There was a figure at the door. More accurately, a woman in a horrible knitted hat. She had both hands and her nose on the glass as she peered inside. Frank was about to shoo her away when the woman started to knock.

'Get rid of her, Sandy,' he ordered.

Mercy nodded to herself. The hat was a nice touch. She'd tell Rose that when she finally got out of there.

'We're closed.' Sandy marched towards the door when the knocker refused to stop. 'We're ... closed,' he repeated loudly.

Because Mercy would get out of there. She knew that now. Rose had provided a distraction and she would take full advantage of it.

'Sort this shit out,' demanded Frank.

'I'm trying,' moaned Sandy, waving his fist at the persistent knocker. 'You're not coming in. Go away ... oh, is she deaf or something?'

Frank walked out from behind the table. He had almost made it to the door when Mercy flew into action.

Picking up her chair, she lifted it above her head and launched it at the window.

I told you I was leaving ...

CHAPTER SIXTY-ONE

The window smashed on impact.

The chair passed through with ease, landing on the pavement outside, surrounded by shards of broken glass.

Mercy was right behind it. Swerving around the table, dodging any protruding chair legs, she sprinted across the length of the café whilst both Frank and Sandy looked on in stunned disbelief. Without breaking stride, she leapt through the open window. Skidded on the glass outside, but somehow kept her balance. She was on the move in no time, refusing to look back at the chaos she had left in her wake. Choosing, instead, to keep her eyes trained on Rose, who had already set off towards the Mini.

Mercy hurried after her.

Back in The Ugly Mug and Sandy struggled with the key as he tried to unlock the door, whilst Frank followed Mercy's lead, albeit not quite so instinctively, as he clambered warily through the window.

By the time both of them had exited the café, Mercy and Rose had reached the car.

Mercy yanked on the handle, but the door refused to shift. 'Open it,' she hissed.

'I'm trying,' mumbled Rose, struggling to get a proper grip of the key.

'Well, try a little harder.' Mercy didn't need to look to know that Frank and Sandy were running towards them. Heads down, fists pumping. 'Just press the fuckin' button!' she yelled.

Right on cue, there was a *click*. The two of them climbed in quickly, slamming their doors shut.

'Where to?' asked Rose, her entire body shaking uncontrollably as she gripped hold of the steering wheel.

'Anywhere,' spat Mercy. 'It doesn't matter ... oh, shit!' She flinched as Sandy threw himself onto the car bonnet. 'Drive, Rose! Drive!'

There was a moment's hesitation before Rose put the Mini into reverse.

'Faster!' cried Mercy.

Rose increased the pressure on the accelerator and the Mini flew backwards. It was enough to make Sandy let go as he rolled straight off the bonnet and into the road.

'Great work,' panted Mercy, trying to catch her breath. 'Now get us out of here!'

Rose straightened up before she turned onto the next street. Mercy silently urged her to put her foot down, but kept that particular thought to herself. The last thing she wanted was to scare Rose so much that she ended up crashing. No, as things stood, they were heading to safety. No need to rock the boat.

Not when Frank was still yet to peel Sandy up off the concrete.

'Keep going, Rose,' she said, resting a hand on her friend's shoulder. 'You can relax now. That was exceptional, by the way. Back there, outside the café. I didn't know you had it in you.'

'I – I – I don't,' stammered Rose. 'It's a miracle we're both still alive.'

Mercy pulled her phone from her pocket and tapped at the screen.

'Who are you calling?' asked Rose, glancing in her rear-view mirror for any sign of their pursuers. Thankfully, the coast was clear.

'Lucas.' Mercy scrolled down her contact list. Prodded his name. 'He's got out. Escaped. We need to find him.'

Lucas answered on the third ring. 'You took your time,' he said slowly. 'Where have you been?'

'No, where have *you* been?' shot back Mercy. 'We'll come and get you.'

'You make it sound so easy,' Lucas muttered. 'I'm in the middle of nowhere. God only knows.'

'Describe it,' snapped Mercy, struggling to hide her frustration. 'Anything stand out?'

Lucas tried to think. 'I'm in a barn. There's a huge white house close to where I am. I was going to make my way there, but there's a man on the lawn and I don't want him to see me. Could be the owner ... maybe a gardener ... I mean, he's got a wheelbarrow. Oh, and a dog. A black Labrador—'

'Wait!' Mercy placed a hand on Rose's shoulder. 'Turn

around. We're going the wrong way.'

'I thought ... you said drive anywhere,' spluttered Rose.

'Things have changed,' said Mercy. 'I know where Lucas is. I think.'

That was half the problem. She wasn't certain. Fifty-fifty at best. And yet there were lives at risk.

'Feel free to fill me in any time you like,' said Lucas.

'Wild Wood Hall,' revealed Mercy, backing her judgement. 'Hang on in there, Lucas. We're coming to get you.'

CHAPTER SIXTY-TWO

Tommy got Miles to get Agatha to get Olaf to pick him up from Peartree Court.

He was about to climb into the Audi when the incumbents of the car did the exact opposite. They greeted him on the pavement. Grimaces rather than grins, no one seemed particularly overjoyed to see him.

'Do we need to go in there and check it out for ourselves?' asked Miles.

'Of course you don't,' snapped Tommy. 'I'm not completely stupid.'

'No one ever said completely. Just eighty per-cent. Maybe eighty-five.'

'Hilarious, Millie. You lot need to start appreciating me a bit more. If you're not careful, I'll run off with another elite team of highly skilled professionals.'

'Another? You've never been in *one* team of highly skilled professionals.'

'Please, you two.' Agatha pressed a finger to her lips. 'Squabbling in the street is so unbecoming.'

'He started it,' said Tommy, eyeballing Miles. His mood soon changed when he opened the door to the Audi and climbed inside. 'This is nice,' he said, running a hand over the leather interior. 'Wouldn't mind a bit of this myself.'

'If I remember correctly, you *had* a bit of this not so long ago,' remarked Agatha, joining him on the back seat. 'Not legally, of course. You took my car without my permission.'

'Also known as stole it,' muttered Miles. He was the last to enter the vehicle, taking his place in the passenger seat. 'Olaf still hasn't forgiven you.'

The driver grunted at the sound of his name.

'Told you,' said Miles. 'He's practically apoplectic.'

'I'll take your word for it,' frowned Tommy. 'Largely because I don't know what apo-whatsit even means.' He leant over and patted the driver on the head. 'Sorry, Olaf, my Scandinavian buddy. There. We're the best of friends now. Besides, if *I* remember correctly, I was saving the day as usual. I had to steal the car to rescue Mercy and Lucas. Some things never change…'

'Give that man a medal,' said Miles under his breath.

'A pay rise will do.' Tommy turned to Agatha and winked. 'But then you know that already, don't you?'

'We had an agreement,' said Agatha. 'I told you I'd raise your expenses—'

'Adult pocket money,' chipped-in Miles.

'If you took care of the dead body,' continued Agatha. 'Which you failed to do. You lost him within minutes of collecting his coffin and still haven't recovered him yet. Not only that, but Lucas has vanished whilst in your company, too. If anything, you owe me money.'

Agatha clicked on her seat belt, all the while resisting the urge to smile at her own comeback.

'I've called an ambulance,' said Miles, glancing over his shoulder. 'Told them Ada Stokes was a neighbour and I haven't seen her for a while. Probably best not to be here when they arrive.'

'So, what now?' wondered Tommy. He stretched his arms out in front of him. Yawned loudly. 'I wouldn't mind putting my feet up if I'm being honest. I've had one hell of a busy day.'

Miles was shaking his head long before he spoke. 'Forty winks can wait. We've located Mercy and Rose.'

'They've gone to Wild Wood Hall,' said Agatha. 'The last known residence of Frank DeMayo. Mercy's been there once today already. Now, why do you think she'd go back again?'

'Memory loss from being punched one too many times in the face?' guessed Tommy.

Agatha shook her head. 'No, I think she's found something. And we're going to find out what.'

CHAPTER SIXTY-THREE

Lucas ended the call.

Closed his eyes and rested his head against the barn wall. The end was in sight. Mercy and Rose were coming. It was over. A calmness settled upon him. It was a calmness he hadn't felt for a long time. Not since the days before the car crash. The crash that, to all intents and purposes, had ended his life.

It was a calmness that lasted approximately four seconds.

Lucas sat up, eyes wide, body rigid. He had sensed a presence in the barn. His gaze fell upon Maurice. He was yet to move, though. Still out cold. Still naked. Still wearing the belt around his neck instead of his waist. Lucas looked elsewhere, but there was nothing or nobody lurking in the shadows.

With his mind racing, Lucas shuffled across the wall until he reached the doorway. Turned his head and peeked outside. At first glance, all was still. The man with the wheelbarrow and his dog, however, were nowhere to be seen. Clocking off time must've been and gone. Lucas couldn't believe his luck. With nobody about, Mercy and Rose had an unobstructed path all the way to the barn.

Sure enough, a set of headlights illuminated the mid-afternoon gloom. There was a car coming along the lane. Approaching the house. Uncharacteristically fast. Not Rose then. She tended to drive at half the speed limit. That just left Mercy.

This was it.

Lucas watched eagerly as the car drew closer. And then it hit him. Hard. Like a hammer blow to the chest. A soul-destroying realisation that he had seen the car before. Sat in it alongside Sandy and Maurice.

A black Ford Focus.

He cursed himself. He had waited too long. Switched off when what he really needed to do was stay focussed. Now he was trapped. Frank and Sandy would undoubtedly find him. See what had happened to Maurice.

There would be repercussions.

Not necessarily ...

Lucas picked himself up, his teeth clenched, fearful of shouting out in agony. He used the wall to keep him upright as he shuffled towards the doorway. He had come to a decision. He knew what he had to do.

The Focus skidded to a halt right outside the house.

Lucas didn't notice. He was already on his way. Heading in the opposite direction.

Destination the woods.

CHAPTER SIXTY-FOUR

Frank slammed on the brakes.

'Calm down,' said Sandy, gripping hold of his seat. 'Don't do something you might regret.'

'Not possible.' Frank smashed his fist down on the steering wheel. 'Who do these fuckers think they are? They're playing games with us. Well, no more. This ends now. And it ends badly.'

Frank yanked on the handle and the door swung open. He climbed out, only to be confronted by his groundsman.

'We had a visitor, Mr DeMayo,' said Forbes stiffly. 'A woman. Young. Black. I don't—'

'I do.' Frank's brow furrowed. 'She's been getting in my way all afternoon. She didn't reach the stables, did she?'

'Of course not,' said Forbes. 'I cleared her off the driveway. She wouldn't have seen anything except the house.'

'Good,' nodded Frank. 'Now I'd like you to do the same. Make yourself scarce. I'll pay you regardless. You don't have to worry about that.'

Forbes hesitated. 'As you wish. I was going to check those

traps in the wood, but—'

'Tomorrow.' Frank turned away. Set off towards the barns at the bottom of the garden. 'Enjoy your evening, Forbes. Get a good night's sleep, won't you?'

Sandy locked up the Focus. Took off after the other man.

'You don't think Maurice will have done anything stupid, do you?' he asked warily. 'Yes, he's my brother, but he's also unhinged. It wouldn't surprise me if blood's been spilt whilst we've been away.'

'It better not have,' muttered Frank. 'That's my job. I've been looking forward to releasing a little bit of tension ever since that bitch scarpered from the café.'

'Listen, don't go in all guns blazing, will you?' said Sandy, fearing the worst.

Right on cue, Frank removed a handgun from inside his coat. A Beretta 92. Worst fears realised. 'Neat party trick,' he remarked. 'Reading my mind like that. Next time I want your advice, though, I'll ask for it.'

Sandy fell silent. There was no point digging his heels in and causing an argument. Instead, he slowed his step. Tucked in behind his boss. Know your place, soldier. Second in line for the second in command.

Frank had barely entered the barn when he came to a sudden halt. 'What the—?'

Sandy followed his gaze. Frank was staring at the first of the stalls. The door was wide open and there was a body on the ground. It wasn't the prisoner.

It was Maurice.

Laid out in the doorway, he was all but naked except for a belt – his own at a guess – pulled tight around his throat. That probably explained why he was currently out cold.

Without another word, Frank wandered over to a bucket of water in the corner of the barn. He picked it up, turned back to the unconscious man and poured it slowly over his face.

It took less than half a bucket before Maurice spluttered and coughed. Sitting up, his fingers clawed at his throat as he struggled to remove the belt. 'Hey ... wait ... what's going on?'

'You tell me,' frowned Frank. 'Where's the prisoner?'

Maurice looked behind him. 'He was here ... in the stall—'

'And now he's not,' replied Frank.

'What you getting at?' scowled Maurice. He tossed the belt to one side and grabbed at his clothes.

'What am I getting at?' Frank threw back his head and laughed. 'What do you think, Maurice? Not only has the prisoner vanished, but you were sprawled out on the floor, dead to the world, with nothing on. Listen, it's bad enough that Lucas has found a way to escape. What I can't figure out, though, is why he'd strip you naked before he did so?'

'And I can?' Maurice was practically frothing at the mouth. 'If you're trying to say something, then just say it.'

'Okay, you two. Cool it.' Sandy wandered over to the barn door and poked his head outside. 'He can't have gone far. He's had the shit kicked out of him, remember? If he'd headed back towards the house and beyond, we'd have seen him. And, if not us, then Forbes. No, he must've made his way into the woods. That way he could lie low.'

'At last. Some common sense.' Frank shot Maurice an accusing glare. 'Get yourself dressed and then meet us outside. Looks like we're going hunting.'

CHAPTER SIXTY-FIVE

Crouching down in the undergrowth, Lucas watched as Frank and Sandy made their way into the barn.

They would find Maurice first, probably before they even realised that he was gone. He would still be laid out on the ground, unconscious. Naked but for the belt around his neck. That would be one hell of a curveball. It wouldn't hold them up for long, though. Soon, they would regroup. Be back on the move. Hopefully towards the house. That was the obvious place for Lucas to escape to. Surely not the woods. It was getting dark. Colder by the second. Who in their right mind would hide out there?

Still, no point hanging around for the sake of it.

Lucas tried to stand, but only got so far before his legs buckled beneath him and his head started to spin. He had barely slept in the last few days. Just a few hours at most. He'd drunk and eaten practically nothing. Throw in all the mental and physical abuse he'd suffered – largely at the psychotic hands of Maurice – and he was more than just walking wounded; he was lucky to be alive.

He steadied himself on a tree trunk. Closed his eyes and took a breath. Followed it up with another. He was okay. He silently repeated that again and again. He wasn't going to pass out. Not yet, anyway. He'd save that until he was safe.

If he was ever safe.

Don't think like that. Mercy was on her way. He had hoped she would've arrived before Frank and Sandy, but that ship had already sailed. Not the end of the world. Not in the big scheme of things. At least Mercy wouldn't be alone. She'd definitely have Rose, maybe Tommy. Fingers crossed, she might even have Agatha and Miles and enough back-up to get him out of there unharmed.

Practically unharmed.

Pushing himself away from the trunk, Lucas half-stumbled, half-staggered as he set off deeper into the woods. It was far from easy going, especially once he moved away from the natural path to battle his way through something impossible to penetrate. A tangled mass of thorns and brambles, he could feel it ripping at his clothes, piercing any exposed skin. It was a strength-sapping exercise. He had started at a low ebb and descended ever since. The desire was still there, but the body wasn't playing. Not anymore.

A scorching pain stopped Lucas in his tracks. He tried to take another step, but his foot refused to shift. There was something pressing down on it, preventing it from moving. He shuffled backwards in an attempt to free himself, but it was no use. As a last resort, he bent his knee and pulled his leg up. His foot stayed exactly where it was.

Bending over, he brushed the leaves to one side and realised there was something clamped around his ankle. A closer inspection revealed steel jaws with a serrated edge. It was an animal trap. Inhumane. Illegal even.

He turned back towards the barn. There was movement there. Frank and Sandy had stepped out into the open. They were side by side, heads pressed together, conspiring. They were looking in his direction. Not at him, but close. Maurice soon joined them, buttoning his shirt as he wandered out of the stables. Without another word, they set off towards the woods.

No. No. No.

Lucas blinked away the tears. All three of them were armed. Handguns, at a guess. It was hard to tell from distance. Not that it mattered. Fact was they shot bullets.

If the trap had slowed him down, then Frank and the Maddison twins would go one step further.

They would stop him once and for all.

Lucas collapsed, slumping to the ground as he tried to catch his breath. He was all out of everything. Strength. Time. Luck. Mould the three together and there was only one possible outcome.

He was fucked.

Well and truly so.

CHAPTER SIXTY-SIX

'Stop!'

Rose winced as she pressed down on the brakes with an uncomfortable degree of force. As expected, the Mini Clubman skidded spectacularly in the middle of the road.

'Down there,' said Mercy, pointing out of the window at the turning for Chambers Lane.

Rose steered the car in the right direction. She came to a halt when she saw the swinging sign blocking her way. 'No entry,' she shrugged.

Mercy scrambled out of her door without another word. Unclipped the metal chain from both wooden posts and then tossed it into the bushes. 'First you see it, then you don't,' she said, climbing back into her seat. 'Onwards. And this time, put your foot down.'

'I'm trying,' insisted Rose, slowly increasing her speed as she made her way along the lane. 'Driving fast doesn't come naturally to me, though. It makes me nervous ... what's that?' She stopped abruptly. There was something coming towards them. A shape in the gloom. 'It looks like a—'

'Forbes,' said Mercy.

'Well ... I mean ... I was going to say a man, but you know best,' muttered Rose under her breath. 'I'll just get on with my inadequate driving, shall I?'

Forbs, however, had other ideas. The closer they got, the more he drifted from one side of the lane to the other. He was intentionally blocking their way, no doubt about it. It left Rose with little choice but to ease the Mini to a complete standstill.

'I'll deal with him,' said Mercy firmly.

Rose didn't like to ask. Didn't like to ... but had to. 'How?'

'Verbally,' said Mercy, as she exited the car. 'Then physically. One way or another, he'll move.'

Forbes greeted her with a suspicious frown. 'You're back?'

'I'm back,' nodded Mercy. 'I wanted to take another look at the house. I'm thinking about putting an offer in. See if I've got a spare million or two lying about in loose change.'

Forbes slowly shook his head. 'Try again. And this time tell the truth.'

Mercy weighed it up. Yeah, why not? She had nothing to lose. 'We're here to rescue someone. A friend of ours. We think he's being held hostage. Not in Wild Wood Hall itself, but close by. Frank DeMayo kidnapped him.'

Forbes avoided eye contact as he leant over and stroked Benton. 'Right ...'

'You don't seem that surprised.'

'I'm not. It'd take a lot to shock me nowadays. I've seen things you can't imagine.'

'I've not exactly led a sheltered life myself.'

'Given the choice, I'd rather turn a blind eye and get on with my job,' said Forbes, standing up straight. 'Pretend it's not happening.'

With that, he pulled on the lead and the two of them, man and dog, set off again. Past the Mini and along the lane. Towards the road.

'You're not going to try and stop us?' Mercy called out.

'Doesn't look like it,' shouted Forbes. 'I'm not at work again until tomorrow morning. Let's hope you're not still here when I return, eh?'

Mercy watched him for a moment before she got back into the car. 'Only verbal,' she said. 'No fists required. I'll save that for later.'

Rose drove the rest of the way to Wild Wood Hall in silence. She parked by the front door. Beside a black Ford Focus. 'Isn't that the car that grabbed Lucas at the hospital?'

Mercy nodded as she climbed out of the Mini. Took in her surroundings. 'Lucas said he could see the house from where he was. There are some barns around the back. I'm guessing that's where he is.'

Rose mumbled a reply, but she was barely listening. She had tried to keep her cool, especially in front of Mercy, but her nerve was failing her. What if Frank was already here? She couldn't fight. She couldn't even run. Not fast, anyway. Yes, she could always scream, but what good would that do her? She was in the middle of nowhere. You could scream all you liked out here.

No one would ever come to investigate.

'Relax, Rose,' said Mercy quietly. 'I can hear your heart beating from here. You're panicking over nothing. All we have to do is ...'

Mercy ended her sentence at the same time as she slowed her step. She had spotted movement in the distance. Two shadowy figures coming out of one of the barns. No, make that three. They were on the move soon after. Not back up to Wild Wood Hall, but towards the trees that ran around the edges of the property.

One quick glance, however, and they would change direction.

Pressing a hand over Rose's mouth, Mercy pushed her against the side of the house and kept her there, hidden from view.

She gave it ten seconds before she let go.

'What is it?' breathed Rose, shaking with shock.

'Not what – *who*,' said Mercy. 'Frank and his boys. They're heading into the woods. And why do you think that is?'

She didn't wait for a reply. Once the three men were out of sight she set off across the lawn.

'Where are you going?' whispered Rose, trying not to raise her voice as she scurried after her friend.

'Into the woods,' replied Mercy.

Rose threw up her hands in despair. 'But that's where Frank is?'

'Exactly,' said Mercy. 'We need to get to Lucas first. End of conversation.'

CHAPTER SIXTY-SEVEN

Lucas stayed out of sight, concealed by the undergrowth.

Not exactly camouflaged, but as good as. Like hide and seek with potentially life-threatening consequences.

Don't breathe. Don't blink. And certainly don't move. Not even an inch.

Funnily enough, he couldn't have even if he wanted to. No, forget that. It wasn't funny. Not in the slightest. It was absolutely devastating. The last few days hadn't just caught up with him; they had tripped him up and then trampled all over him like a herd of psychotic elephants. There were only so many times you could take a beating. Only so many hours you could survive without food and drink. The final push into the woods had used up his last reserves of energy. The *last* of the last. He had thought that before, of course. Now he was certain. His only wish was to close his eyes and drift off to somewhere else entirely. Sleep would bring a peace that he desperately craved. A resolution, albeit temporary.

Without realising it, Lucas found himself laid flat on his back. How did that happen? He didn't question it for long. Instead, he let his eyes fall shut and his mind slip away into oblivion ...

A *crack* brought him out of his thoughts and back to reality.

Lucas opened an eye just a fraction. There was a figure stood over him. It looked like Maurice, but it couldn't have been. If it was, Lucas would almost certainly have been dead by now. Which meant it was someone else. Someone similar, just not quite so deranged.

Sandy.

Lucas laid still. Tried to fake unconsciousness. Not that hard, really. He was practically there already. It was either that or come out fighting, and that wasn't going to happen.

The next thing he knew, he was being slapped on the cheek. Not an attack on his senses as such. More a gentle reminder.

'Wakey-wakey,' said Sandy. 'I've found you.'

Lucas refused to react. He was cornered, but that didn't mean he was going to make it easy.

It was a thought that Sandy shared. How could he get this man, this dead weight, out of the woods? The truth was he couldn't. Not on his own. He needed help.

He needed Frank and Maurice.

Sandy was about to reach for his phone when a woman's voice caught him off-guard.

'Hey! Over here!'

He didn't have to look too hard to find her. Less than twenty feet from where he was stood, her head and shoulders were clearly visible whilst the rest of her body was hidden behind a thick clump of unruly bushes.

Without warning, the woman ducked out of sight.

Sandy was still trying to make sense of it when her head reappeared. The woman was staring straight at him. He met her eye. Recognised her immediately from the Ugly Mug café.

The woman had been hammering on the door, distracting them before Mercy had launched the chair through the window. Yes, she looked different without the knitted hat, but it was definitely her.

And now she was back. Distracting him again.

The woman ducked down for a second time, disappearing from view.

Sandy dropped his gaze to Lucas. Sprawled out by his feet, the prisoner was now a shell of a man. An empty carcass. Threat level at a minimum. With that in mind, he switched his full focus onto the woman. The soon-to-be dead woman.

No more distractions.

Removing his gun, Sandy held it at arm's length and took aim above the bushes. He would fire off a shot when the head reappeared. History dictated that he wouldn't have to wait for long.

And he didn't.

The head popped up and Sandy pulled the trigger.

The lights went out soon after.

CHAPTER SIXTY-EIGHT

Mercy had wielded the fallen branch like a baseball bat.

A two-handed grip. Good back swing. A smooth, flowing action.

And if the branch was a bat, then Sandy's head was the ball.

Mercy had made her move the moment he had aimed the gun at Rose. That had been their plan all along. To split up. One at the front, one at the back. Rose would distract him whilst Mercy crept up behind and took him out. Her initial preference had been to use her fists, but then she tripped over the branch. A lucky accident, perhaps.

Not quite so lucky was the fact that Sandy had beaten her to it. He had fired off a shot before she had chance to strike. He had fired and Rose had vanished.

Now Sandy was face down in the earth. A crumpled heap in a large overcoat. His hands were empty, which meant he must have dropped the gun. Mercy looked a little harder and spied it near to where he lay. It got her thinking.

A plan was taking shape …

'I knew you wouldn't let me down,' gasped Lucas, forcing

a smile. It turned to a grimace, however, when a sharp pain erupted in his jaw. He would add that to all his other injuries. Put it at the bottom of an ever-lengthening list.

Mercy smiled back at him. Rested a hand on his shoulder. Lucas winced at her touch, but nothing more. He was fine. He would survive. Which just left one ...

Careful not to reveal herself, Mercy crept forward and cast an eye over the dense bushes that Rose had hidden behind. She wanted to call out, but it was too big a risk, especially with Frank and Maurice lurking somewhere nearby. Instead, she kept on searching. Dark thoughts started to descend. Why hadn't Rose shown herself yet? Ignore the obvious reason. That she had taken the bullet. That she was injured. Or worse.

A frantic Mercy was all set to battle her way through the bushes when a rustle of leaves preceded the arrival of a head and shoulders above the greenery.

'Did ... you ...you ... get him?' stammered Rose, the words stumbling out of her mouth in a staccato blast.

'I got him,' mouthed Mercy. She urged Rose to join them before she dropped down and spoke to Lucas. 'Do you need to go to hospital?'

'Probably, but I can wait,' he replied. 'We need to sort this mess out first. What now?'

Mercy pretended to think. It was all an act, though. She already knew what she had to do. Just her. Nobody else. And sooner rather than later if they were going to get out of there alive.

Rose finally emerged through the undergrowth. She took one look at Lucas and fell to her knees beside him. 'You look terrible,' she said, pressing a hand against his forehead.

'Don't hold back, will you?' moaned Lucas. 'Still, at least you're both here now—'

'Not for long.' Mercy picked up Sandy's gun from the ground. She had wanted to do that ever since she had first clapped eyes on it. 'Take care of Lucas and keep out of sight,' she said, turning to Rose. 'I'll be back before you know it.'

'What? Wait! Where are you going?'

'Frank will have heard the gunshot,' said Mercy. 'If we stay here for too long, he'll track us down. I can change all that, though. I can get to him first.'

Rose screwed up her face. 'What do you mean, *get to him first*?'

'I'm sick of running away,' remarked Mercy, heading back the way she had come. 'It's time the hunted became the hunter.'

CHAPTER SIXTY-NINE

Tommy had only just climbed out of the Audi when he heard the gunshot.

It was close ... but not that close. He looked past Wild Wood Hall and saw a number of barns at the foot of the garden. And, beyond that, the woods that had given the house its name.

That was where the gunshot was coming from.

'Don't,' said Agatha, reading his mind as she joined him on the driveway. 'Leave this to the professionals.'

Professionals. Tommy glared at Miles. Do me a favour.

And, with that, he set off towards the woods. Head down, he broke into a sprint, his pace increasing with every stride as he raced across the lawn.

Why was he running?

No, seriously.

Lucas couldn't stand him. Mercy barely tolerated him. And Rose was far too polite to tell him that she didn't like him, even though, let's be honest, she probably didn't. They weren't friends. None of them. They were just trapped together in this parallel universe. Overworked and underpaid.

So, say it again. Loud and clear. And this time answer the question.

Why was he still running?

Tommy couldn't put it into words. None that he knew, anyway. But there was something there, inside of him, urging him on. An invisible force dragging him towards the woods.

A desperate desire to save the day.

Is that what this was? Some kind of super hero trip? Tommy didn't dwell on it for long. Instead, he slowed his speed. He was there.

Close up, the woods were an impenetrable mass of greenery. Straddling a thorny bush, he was suddenly aware of the noise he was making. From now on, he would move on tip-toes. It would slow him down, but so be it. Surely it was better to arrive late than never arrive at all.

Slowly, slowly, catchy monkey, as the saying goes.

It was just a shame the monkey had a gun.

Mercy's knees were aching from the strain.

The strain of being stuck in the same crippling position for several minutes. That position was an awkward, lop-sided crouch. Before that, she had wandered unknowingly into a clearing in the woods. Fearful of being spotted out in the open, she had stepped back until she found a suitable hiding place on the periphery. It gave her a perfect view of anybody approaching.

Anybody being Frank DeMayo.

He was in her sights. Coming from the opposite direction, his head was bobbing up and down as he fought his way through the foliage. Any second now his whole body would appear in the clearing. Mercy gripped the gun that she had taken from Sandy in both hands. Tried to steady her nerve. There was nothing obstructing her from where she was crouched. She didn't have to shoot to kill; just wound. A leg shot, perhaps. In the thigh. Or the knee. All small targets, though. Much easier to aim for the chest. Easier with added consequences.

What if she killed him in cold blood?

The thought of it made Mercy's hands shake. There was another way, of course. Ditch the gun and use her fists. Her weapon of choice. Yes, he was armed, but the element of surprise was everything. That was how she had dealt with Sandy, after all.

Mercy was still mulling things over when Frank burst into the clearing. He stopped. Looked around. She had seconds at most.

Or less ...

She was all set to fire when something smashed into her from behind. It was enough to send her stumbling forward until she hit the ground, landing heavily on her front. Heavier still was the boot that caught her in the midriff. The pain struck at once, momentarily paralysing her. A fist to the side of her head was another blow that she couldn't prevent. She tried to roll over, desperate to fight back. There was a man stood behind her. Not Sandy, because he was currently sleeping somewhere else in the wood. But it looked like him. Identical, in fact.

Like a crazy twin brother.

Rose couldn't remember the last time she had blinked.

Eyes fixed on her surroundings, she was fearful of what, or who, might appear at any moment. Mercy had gone off to find Frank, but what if she didn't? She could easily take a wrong turn and only realise her mistake once it was too late.

Rose was still staring into space when Lucas nudged her in the ribs. He followed it up with a frantic nod towards the man at their feet.

Sandy had begun to stir.

The fear was closer than Rose had imagined.

Letting his arms take his weight, Sandy raised himself up off the ground until he could shift onto his knees. His eyes were yet to open, not fully at least, but that would soon change.

'Rose.'

She snapped out of her trance when she heard her name. Lucas was nodding again, this time at the fallen branch that Mercy had used with great success only minutes before.

'Do it,' he whispered. 'Hit him.'

Sandy let his fingers brush over the ground. He was searching for his gun. Not that he would find it, thought Rose. Mercy had seen to that. But what then? He was growing stronger by the second. Soon he would be back on the move. In pursuit of Mercy. Or the alternative, of course. He didn't need a gun for that. At a guess, he could probably kill both Rose and Lucas with his bare hands.

The prospect of that alone was enough to shock Rose into action.

In one swift motion, she lifted the branch and cracked it over Sandy's head with as much force as she could muster. He wobbled for a moment and then fell forward, landing face-first by her feet, back where he had started. Rose waited, branch in hand, to see if he would get up again. He didn't. Thank goodness for that.

Lucas smiled at her. 'Remind me never to get on your wrong side ...'

Panic over, Rose got back to staring into space. The fear was still out there. Somewhere. Ready to pounce. Just not so close anymore.

It seemed to take forever, but Tommy eventually forced his way through the knotted undergrowth.

He found himself in a clearing in the woods. His heart leapt when he spotted Mercy.

And then sank when he saw that she was neither alone nor standing up.

Laid flat on her back, Maurice was sat on top of her, his knees pinning her arms to the ground.

Tommy rushed forward. He had barely shifted, however, before the sight of another man made him stumble to a halt.

'Stay where you are,' ordered Frank. The persuasive powers of having a gun pointing straight at you was enough to make Tommy do as he asked. 'Looks like we've got ourselves a little party. So, I'm guessing it was Sandy who fired just now. Where is he?'

Mercy squirmed under Maurice's weight. She tried to spit out a reply, but his hands had moved to her throat, pressing against her windpipe. Breathing had suddenly become a whole lot more difficult.

'Take it easy,' said Frank. 'You're going to choke her.'

But Maurice wasn't listening. Instead, he tightened his grip. Applied more pressure. He was enjoying himself. Why stop now?

'Get off her!' Frank took a step towards them. 'I'm warning you.'

'You're warning me?' Maurice glanced up, eyebrows raised, a curious smirk plastered across his face. 'Say that again.'

'I'm warning you,' repeated Frank.

Mercy gasped as Maurice finally eased the pressure. First his hands and then his entire body as he leapt to his feet. 'You've never warned the Imp,' said Maurice, shifting his attention onto the man at the opposite end of the clearing.

Frank shrugged. 'What's that supposed to mean?'

'What do you think?'

'I don't know,' said Frank, fighting to hide the frustration in his voice. 'Why don't you stop fooling about and tell me?'

'We've been searching for that little fucker for days now,' blurted out Maurice. 'We've risked everything. And for what? Go on. Tell me.'

'Impetus is one of us,' insisted Frank. He pointed his gun at

Mercy and then Tommy. 'These two know where he is. They're going to tell us. And that's why I don't want you to kill them.'

'Bullshit!' shouted Maurice. 'They won't tell us anything. And I don't want them to, anyway. I hate Stokes. Hate him with a passion. Forget all that fake death crap. I wish he really was dead!'

'What's wrong with you?' Frank marched forward. Stopped suddenly a few strides later when he realised Maurice had removed his gun. 'Seriously, what's wrong with you?' he repeated. His voice had lost its edge, though. A wariness had kicked in. Fear of the unpredictable.

'Oh, there's everything wrong with me,' spat Maurice, shaking with rage. 'I'm Mad Mo, aren't I? The lunatic. Well, not anymore. Things are going to change. You can't keep telling me what to do.'

'Oh, I think you'll find I can,' said Frank matter-of-factly. He ended his sentence with a wry smile.

It was a smile that tipped the scales.

Maurice tensed up. His mind was muddled, but he had come to a decision.

A second later, he pulled the trigger.

CHAPTER SEVENTY

Maurice couldn't really miss.

Not from close range. Hit the target and it was an instant fatality. He knew that. Of course he did. But this had been building up inside of him for years. Think hard enough and he could probably pin-point the exact moment the anger had taken root and started to grow. The day Impetus Stokes had shuffled uninvited into their lives. Frank's new best friend, he gave that little shit more respect than any man had ever deserved. Put him on a pedestal like some kind of shrivelled-up king. Let him eat at the top table. *Their* table. Well, things had changed. Now it was Maurice's table. And Maurice had altered the seating plan.

Poor old Frank DeMayo. He wasn't going to sit anywhere ever again. Not now he was dead.

'Whoa! Don't do anything stupid,' said Tommy, raising his hands in cartoon horror, his eyes fixed on the gun in case the demented twin had gone trigger-happy.

'Bit late for that now,' muttered Mercy under her breath.

Maurice was raging. All sense had deserted him, leaving behind a pent-up volcano, ready to erupt without thought or feeling. 'Oh, yeah, that's me alright,' he snorted. 'Mad Mo. Unhinged. Crazy. Well, I'm sick of it! People treating me like I'm nothing ... putting me down ... belittling me. Well, who's laughing now? Answer me that. Who's ... laughing ... now?'

Birds flew and wildlife scattered as Maurice's cry echoed around the woods. Tommy glanced at Mercy, who returned it with a side-eye. He guessed they were thinking the same thing. That this could easily go either way. Bad or very bad. One wrong move and Maurice would have no hesitation in putting a bullet between their eyes. He had killed Frank, after all, and the two of them were close. What would he do to a pair of major irritations who had done nothing but escalate the problem these past few days? They were the catalyst for everything that had gone wrong. If Maurice figured that out for himself, they were in the shit. Big time.

Tommy felt his stomach turn. They were perched on the precipice of life, rocking back and forth, their mere existence in the hands of a self-confessed maniac.

'We used to be the best.' Maurice gently shook his head as he walked around the dead body. 'Back in the day. We were unstoppable. Things could've stayed that way. They didn't have to change.' He stabbed a finger at Frank. 'Your fault. You let Stokes in. Opened the door to outsiders. You even called him the brains to our brawn. Well, smarts only get you so far, don't they? Stokes will still rot in prison, when he gets caught again—'

'And how do you think this is going to end for you?' asked Mercy. 'You've just murdered a man in cold blood. That's a life sentence right there.'

'A life sentence?' Maurice stopped moving. Holding the gun still, he aimed it at Tommy's chest. 'Why stop at one, then? Maybe I've got a taste for it now. Maybe Mad Mo wants to live up to his nickname.'

Agatha decided against taking another step for fear of treading on something she'd rather not.

The woods were a trip hazard. Protruding roots and fallen branches, both of which snatched at dangling legs with joyful abandon. Twigs and leaves were hardly any better, either. Hover your foot anywhere near them and they snapped and cracked and rustled. Best not to move. Don't make a sound.

Agatha used one hand to steady herself against a tree trunk. The other she rested on Miles's shoulder. Whispered in his ear. 'Have you got a clear shot?'

'As good as.' Miles was holding his trusty Glock 17 in both hands, body bent forward at the waist. He had positioned his feet in a boxing stance, his non-shooting side foot slightly ahead of the other. 'Just give me the word.'

Agatha glanced up at the sky. 'It's getting dark.'

'And?'

'You might miss.'

'I never miss.'

'You're going to look pretty silly if you do.'

'Well, that's a risk I'm prepared to take.'

Agatha hesitated. 'No chance of anybody else getting caught

in the crossfire?'

'Zero.' Miles took a slow, steady breath. 'Time's ticking. Maurice has gone off the rails. Frank's dead and, at this rate, he won't be the only one. If I don't put him down now, the Nearly in your Nearly Dearly Departed Club will no longer be required—'

'Take the shot,' said Agatha calmly. She edged away from him before she spoke again. 'End this nonsense once and for all.'

Maurice was about to pull the trigger when his own head exploded.

Blood and brain matter splattered over the nearby foliage, dripping from the leaves, staining the undergrowth. His body dropped a moment later. His legs folded and he landed in a crumpled heap. There was no chance of him getting back up again.

Not now Maurice Maddison was a dead man.

'No ... fuckin' ... way!' Tommy staggered backwards with his hands up to his face, unsure where the shot had come from. A second after that, shock gave way to revulsion and the contents of his stomach escaped from his mouth.

Mercy simply held her ground, stared in disbelief. Silence had returned to the woods. And with the silence, a sudden calm. Mercy felt nothing as she looked upon the dead bodies. Frank and Maurice were both wicked men. They had done bad things, probably since childhood. Everybody's luck had to run out eventually. They weren't fools. They knew the risks when they started.

The same risks that had finally finished them off.

The same risks that still hung heavy in the air. Maurice had killed Frank. They had seen that with their own eyes.

But who had killed Maurice?

Mercy was still rooted to the spot when her phone vibrated. She pulled it out robotically. Answered without looking. 'Hello.'

'How is he?' It was Miles.

He had to be Maurice. 'Not good.'

'Dead not good?'

'Yeah, dead not good,' repeated Mercy. 'I'm guessing that was you.'

'You guess correctly. We know Frank's dead, but what about the other one?'

'Out cold the last time I saw him.'

'Almost the perfect hat-trick.' Miles checked himself. 'Sorry. Old habits die hard. I shouldn't make light of it. How's Lucas?'

'Battered and bruised, but nothing that a stiff drink and a good night's sleep can't fix,' said Mercy. 'Tommy And Rose are fine, too. Well, fine-ish. We're coming out now. Probably leave the bodies where they are if that's alright with you.'

'Hopefully the earth will swallow them up.' Miles ended the call. Smiled at Agatha. 'Job done.'

'Job done,' she nodded. 'Just not the job we were assigned to do. Still, beggars can't be choosers, I suppose.'

It was several minutes before the four of them emerged from the woods.

One by one. Scratched and scarred. Mercy first. Then Tommy. Then Lucas, with Rose stood behind him. An arm supporting his elbow, the other around his waist.

Agatha rubbed her hands together as she waited for them to join her. She had moved back towards the house. It was no warmer up there, though. It was time to wrap this up before the chill set in and get back to the Nightingale Hotel. Her closest thing to home. Without being homely.

'Congratulations,' she said, nodding at each and every one of them. 'I see you're all still standing. '

'Don't know how,' muttered Mercy. 'People have died.'

'Not *my* people,' shrugged Agatha.

'And Impetus Stokes has vanished,' added Tommy.

Agatha shrugged again. 'Good for Impetus Stokes. He's not my concern. You are. And, like I said, you're all still standing.'

Lucas groaned. 'Doesn't seem like much of a victory.'

'True,' nodded Agatha. 'Let's call it a draw, shall we?'

'A score draw,' chipped-in Miles. 'Not quite so boring.'

'I suppose this is a crime scene,' said Agatha, casting an eye over her surroundings. 'I'd better call it in—'

'Looks like you won't have to.' Tommy gestured towards a row of flashing lights coming along Chambers Lane. Sirens soon followed. 'We should leg it,' he said, turning his attention to the woods. 'Hide out in there. No one would find us for weeks.'

'I don't think I'm cut out for a life on the run, do you?' Agatha sighed. 'No, leave this to me. I'm sure we can come to an amenable conclusion.' With that, she turned around and walked towards the flashing lights. 'My name is Agatha Pleasant,' she called out, hands raised above her head. 'I come in peace ...'

CHAPTER SEVENTY-ONE
WEDNESDAY

Olaf eased the Audi to a gentle halt on the patch of wasteland behind the railway station.

It was early morning. Just before seven. Still as dark as the dead of night and predictably cold. The hint of a slight frost coupled with a bitter wind. Nothing that a thick coat and even thicker gloves couldn't deflect, though.

Olaf had two passengers in the back of the car. Miss Pleasant and Miles. The boss and her capable assistant.

'We're early,' muttered the latter of the two.

'We're *always* early,' replied Agatha, gazing out the window at nothing in particular. 'It's why we're the best.'

Miles snorted. 'So, why are the best currently stuck in Stainmouth? Also known as the arse end of the world?'

Agatha greeted that with a frown. 'You're very grumpy these days. Something bothering you?'

'Not something – the *same* thing.' Miles rubbed his eyes with a fierce intensity. 'That bloody hotel. I swear I saw two mice in the corner of the room last night, heads together, chatting away.'

'Speak mouse, do you?'

'I might have been hallucinating. I even imagined one of them had crawled into bed with me. Started nibbling my toenails.'

Agatha smiled. 'That'll be all the cheese you eat before bedtime.'

'I can't help it. I've had more pizzas this last month than I've had in my entire life. Step foot outside the hotel and there are at least five takeaways right on the doorstep. I've got to eat something.'

'The food at my hotel's very nice.' Agatha winced. That had slipped out by accident. 'I'll sort out your living arrangements,' she said hastily. 'I promise. It's the least I can do.'

She stopped talking as headlights appeared on the horizon. They drew closer until, eventually, a van skidded to a halt directly in front of them. It was a white Mercedes Benz-Sprinter adorned in blue and yellow checks. No need for sirens. The driver killed the engine, but left the lights on full beam. A second later, the passenger side door swung open and a man appeared. No uniform. Just a badly fitted suit and crooked tie.

Olaf watched as the man slammed the door shut with unnecessary force. Walking around to the front of the vehicle, he crossed his arms and fixed the Audi with an impenetrable stare.

'I'm waiting,' he shouted.

Olaf had never met the Chief Constable before, but then didn't need to. He could tell at first glance that the man was untrustworthy. A snake who had risen to the top by foul and unfair means. He hoped Miss Pleasant knew that, too. That she hadn't swallowed his lies and bowed down to his rank.

'Just look at the state of him,' said Agatha, breaking Olaf's train of thought. 'He's like a bloated weasel stuffed inside a bin bag.'

Olaf fought the smile that attempted to creep up on his face. It didn't do to show your emotions. Behind closed doors, perhaps. In the privacy of your own home. Not whilst at work.

'And here's me thinking Goose was boyfriend material,' grinned Miles.

'I'll pretend I didn't hear that.' Agatha pushed open the door. 'This shouldn't take long ...'

'Do you want me to come with you?' asked Miles.

'I've dealt with bigger men than Clifford Goose,' Agatha insisted. 'There's nothing about him that scares me. Well, only his breath, but I'll keep my distance.' With that, she exited the Audi and made her way slowly towards the Chief Constable, swerving any mounds of rubble or broken bricks she came across in the dark. 'Good morning, Clifford.'

'You've got a bloody cheek, woman,' he scowled. 'I said six and you switched it to seven. Who do you think you are? I make the rules around here. I lay down the chuffin' law. I told you that yesterday in The Wild Boar. Why don't you listen? Why do you always think you can do what you want?' Goose stopped ranting. Looked over his shoulder. 'Where is he? The Imp? That's what this is all about, right?'

'Mr Stokes isn't here,' said Agatha. 'We don't know where he is.'

'You bloody what?' Goose slammed his hand down on the Mercedes' bonnet. 'How the hell have you managed to lose a dead body?'

'Oh, we didn't lose a dead body,' began Agatha calmly. 'We lost a body that was perfectly alive. That broke out of a coffin and ran into the road. That vanished from the hospital in plain sight. That watched his own mother die before escaping through a ready-made tunnel in the ground.' Agatha took a breath. 'Anything to say, Clifford? I'm guessing all that might not come as a complete shock to you.'

Goose's jaw dropped. 'Bollocks.'

'Bollocks indeed,' nodded Agatha. 'Whatever possessed you to start dealing drugs to prison inmates?'

'Who told you that?' frowned Goose. 'Not the Governor? Bridget the ballbreaker? Wouldn't say that to her face, mind. Only behind her back.'

Agatha sighed. The Chief Constable had no filter. Or just no common sense. Either way, it was a miracle he was still in the job. If he had been a woman, people would've questioned who she'd had to sleep with to climb the ladder. No one would want to sleep with Goose, though. Not even his own duvet. 'It wasn't the Governor,' lied Agatha, sticking to her promise. 'My source was good, though. I know everything. The whole sordid affair.'

'Sordid, my arse!' blurted out Goose. 'Stokes wanted to be with his mum when she kicked the bucket. And, by the sound of things, he was. You should be calling me a good Samaritan, not making me out to be some kind of pill pusher. It's not my fault things went tits up. I blame Frank DeMayo.'

'The *late* Frank DeMayo,' said Agatha. 'He died last night. I thought you would've heard.'

Goose seemed to perk up a little. 'Bugger me. That's a turn up for the books. How did he croak it?'

'He was killed by one of his own men.'

'Even better,' said Goose, trying not to smile. 'Any other casualties?'

'One. Maurice Maddison. None of my team, though. Thanks for asking.'

Goose pretended to wipe his brow. 'That's a relief. As for the passing of Frank DeMayo, that closes one particular door that's been jammed for years. You can't lock up the dead, can you? No need for the Imp to fill in the gaps any more. Talking of which, do you really not know where he is?'

Agatha shook her head. 'Would I lie to you? He could be anywhere by now, though. Probably not worth the resources trying to track him down.'

'We can't just let him walk away scot free,' protested Goose.

'We're not – *you* are,' said Agatha. 'You're the one who let him out of prison. If you want him back, you find him.'

'No harm done, I suppose,' muttered Goose. 'Everyone thinks Stokes is dead, anyway. Why rock the boat and bring him back to life?' He shifted his weight and farted. He expected Agatha to react, but she didn't. 'Right, is that it? Bollocking over?'

'Not quite,' said Agatha. 'In the future, don't keep me in the dark. Tell me everything. And I mean everything. We're a team now ... whether I like it or not.'

Goose nodded. 'Like husband and wife?'

'Not in your wildest dreams,' said Agatha, turning away. 'I'm leaving now. I'll be in touch soon.'

'Can't bloody wait.' Pushing himself off the bonnet, Goose climbed back into the van. It was on the move before he had even strapped on his seat belt.

'All sorted?' asked Miles, once Agatha had returned to the Audi.

'As good as,' she replied. 'I don't trust him, though. Not in the slightest. From now on, we keep Clifford Goose on a very short leash. Choke him if need be.'

Olaf started the engine without instruction. He was relieved that Miss Pleasant knew what kind of person she was dealing with, not that it came as a huge surprise. You didn't need to be an excellent judge of character to have doubts about the Chief Constable. You just needed eyes and ears and a modicum of common sense.

'What do you think, Olaf?' asked Agatha, out of the blue.

He grunted. Just the once. As usual, he was fully in agreement.

CHAPTER SEVENTY-TWO
SOME TIME LATER...

Lucas kept his distance.

He was stood at a bus stop. Hands in pockets, shoulders slumped, head down. Eyes, however, trained on the school across the road.

A bus slowed until he casually waved it on. He had been there almost five minutes now. Under the circumstances, that was at least four-and-a-half minutes too long. If he wasn't careful, curtains would twitch and tongues would start to wag. People with too much time on their hands would question his motives.

A strange man lurking outside a school.

No, make that a strange black man. Double jeopardy.

Lucas could hear the alarm bells already. Thankfully, they were drowned out by the sound of a real bell. The bell for lunch time. Seconds later, hordes of children poured out into the playground. Running and skipping. Pushing and shoving. Desperate for fun of any kind to break the monotony of the classroom.

It took Lucas a while, but eventually he spotted her. At first glance, she would've passed for a completely different child, a child who could blend in effortlessly with all the other girls and boys. Look a little closer, however, and the warning signs were still there. The straggly blonde hair and dark eyes. Dangerously thin beneath her school uniform. Still, it had only been a week or so. Some things take a while. You can't fix everything at once.

This was a start, though. And any improvement was a damn sight better than the life that Ellie had lived before.

She had been taken in temporarily by a foster family in the village of Ashton Burns. A family who had experience of this kind of thing. Knew the processes. Deliver the basics and go from there. Hot running water, clean clothes and three-square meals a day. She deserved that, at the very least.

Lucas let his mind wander whilst his eyes stayed glued on the child. It was incredible to think that someone so small, so innocent, could've saved his life. She had, though. That was a fact. Ellie had done everything he had told her to. She had got word to Agatha. They would never have found him without that. At a guess, he'd be dead by now.

And, this time, he'd have stayed dead.

Ellie moved closer to the fence. She was playing with two other girls. Spinning around in circles. Lucas felt the urge to go over there and say hello. Thank her for all she had done. No, that didn't seem like enough. He owed her everything. How could he put all that into a single sentence?

Not that it mattered. If he was being honest, Lucas had no

intention of going anywhere. If a strange man hiding by the bus stop was one thing, then a strange man hovering by the school gates was something else entirely. Suspicion would be aroused which would, inevitably, lead to a frantic call to the police. Then what? A barrage of awkward questions he had no wish to answer. Besides, would Ellie even remember him? Mister Poo-Poo? Maybe. Maybe not. If anything, he would probably freak her out. The scars across his cheeks and forehead, the result of repeated beatings from Frank and company, were still yet to heal properly. A face like his could easily give a young girl nightmares. And she'd had enough of those already, poor kid.

An elderly woman in a striped headscarf stepped in front of him, blocking Lucas's view. She tilted her head, glared at him out the corner of one eye, her mind turning over with tabloid tales.

Time to leave.

Lucas set off in the opposite direction. He had seen enough. Enough to leave him satisfied. Reassured even. When all was said and done, the only thing that really mattered was that Ellie was happy. Everything else would take care of itself.

Lucas pressed on. Nothing to see here. Just a strange man walking away from a school. No, a strange black man.

So long, Ellie. Have a nice life.

CHAPTER SEVENTY-THREE

The trapdoor opened and a head popped up from down below.

The eyes looked around to see if the coast was clear. And it was. Everything in the sitting room was just how he had left it, in fact. Minus the body.

The body of his mother, Ada Stokes.

Impetus tried to push that to the back of his mind as he crawled out of the hole. He stopped once he was out. Listened. Convinced that he was alone, he shifted to one side and lowered the trapdoor. The carpet that was stuck to the top blended effortlessly with the rest of the room. He had made a good job of that, even if he said so himself. Very neat and tidy. Forward planning of the highest order.

Forward planning ...

As an afterthought, Impetus lifted the trapdoor and propped it back up again. Better to be safe than sorry. There'd be no time to waste if he needed a quick escape.

He turned his attention to the rocking chair. He wanted to sit in it, but to do such a thing felt wrong. Disrespectful. He had sat on it many times before, but that was then. In the not-so-distant past. Now the chair had lost some of its charm. It looked cold and hard. Appeared practically unfit for purpose. Destined for the rubbish dump.

Thanks for the memories. I'll never forget you.

That wasn't the chair, though. That was the person who had sat in it right up to her dying day.

Impetus always knew he would return to the house. He had been gone for a week. Long enough for the relevant authorities to clear the place and stop coming around. Now it felt empty. Soulless. Still, at least Ada had got her last wish. For him to be there when she finally passed.

His mind shifted, enough to reawaken those dark thoughts that attacked with such disturbing regularity. He had let her down. Been a huge embarrassment for much of her later life. Maybe being present at the end would've made up for it. Did he really believe that, though? That a few hours could make amends for a lifetime of disappointment? No, he may have been there when she had died, but he had still been a criminal. There was no way around that. No clever deception. No cunning cover-up.

Impetus slumped forward as an overwhelming wave of sorrow took him by surprise. As if all the strength had been sucked out of him, his legs gave way and he dropped to his knees. Burying his head in his hands, he started to cry. The tears flowed freely between his fingers. There was no holding them back. Not that he wanted to.

Ada Stokes was gone forever. The woman who had cared for him all his life. His one true ally in a world that didn't quite understand him.

Impetus tried to breathe, but it came in short, ragged bursts. At the same time, he endeavoured to steer his thoughts in a different direction. A positive path he was yet to tread. He was still alive, after all. He had a future. A future that, with any luck, didn't involve being locked up. Maybe he could head to warmer climes. Or switch the heat for somewhere colder. Remoter. More desolate. He would fit in there. No one would suspect a thing. Once settled, he could even make friends. Find a wife. There had to be a woman out there somewhere who could see beyond his height. Who preferred brains to inches.

There was always another option, of course. Where he could stay hidden in plain sight. Live the life that he had been destined for until Frank DeMayo and a career in crime had knocked him off course.

A curious shuffling sound brought him back to reality.

Impetus wiped his eyes. Climbed up off the carpet. The shuffling was coming from the hallway. Footsteps, at a guess. Like an intruder on tiptoes.

He weighed up his options. Fleeing was the most obvious thing to do. Through the trapdoor, down the tunnel and back the way he had come. And yet ... what was he fleeing from? An unknown noise that could've been anything from next door's cat to his own pounding heart beat? No, it made little sense to run. He was rational, not impulsive. First, he would investigate.

Creeping towards the door, Impetus gently lowered the handle. Pushed it slightly to one side. Leaning forward, he poked his head out into the hallway. Looked left towards the front door. Right towards the bedrooms. There was nobody there. Nothing was out of place. Had fallen or smashed. He held his breath, soaked up the silence. The house was quiet, as was the street outside. He repeated the process. Just to be sure. The silence persisted, refusing to be disturbed by either mouth or movement.

Reassured that there was no one there, Impetus closed the door and turned back into the room. He froze when he saw a woman sat in his mother's favourite chair, rocking back and forth.

'Seems as if we both have something in common, Mr Stokes,' she said. 'Turns out that I'm quite sneaky as well.'

Impetus's gaze drifted towards the trapdoor. Without missing a beat, the woman slammed it shut with her foot. 'Whoops. How clumsy. And don't think about leaving through the door either. You could probably outrun me, but I doubt you'll be anywhere near as successful if you go head-to-head with my men. They've got the house surrounded.'

Impetus hesitated. 'It seems you have me at something of a disadvantage. You know who I am and yet ...'

'Agatha Pleasant,' said the woman.

Impetus racked his brain, but the name meant nothing. 'Police?'

Agatha shook her head. 'Certainly not. I'm a little more

unorthodox in my methods, shall we say? Please make yourself comfortable. This shouldn't take long.'

Closing the door behind him, Impetus sat down on the sofa. 'I suppose you're here to kill me.'

'Bit dramatic,' frowned Agatha. 'No, I'm here to pass on information. Frank DeMayo is dead. As is Maurice Maddison. Sandy, his twin brother, will be heading straight to prison when he comes out of hospital. They're no longer a threat.' Agatha paused. 'You don't seem particularly overjoyed.'

Impetus stared at her for longer than intended as he tried to process the news. 'I am ... I mean ... I should be. Sorry. It's come as quite a shock. If I'm being honest, I don't know what to feel.'

'Relief?' suggested Agatha. 'A sense of freedom?'

'Perhaps. It's hard to explain, but Frank has been a part of my life for a considerable period of time. I feared him, yes, but I didn't hate him. If anything, I wanted to impress him. Show him how clever I was. He always treated me well when things went smoothly.'

'And when they didn't?'

'He largely took it out on Maurice. He was always the scapegoat. Frank only persisted with him because of Sandy.'

Agatha nodded to herself. That made sense. No wonder Mad Mo had finally flipped out in the woods.

'How did you know I'd be here?' asked Impetus, studying her with intent. 'I've only been in the house a few minutes.'

'Let's call it a lucky guess,' Agatha admitted. 'I had a feeling.'

'And how did you get in?'

'Now, that would be telling, wouldn't it?' Agatha stopped rocking and stood up. Moved swiftly towards the door. 'Goodbye, Mr Stokes.'

'What? Is that it?' asked Impetus, taken aback.

'I don't see why not.'

'I thought ...' Impetus stopped mid-sentence. And then started again. 'I thought you'd be taking me back to prison. That's why you're here, right?'

'Wrong,' replied Agatha. 'Like I said before, I'm not the police. Which means you're not my problem.'

'So, I'm free?'

Agatha shook her head. 'I doubt that very much. You're currently on the run. You're a wanted man. Just not wanted by me. Any idea where you might slip off to whilst my back is turned?'

'I was thinking about staying put,' revealed Impetus. There. He had said it out loud for the first time. 'Right here. Fourteen Peartree Court. It can't be that difficult to hack into the system and change all the deeds and records. I could even give myself a new name. Something sophisticated. Something like—'

'It's probably best that you don't tell me.' Agatha opened the sitting room door and stepped outside. 'What I don't know can't hurt you.'

Impetus hurried after her. 'Won't your men be suspicious? You know, when you leave here without me?'

'Men?' Agatha kept on walking. 'What men?'

And, with that, she was gone. Out the door. Out of the

house. Out of his life.

A life that had only just begun.

Goodbye, Impetus Stokes. It's been nice being you.

CHAPTER SEVENTY-FOUR

Mercy was upstairs in her room at Cockleshell Farm when it happened.

Somebody knocked on the door.

No, not somebody. Somebody suggested that you didn't know who it was. Just a random caller. An uninvited guest. But Mercy *did* know. She knew exactly who *this* was. If she was being honest, she had been expecting a call like this ever since that fateful night on Bartholomew Street.

The night that Errol Duggan had met his unfortunate death.

The knock came again. Four raps. Short. Sharp. Sonically effective. Enough to strike fear into the hearts and heads of criminals up and down the land. Except she wasn't a criminal, was she? Not really. She had lied, yes. She had covered up for Solomon. No denying it. But that was for the greater good.

At least, that was what she kept telling herself. Over and over. On repeat.

They didn't know that, though.

Mercy walked out onto the landing and listened. She

wondered who would answer the door. Lucas was out and about somewhere, whilst Proud Mary was tending to the pigs. That just left two. Tommy and Rose.

Tommy was the first to react. 'Somebody get that 'cos I'm not.' His voice was coming from the sitting room. He'd be sprawled out on the sofa watching some daytime crap on the television. One hand behind his head, the other down his pants.

The knock came again. Just as short. Just as sharp. Just as sonically effective. Third time lucky.

'Oh, for crying out loud!' barked Tommy. 'Do I have to do everything in this bloody house?'

A dull *thud* and he was on his feet, grumbling and groaning with every step. Mercy ducked out of sight as he appeared in the hallway. She didn't want to be seen. Not if she was proven correct.

Tommy opened the door. He made a peculiar noise – a kind of high-pitched squeak – before he spoke. 'Hey, it's ... it's Sarah and Alan, isn't it? Oh, and the entire Stainmouth police force as well. You should've told me you were coming en masse. I'd have got the beers in.'

Mercy gripped hold of the banister. Sarah and Alan. Also known as PC Burrell and PC Tuffers. It couldn't have been anybody else.

'This isn't a personal call, sir,' said PC Tuffers stiffly. 'May we come in, please?'

'What? All of you?' replied Tommy. 'Proud Mary will lose her wig if you stomp mud all over the carpet.'

Mercy crept across the landing. Made her way into Lucas's room. His window looked out onto the driveway. Sure enough, there were three police vans parked in a row.

This isn't a personal call ...

'We don't all have to come in,' remarked PC Burrell. 'The rest of them are here purely as a precaution.'

Mercy knew what Tommy was thinking. He would assume the police were here for him. The guilt complex of a shady past. He was wrong, though. 'What's all this about?' he asked.

Mercy could picture him now. Blocking the doorway. Sticking his chest out. God bless you and your bloody awkwardness, Tommy O'Strife. Without knowing it, he had bought her some time.

'We're looking for one of the other lodgers who are staying here,' began PC Burrell. 'Mercy Mee. We'd like to have a chat with her about an incident several weeks ago. A murder ...'

Mercy had heard enough. Tiptoeing back into her room, she grabbed a pair of trainers from the wardrobe and pulled them on over her feet. She didn't bother with a bag. No time to consider a coat.

She could hear the police entering the farmhouse as she quietly opened the window. Without over-thinking things, she climbed out onto the ledge. Carefully, she lowered herself down, gripping on with both hands whilst her legs dangled in mid-air. For a moment she just hung there, face against the wall, her arms stretched above her head.

The moment passed and she let go.

Her landing was smooth. A quick breath and she was off. Running at speed across the grass. Past the barns. Over the wooden fence at the foot of the garden.

Nobody had seen her. She was sure of it.

She made her way over open fields, maintaining her pace at all times. Slowing down wasn't an option. Not unless she wanted to get caught.

Because getting caught meant being arrested.

And being arrested meant being charged for the murder of Errol Duggan.

She was the mystery intruder. But now it wasn't a mystery anymore. Someone must've seen her getting into the Mini Clubman. Filmed it. Put it on social media. Shown it to the police. She had no explanation, no reason as to why she was there on Bartholomew Street.

Only the truth.

And she couldn't do that to Solomon. He didn't deserve it, not after everything he'd been through. Prison would ruin his life. Destroy him.

No, Mercy would keep that secret to herself.

She came to another wooden fence and began to climb over it. Pausing at the top, she glanced back at Cockleshell Farm. Would the police have realised she wasn't there and left by now? Not a bad thing, of course. She was allowed to leave the premises. Nothing suspicious about that. They would just come back later on that day. Tomorrow even. Or the day after. If nothing else, it gave Mercy a head start. For the time being at least, she was the one in control.

Hopping down from the fence, she quickly regained her footing and set off again. What about the rest of them? Rose, Lucas and Tommy? Even Proud Mary? How long would it take them to realise that she was never coming back? Because that's what this was. A last farewell to a life that she had stumbled into.

She was no longer nearly dearly departed.

She was just gone.

Gone forever.

NOTE TO READER

Thank you for getting this far. If you've read the whole book then you deserve a medal. Just don't ask me for one because I haven't got any. But I am extremely grateful. And do feel free to leave a review on Amazon if leaving reviews on Amazon is your kind of thing. It's not easy for a new author so please be kind.

Big thanks to Stuart Bache for the cover. Excellent work as usual.

Until the next time ...

OTHER BOOKS IN THE SERIES

THE NEARLY DEARLY DEPARTED CLUB (BOOK 1)

Meet the Nearly Dearly Departed Club. Four random strangers with one thing in common. They're all dead. Deceased and departed. No longer with us.

Or maybe not ...

Teenager Benji Hammerton has gone quiet. Worryingly so. Fearing the worst, his parents turn to the one person who might be able to help – Agatha Pleasant, an ageing secret agent who operates largely in the shadows, unburdened by rules and regulations. As luck would have it, Agatha has a batch of new recruits at her disposal. Untapped potential desperately in need of work experience.

Enter the Nearly Dearly Departed Club.

Their search takes them to Stainmouth, a grim Northern town with little to offer except bitter winds and a toxic atmosphere. With a life hanging in the balance, they hunt tirelessly for the missing boy. They make friends along the way, but also enemies. The kind of enemies who think nothing of taking a life if the need arises. As tensions mount, and the risks start to outweigh the rewards, the team question their involvement. Their purpose. Their future. Is any of it really worth dying for?

Especially when you're dead already ...

Printed in Great Britain
by Amazon